continued . . .

"Melanie Turner may well be one of the most exciting, smart, and funny heroines currently in any book series. . . . There's enough excitement to keep you reading until late in the night."
—Fresh Fiction

THE WITCHCRAFT MYSTERIES

Hexes and Hemlines

"This exciting urban fantasy murder mystery . . . is an entertaining paranormal whodunit. . . . Her familiar, Oscar, half goblin-gargoyle, becomes a cute potbellied pig who adds jocularity to the fast-paced story line as part of the quirky cast (benign, kind, and evil) that help make this spellbinding tale a fun read."
—Genre Go Round Reviews

"*Hexes and Hemlines* carries you along with an unconventional cast where nothing is out-of-bounds. Extraordinarily entertaining."
—*Suspense Magazine*

"This is a fun and totally engrossing series that hooks you instantly and makes you want more. . . . I love the mix of vintage clothes, magic, and a lingering possibility of romance combined with mystery."
—Fang-tastic Books

"Juliet Blackwell has created a series that will appeal to mystery fans as well as paranormal enthusiasts."
—Debbie's Book Bag

A Cast-Off Coven

"If you like your mysteries with a side of spell-casting and demon-vanquishing, you'll enjoy the second title in Blackwell's Witchcraft Mysteries."
—*Romantic Times*

"This awesome paranormal mystery stars a terrific heroine."
—Genre Go Round Reviews

Secondhand Spirits

"Juliet Blackwell provides a terrific urban fantasy with the opening of the Witchcraft Mystery series."
—Genre Go Round Reviews

"An excellent blend of mystery, paranormal, and light humor, creating a cozy that is a must read for anyone with an interest in literature with paranormal elements."
—The Romance Readers Connection

"It's a fun story, with romance possibilities with a couple hunky men, terrific vintage clothing, and the enchanting Oscar. But there is so much more to this book. It has serious depth."
—*The Herald News* (MA)

Also by Juliet Blackwell

MURDER ON THE HOUSE

A Haunted Home Renovation Mystery

Juliet Blackwell

AN OBSIDIAN MYSTERY

OBSIDIAN
Published by New American Library, a division of
Penguin Group (USA) Inc., 375 Hudson Street,
New York, New York 10014, USA
Penguin Group (Canada), 90 Eglinton Avenue East, Suite 700, Toronto,
Ontario M4P 2Y3, Canada (a division of Pearson Penguin Canada Inc.)
Penguin Books Ltd., 80 Strand, London WC2R 0RL, England
Penguin Ireland, 25 St. Stephen's Green, Dublin 2,
Ireland (a division of Penguin Books Ltd.)
Penguin Group (Australia), 250 Camberwell Road, Camberwell, Victoria 3124,
Australia (a division of Pearson Australia Group Pty. Ltd.)
Penguin Books India Pvt. Ltd., 11 Community Centre, Panchsheel Park,
New Delhi—110 017, India
Penguin Group (NZ), 67 Apollo Drive, Rosedale, Auckland 0632,
New Zealand (a division of Pearson New Zealand Ltd.)
Penguin Books (South Africa) (Pty.) Ltd., 24 Sturdee Avenue,
Rosebank, Johannesburg 2196, South Africa

Penguin Books Ltd., Registered Offices:
80 Strand, London WC2R 0RL, England

First published by Obsidian, an imprint of New American Library,
a division of Penguin Group (USA) Inc.

First Printing, December 2012
10 9 8 7 6 5 4 3 2 1

ALWAYS LEARNING   PEARSON

To Pamela Groves:
My heart is with you.

Acknowledgments

Thanks are due, as always, to my wonderful editor, Kerry Donovan. You are a woman of great patience, keen intelligence, and obviously of *fabulous* taste!

Many thanks to Jeri Hoag and her husband, Paul, for answering all sorts of gruesome questions about carbon-monoxide poisoning. And to the citizens of San Francisco's Castro District, past and present, for laying the groundwork for such an incredible, diverse, and vibrant neighborhood.

A special shout-out to my sister Carolyn, who always offers such incredible insights, suggestions, and ideas. To Jace for allowing me to bore you with endless plot problems. To Shay, Suzanne, Kendall, Susan, Chris, Casey, Anna, Mary, Sara, Dan, Karen, and the entire Mira Vista Social Club (and annex) — thank you for being there!

To my father for being such an inspiration in these

novels and in life. To my sister Susan for all your support and cheerleading!

Thanks to all my writer pals, especially Sophie Little-field, Rachael Herron, Nicole Peeler, Gigi Pandian, Victoria Laurie, Adrienne Miller, Martha Flynn, Lisa Hughey, L. G. C. Smith, Mysti Berry, and Steve Hockensmith. You all keep me sane . . . or at least as close as I'm going to get.

Chapter One

What makes a house look haunted?

Is it enough to appear abandoned, run-down, bleak? To creak and groan when long fingers of fog creep down the nearby hills? Or is it something else: a whisper of a tragic past, a distinct but unsettling impression that dwelling within is something indescribable—and perhaps not human?

Beats me. I'm a general contractor with a well-earned reputation for restoring and renovating historic homes in the San Francisco Bay Area, and an abiding desire to chuck all my responsibilities and run off to Paris. Reconciling those two imperatives has been hard enough, but recently my life was made even more complicated when *Haunted House Quarterly* named me "California's most promising up-and-coming Ghost Buster."

A misleading moniker if ever there was one. When it comes to ghosts, I'm pretty clueless. Not that I let that stop me. Recently ghosts had appeared on a couple of my jobsites, and I'd done what any really good contractor would: I handled them as best I could, and got back to work.

But at the moment I was standing — on purpose — on the front stoop of an alleged haunted house in San Francisco's vibrant Castro District.

The graceful old structure didn't *look* haunted, what with the cars parked in the drive, the cluster of red clay pots planted with marigolds on the porch, ecru lace curtains hanging in the front windows, and a folded newspaper on the sisal doormat. But the current residents were certain they weren't the only ones inhabiting the place — and they liked it that way. In fact, they planned to renovate it and transform it into a haunted bed-and-breakfast.

The house was massive, built in a neoclassical revival style with Italianate flourishes. The street-side facade was symmetrical; the peeling paint on trim and walls alike was a traditional monochromatic cream. There were long rows of tall, narrow windows with ornamental lintels, and the low-pitched roof was supported by ornate corbels that marched along the underside of the eaves with military precision. Where the city's famous Queen Anne Victorian homes were decorated with scads of elaborately painted and gilded gingerbread flourishes, the neoclassical style was understated, its only frills the "wedding cake" effect of the lintels and corbels, and the Corinthian columns supporting a demilune roof over the front-door portico.

As usual when facing a magnificent structure, my heart swelled at its history, its artistry . . . and its needs.

My practiced eye noted a host of problems: One corner under the roof overhang gaped open, inviting vermin. The gutter had detached in a few spots, and the roof displayed long streaks of bright green moss that hinted at water issues. Window sashes sagged, indicating rot. Such obvious signs of neglect meant a thousand other problems would be uncovered once the walls were opened.

And then there were the purported ghosts.

I took a deep breath and blew it out slowly. *Here goes*. Looking around for a bell or knocker, I found an ancient intercom system to the right of the front door. A quick press of the button was greeted by a burst of static.

I had just reached out to knock on the door when it swung open.

I squeaked and jumped in surprise, my hands flailing.

This was another glitch in any of my ghost buster career aspirations: I'm not what you'd call cool in the face of ... well, much of anything. At the moment, for instance, I appeared to be at a total loss when faced with a rosy-cheeked little girl, with long chestnut hair and big eyes the deep, soft brown of milk chocolate.

As I tried to pull myself together, she giggled.

"Sorry," I said, taking a deep breath and striving to regain my composure. "My mind was somewhere else."

"My mama does that all the time," the girl said with an understanding little shrug, displaying a preadolescent sweetness of a child who was oh-so-familiar—and patient—with the mysterious ways of adults. Though she held herself with great poise, I pegged her age to be ten or eleven. Give her a couple more years, I thought, and she'd be as snarky and sullen as my teenage stepson.

She stepped back. "Do you want to come in?"

"Yes, thank you. I'm Mel Turner, with Turner Construction. I have an appointment with Mrs. Bernini.... Is she your grandmother?"

The girl laughed and shook her head. "No, of course not. I'm Anabelle. Anabelle Bowles. I'll take you to the parlor. Follow me."

I stepped into the front foyer and paused, savoring the moment.

In the old days all buildings were custom-designed and custom-built, so each historic house is unique. My favorite part of my job, bar none, is stepping into an old structure for the first time; one never knows what to expect.

Although the lines of this house were neoclassical, the interior details were eclectic. The front entry was airy and open, the intricate woodwork painted a creamy white throughout, rather than stained or shellacked. The brightness was a welcome change from the dark woods so characteristic of the Victorian style, as in the house I was finishing up across town. These walls were lined in high bead-board wainscoting. Tall sash windows allowed sunlight to pour in, giving the home an airy, sunny feel. An enormous fireplace, missing several of its glazed blue green tiles, was flanked by built-in display cases. Each newel post on the banister leading upstairs was carved in a different pattern: One was a series of different-sized balls; another was geometric boxes; yet another sported a face carved into the lintel.

In marked contrast with the home's exquisite bones, the interior decorating was appalling. Everywhere I looked there was a pile of clutter: a sagging floral sofa sat along one wall, one missing leg replaced with a stack of old magazines, and an overstuffed velvet armchair was covered with a faded Indian-print cloth. The walls and shelves were lined with children's school photos, several slipping and crooked in their cheap plastic frames. Newspapers were piled in one corner, and flyers from local merchants littered a scarred maple coffee table from the 1960s. Shreds of discarded paper and a pair of scissors suggested someone had been clipping coupons. And there was a distinct chill to the air, so it felt almost colder than the winter afternoon outside—I imagined the windows were single-paned and leaky, or the heater was broken. Or both.

It got worse as I studied the walls and ceiling. Rather than strip the faded wallpaper above the old wainscoting, someone had simply painted over it; it was pulling away from the walls and hung in crazy-quilt patches. Rusty water stains bloomed in several spots on the peeling ceiling, and the broad-planked oak flooring was warped and discolored in several places.

Beneath the papers and layers of grime that had settled across everything, I thought I spied a marble-topped antique credenza as well as a few light fixtures that appeared to be original handblown glass. In general, though, the turn-of-the-century home's ambience was, by and large, twenty-first-century Frat Boy. It would require a lot of work, both structural and cosmetic, to transform this historic home into a welcoming B&B.

Haunted or otherwise.

"Have you happened to see our dog?" asked Anabelle. "A little cocker spaniel puppy?"

"No, I'm sorry."

"I've been looking for it. I'm sure it must be around

here somewhere. This way." She led the way down the hall to the left.

Several broad corridors spiraled off the central foyer. The hallway we walked down was lined with so many identical cream-colored doors the place felt a little more like a hotel than a private home. We passed a formal dining room with a built-in china hutch, a carved marble fireplace, and two impressive crystal chandeliers hanging from the coffered ceiling.

The size and grandeur of the room was compromised by the delaminating linoleum-topped table surrounded by at least a dozen mismatched chairs.

"I like your dress," said Anabelle, glancing over her shoulder. "You look like you could be in Ringling Brothers. We saw them when they came to town. They say it's the greatest show on earth."

I looked down at myself. It's true, I have a tendency to wear offbeat clothing. Nothing inappropriate, mind you, just . . . unexpected. I chalk this up to the years I spent in camouflage when I played the role of respectable faculty wife to a respectable Berkeley professor who turned out to be a not-so-respectable, cheating slimeball. The minute the ink was dry on my divorce papers, I yanked every scrap of my expensive Faculty Wife Wardrobe out of my closet and drove the whole kit and caboodle over to a women's shelter.

Once freed from my "respectable" constraints, I indulged my fondness for spangles and fringe with the help of my friend Stephen—an aspiring costume designer and the much-loved only son of a Vegas showgirl. It started as a joke, sort of, but soon became a "thing." My unconventional wardrobe inspired good-natured ribbing on the jobsite, where denim rules the day, but I'm serious about my profession: I always wear steel-toed work boots and bring along a pair of coveralls so as to be ready for any construction-related contingency.

But today I was meeting a client for the first time, so I had left the sparkles shut away in my closet in favor of a simple, above-the-knee patterned dress topped by a cardigan. Although an odd ensemble for *me*, to my eyes at least nothing about the outfit screamed "circus." Then I reminded myself that the residents of the Castro were famous for their outré fashions. Perhaps Anabelle wasn't accustomed to such uninspired attire in this neighborhood.

"I like your dress, as well," I said. "Especially the matching ribbons in your hair."

"It's called peony purple," she said, clutching a bit of the skirt in each hand and holding it up as though ready to curtsy. She gave me a big smile and turned down a narrow passage to the right.

Known locally as the Bernini house, after the family that had lived here for the past several decades, the building was exceptional not only for its square footage but also for its extensive grounds, which took up half a city block. The spacious courtyard garden stretched clear to the next street, where two outbuildings formed a border. This house was a stunner as it was; once renovated, it would be a rare gem. A landmark, even.

I wanted this job so much I could taste it. But there was no guarantee it would be mine.

The clients were also meeting with one of my competitors, Avery Builders. They were good—almost as good as Turner Construction, though it galled me to admit it. Avery and Turner had similar portfolios, and comparable track records for keeping on budget and on schedule. When competition for a job was this tight, the decision usually came down to whomever the clients liked more. Whom they felt more comfortable having in their homes, day in and day out, for months on end.

Client relations make me nervous. I'm a whiz at construction, and understand the ins and outs of buildings and architectural history as if they were in my blood. But when it comes to dealing with people, well . . . I'm fine. Up to a point. Mostly if they let me do what I want, and what I know is right for the house. Diplomacy is not my strong suit.

I did have one distinct advantage: As far as I knew, Avery Builders didn't have a ghost buster on staff, whereas Turner Construction could boast a real "up-and-comer" in the field of talking to the dead. Just ask *Haunted House Quarterly*.

Anabelle hummed as she walked ahead of me, finally breaking out into song: *"With garlands of roses, and whispers of pearls . . ."*

She glanced over her shoulder and smiled, displaying deep dimples. "Do you know that song?"

"I don't. But I'm no good at music."

"You don't play? I'm learning to play the piano."

"I tried my hand at the clarinet in the fifth grade. It wasn't pretty."

Anabelle gave me a withering look, as though I'd suggested she make mud pies in her nice purple dress. Usually I'm good with kids, because I don't take them—or myself—too seriously. My stepson, Caleb, and I had gotten off to a famously good start because I had immediately grasped why he felt compelled to wear his pirate costume and remain in character for more than a year before graduating, in a manner of speaking, to pretending to be the more "grown-up" Darth Vader. But then I have a flair for sword fights and laser battles, if I do say so myself.

"*. . . and gardens of posies for all little girrrrrls . . .*"

Anabelle resumed singing, slightly off tune, and stopped in front of a door that stood ajar. "Here we are. Have a seat, please, and I'll let them know you're here."

She skipped back down the hall, calling over her shoulder, "Good-bye. It was nice to meet you."

"Nice to meet you, too," I said, watching her go and marveling at the energy of youth. When was the last time I had skipped somewhere?

I pushed open the parlor door.

The room was empty.

Not just empty of people; it was vacant. No furniture, no rugs, no lights, no knickknacks. Nothing but a heavy coating of dust, a few scraps of paper on the floor, and a pair of shredded curtains on the large windows that overlooked a huge courtyard and garden. Through a cracked windowpane I could see a tall, rotund man in overalls, hard at work trimming a tall rosebush. Upon noticing me he stopped abruptly, staring, the pruning shears falling from his hand to the ground. I lifted my hand in greeting, but let it drop when he didn't respond. I felt a frisson of . . . *something* marching up my spine.

The afternoon sun sifting in through the antique wavy glass illuminated cobwebs in the corners, and a single paneled door I assumed led to a closet. I didn't see so much as a footstep—other than my own—in the dust on the floor, and the musty smell indicated the room hadn't been aired out for a very long time.

"Wait, Anabelle! I don't think . . ." I poked my head through the open door and peered down the long corridor, but the girl was gone.

Then a sound came from the opposite direction.

Clank, shuffle, clank, scrape.

I caught a glimpse of something passing in front of the arch at the end of the hall.

Some*one*, I reminded myself. *Get a grip, Mel. The child is playing a joke.*

"Hello?" I called out as I started down the dim corridor. "Anabelle?"

I heard it again: a slow step, a shuffle, a clank. My mind's eye conjured a picture of a ghost in chains. But that was an old Hollywood convention, not reality. I hoped.

Clank, shuffle, clank, scrape.

What *was* that?

And if this truly was a restless spirit, why should I be so surprised? I had been asked to the Bernini house to help broker a deal with the resident ghosts, after all. I just hadn't expected to see anything right off the bat, much less in the middle of a sunny afternoon.

I took a deep breath and fingered the simple gold band I wore on a chain around my neck, centering myself. All right, *fine.* If this was a ghost, so be it. It was essential to maintain one's resolve when going up against them. I'd learned that much, at least. Also important to keep in mind was that ghosts, being immaterial, can't physically harm a person. I was pretty sure. Actually . . . maybe I should double-check that little factoid. Despite my so-called "promising ghost buster" status, I'd encountered only two situations involving ghosts, and to be honest they still scared the you-know-what out of me.

Slowly, cautiously, I continued down the hallway to where it ended in a T, the sound growing louder with each step. *Clank, shuffle, clank, scrape. Clank, shuffle, clank, scrape.*

I took a deep breath, screwed up my courage . . . and peeked around the corner.

An old woman hunched over an aluminum walker was slowly making her way down the corridor. Her hair was a blue gray mass of stiff-set curls, and she wore an orange and yellow crochet afghan draped over her narrow shoulders. With each laborious step-push-step she made, her slippered feet and the walker sounded off: *clank, shuffle, clank, scrape.*

"Hello?" I said.

"Oh!" She let out a surprised yelp, one blue-veined hand fluttering up to her chest. "My word, you gave me a fright!"

"I'm so sorry," I said, still basking in relief at the sight of a flesh-and-blood woman instead of a spectral presence. "I'm Mel Turner, from Turner Construction?"

"Oh yes, of course. How do you do? I'm Betty Bernini."

"It's so nice to meet you. You have an amazing place here."

"Thank you. Come, we've been expecting you. The Propaks are in the front room." She resumed her slow progress, and I fell in step, resisting the urge to offer to help.

"I'm afraid I didn't hear the doorbell," Mrs. Bernini said as we walked. "Who let you in?"

"Anabelle answered the door, but she showed me to the parlor—the wrong room, I take it."

The clanking stopped as Mrs. Bernini straightened and fixed me with a steady gaze.

"Anabelle?"

"Yes, she's a sweetheart."

"Anabelle let you in."

I nodded, suddenly feeling guilty. Was Anabelle not supposed to answer the door? Had I gotten the girl in trouble?

"Let me show you something." Mrs. Bernini shuffled a little farther down the hall and opened the door to a bookshelf-lined study full of cardboard boxes, stacked furniture, and a cracked old leather couch. She gestured to an oil painting hanging over the fireplace. Done in rich old-master hues of blue, red, and burnt sienna, it featured a girl and a slightly younger boy. She stood with one hand on the boy's shoulder, while he held a cocker spaniel puppy.

The girl had long chestnut brown curls, tied in pretty ribbons.

Peony purple.

A brass plate on the picture frame read:

Anabelle and Ezekiel Bowles. 1911.

Chapter Two

"This is so *exciting!*" said Kim Propak as she placed a tray of packaged cookies on the coffee table and perched on the edge of a worn brocade sofa. Her husband, Marty Propak, Mrs. Bernini, and I had taken our seats in a front room that overlooked the street. "I can't believe they've already made contact! You're *amazing!*"

With her pert blond pageboy and single strand of pearls, Kim Propak reminded me of a fiftyish Doris Day. Hard to dislike . . . but also a wee bit annoying.

I was still reeling from the fact that I'd been met at the door by a darling girl whose only sign of being dead was her old-fashioned dress and—I realized as I thought about it—her button-up shoes. I hadn't had a clue Anabelle was not from our mortal world until after the fact. She hadn't appeared transparent, or hazy, or not entirely "here," like the other ghosts I'd seen. Nor had she floated down the hall, or faded in and out, or appeared in a cloud of black smoke, or in any other way seemed detached from reality.

Seeing ghosts was one thing, but if I couldn't tell the difference between a spirit and a real person ... ? That was truly crazy-making.

Marty Propak seemed to notice my discomfiture at his wife's effusive enthusiasm. No Rock Hudson to her Doris Day, he was a small man with thinning, short-cropped curly brown hair graying at the temples. His mild brown eyes were obscured by the frames of heavy tortoiseshell glasses, which gave him a scholarly air.

"I must confess, we didn't expect you to see anything so, er, soon. Or so easily." Marty sat forward on the old red brocade couch, his hands clasped primly together. "And the ... uh ... little girl ... what did she seem like?"

"Anabelle? She was very polite, very sweet," I replied, taking off my sweater. The front room, unlike the rest of the house, was warmed by a space heater and felt quite snug. Many people with huge houses wound up using only a small percentage of their space—I had the sense this was a truly lived-in room.

"This is so exciting!" Kim repeated with a happy sigh, clapping her hands together as though vowing that she *did* believe in fairies.

But I knew, from my admittedly limited experience, that those reaching out from beyond the veil weren't carnival attractions or exciting oddities to be exploited for the entertainment of live humans. From what I could tell, ghosts were souls in need: usually confused, sometimes angry, and often looking for help.

Which begged the question: What did Anabelle want?

"Mrs. Bernini," I asked, "are you related to the children in the portrait?"

"Oh, no." Mrs. Bernini shook her head. "We found that painting up in the attic. It must have been there since my husband, Angelo, and I moved in years ago. I had half a mind to throw it away—I confess I thought it was a bit insipid!—but my young friend Portia said it was worth money, that it was a portrait of the children of the family who built the home."

"Portia Kirkbride has an antiques store on Castro Street. She's helped us to piece together some of the early history of the house," Marty explained. "It was built in 1901. The original owner was a physician, apparently from a well-to-do family, and respected in the early days of medicine here in the city. He was instrumental in establishing the San Francisco Physicians' College. That's one reason we were attracted to renovating the property."

As I listened to Marty, my attention was focused on Mrs. Bernini. I knew her husband had passed away last year, after sixty years of marriage. The couple had raised numerous foster children in this house. Their finances had taken a turn for the worse when Angelo became ill with cancer, and his final medical bills had eaten through their nest egg. Maintaining a house like this in San Francisco must cost a fortune, which I assumed explained the odd decorating choices, lack of heat, and neglect of basic maintenance.

"Have you seen the ghosts yourself?" I asked Mrs. Bernini.

"I never *saw* any of them, exactly. A glimpse here and there, at most. My Angelo saw things on occasion, and a couple of the children were, well, sensitive. Poor little Homer was quite taken aback—he really found them frightening." She handed me a framed school photo of a redheaded, freckle-faced boy with a rather goofy smile. I couldn't help but think of Howdy Doody.

"So cute," I said.

"He's a man now, of course." Her smile faded, and her eyes appeared troubled. "Lately, though, I think the spirits . . . the haunting . . . has gotten worse."

"Ghosts are often disturbed by changes—especially renovations."

"That's what *I* said!" said Kim, leaning toward me conspiratorially. "I've been boning up. So to speak."

"The neighbors told me there was a tragedy associated with this house," said Mrs. Bernini. "I guess maybe that's why we got it so cheap—well, that and the fact that this area wasn't as desirable back then. But I always loved it here, so I never really believed the stories. But lately . . . I've been hearing terrible sounds."

"Sounds?"

"There's a loud scraping noise overhead." Her thin shoulders rose toward her ears and she shivered. "It happens all the time these days. And then there are occasional horses' hooves outside, and the sound of marbles rolling along the floor. . . . In fact, we have found a number of marbles over the years."

My eyes flickered over to a fishbowl half-filled with marbles. Mrs. Bernini followed my gaze, nodding.

"Also, we used to have an old radio here, which was original to the house. It had a mind of its own: used to play whether it was turned on or not."

Kim blinked. "What did it play?"

Mrs. Bernini shrugged. "Old-timey music. Once when Homer was visiting it started up, and he got so mad he finally took it to the antiques shop—that's how I first met Portia. I liked the music, myself. The sound that really bothers me is the scraping. It sounds like something's being dragged, and then the bed in the master moves."

"Your bed?"

"Used to be, but once Angelo got sick, we moved downstairs. I went up the other day for the first time in years, but my knees protested. The playroom—"

"*I* think we should let Mel discover such things on her own, don't you?" interrupted Kim with a tight smile.

"Oh, of course," said Mrs. Bernini as she nibbled on a cookie.

Kim was probably right—I had purposefully avoided gleaning too much information about the Bernini estate beforehand, preferring instead to come in "cold." Still, something about Kim's officiousness rubbed me the wrong way.

"Where do your children live now?" I asked Mrs. Bernini.

"They've fanned all over the world. That's how it is with foster children—some are here just briefly. The ones that were here longer term, I keep in touch with all of them. I just love e-mail, don't you? And I just learned to Skype. Several of them came for Angelo's funeral; it was lovely. But only Homer's right here in San Francisco. He has his own deli off Bayshore Boulevard, near where Goodman's Lumber used to be? He does very well."

Kim started describing some of her decorating plans, which would be important information when—if—

renovation began. For the moment, though, I was more interested in getting a feel for the home's bones, for the vibrations in the walls.

". . . and then a floral wing, with rooms named after flowers. I was thinking, maybe, the Rose Room, and the Bluebell Room, and the Lilac Room. Oh! The Posy Room! Wouldn't that be *cute*?" She didn't wait for a reply. "And the Rose Room will be pink and red, the Bluebell Room will be blue, the Lilac Room will be shades of purple, and the Posy Room could be . . . hmm. Well, fiddledeedee, we'll work that out. . . ."

I listened with half an ear and studied the room. There were numerous examples of what Realtors referred to as "deferred maintenance" and what everybody else called long-overdue repairs. I noted signs of dry rot around the windows, and a web of cracks in the plaster. The chandelier had pulled away from the ceiling, exposing its wiring, and was missing several of its crystal drops. There was another old water stain on the ceiling, indicating a serious problem with the roof. Over time, water damage could be devastating to a structure.

I knew that Mrs. Bernini couldn't afford to make the needed repairs, and yet she wanted to stay in her home. This was where Kim and Marty Propak, formerly of Fort Wayne, Indiana, came in. They had taken over the house payments, and had agreed to a price for the house upon her death, when ownership would transfer to them.

"We don't want this to be just another bed-and-breakfast." Kim beamed, her eyes sparkling with excitement. "It will be a *haunted* bed-and-breakfast! I'm writing a book about the renovation, with pictures, and plans and everything! It won't be just Marty and me, of course. Betty will live here just as long as she wants. Which I know will be a long, long time!"

Kim smiled and squeezed the elderly woman's thin arm. It might have been my imagination, but I thought Mrs. Bernini looked a little pained at the familiarity. Or perhaps I was sensing her awkwardness at knowing her housemates were waiting for her to die.

"Oh, and I should mention that we're being discreet about our plans for the moment," said Marty. "We want to present the idea to the neighborhood when everything's set to go, to cut down on interference. This neighborhood is very . . . well . . . people have strong opinions."

I nodded. Neighbor relations were always a challenge. Add the prospect of a year or so of construction into the mix, and things could get volatile. It was smart to go in armed with finalized drawings, permits, and work orders.

"We've been working with an architect, but we wanted to settle on a contractor before going any further. Also, Mrs. Bernini's opinion is very important to us. We want her to be happy."

A soft knock on the door cut me off. It was the man in overalls, the one I had seen in the garden from the window of the empty parlor.

"Sorry to interrupt," he said as he set a vase full of roses on a side table. "Just wanted to let you know I finished up trimming those bushes, Mrs. Bernini. I'm going to start on that water feature next."

"Oh, that's lovely. Please come in, Gerald. I'd like you to meet Mel Turner."

I, for one, was relieved to know this fellow was not a specter. I had wondered after I spied him from the empty parlor. He carried pruning shears in one hand and wore a straw hat over his auburn hair. He wasn't chubby, just tall and big-boned, his hands in what must have been extra-large leather work gloves. He had a full beard and a ruddy complexion, and wore a plaid shirt, the combination of which made him look like a lumberjack or a refugee from the Scottish Highland Games.

"Good to meet you," he said. I found his gaze a shade too intense, too demanding, and I wondered what his story was. "I'd shake your hand, but I'm not fit for it at the moment."

"Nice to meet you, Gerald."

"Everyone—except Mrs. Bernini—calls me Mountain."

"I'm Mel," I said. "The gardens are lovely."

"I've been bringing the old perennials back to life, and next I'll be working on the Victorian cutting garden. Are you familiar with cutting gardens?" The Propaks both looked away, as though barely refraining from rolling their eyes. I got the impression that Mountain was more excited about his work in the garden than the home's nominal owners.

I opened my mouth to reply, but Mountain went on without waiting for a response. "They don't require the formal design or layout of a decorative garden, but rather they're planted for efficient use of space and easy harvest of the flowers, which in a climate like ours means that this house can have fresh flowers in vases all year round. I've planted yarrow, phlox, rudbeckia, otherwise known as black-eyed Susans—"

"Gerald, dear, we talked about the cutting garden last time, remember?" Mrs. Bernini interrupted. "Perhaps we can discuss this later."

"Oh . . . sure." He met my eyes and nodded. "Nice to meet you."

"Same here." After he left, I added, "From what I can see from the windows, it looks like he's doing a wonderful job."

"Oh, he's very devoted," Mrs. Bernini said. "He's coaxed the place back to life. I walk in the gardens every evening. You should take a turn through them before you go. . . . But first, I think we should go over the bidding process for the renovation. We have a somewhat unusual proposition for you."

"Unusual?" I asked, wary. Just what I needed in my life. More unusual.

"Mel, we were *so* impressed with your portfolio, and you come so highly recommended!" Kim beamed at me from her perch on the edge of the couch. She seemed anxious to ingratiate herself with me. Or maybe that's just the way folks were in Fort Wayne, Indiana; I'd never been. "But . . . well, you're not going to believe this." She paused dramatically, shaking her head. I couldn't help but notice that her hair didn't move, hinting at an intimate relationship with Clairol Extra Hold. "We've had two other contractors come out, but they were frightened off by the idea of ghosts, if you can believe it. Grown men!"

"I believe it," I said. Despite their macho affectations, a lot of construction workers were highly superstitious. Of course, a lot of them had cause.

"As you know," interjected Marty, and I got the feeling that they'd rehearsed this little duet, "we've contacted Avery Builders, as well. They're quite interested."

"I'll bet."

"So this is what we propose: We'd like you to spend the night here in the house. It's important that you be able to work with all the home's residents, the living as well as the departed. We're hoping you could speak with them, explain what we're doing, and communicate that we're happy to have them here."

"You want me to negotiate the renovations . . . with the ghosts," I clarified.

The Propaks nodded. Mrs. Bernini looked uncomfortable.

"Tell me—did you also propose this arrangement to Thomas Avery?" I smiled at the thought of the head of Avery Builders—a humorless sort if ever there was one—fleeing in terror from a spirit.

"Thomas Avery isn't the one interested in the project. It's his nephew, Josh."

"Josh Avery? I don't know him."

"Apparently he's working with his uncle to learn the skills of the trade, with the intention of taking over the business. One generation passing the torch to the next."

"Ah. And can this Josh fellow communicate with ghosts?"

Kim and Marty exchanged a glance.

"Not that we know of," Kim replied. "Maybe!"

"Even if he can't," Marty said, "at the very least, we want the contractor we select to be able to deal with whatever . . . encounters . . . they might experience in the house. Like the odd sounds, and the furniture moving."

"I see," I said.

"There's one more thing," Marty said, and paused for effect. "Kim and I are committed to bringing the house back to its former glory. We'd like to incorporate a few new items, such as a decent heating system and Internet wiring, and plumbing in some private bathrooms for the guests. But overall, we'd like to restore its historic character, use vintage items, that sort of thing."

Words like that made my heart sing. This was my passion.

"As I'm sure you know," Marty continued, "my brother serves on the board of American Architectural Design. He and I think this house would be a great candidate for the AIA award for historic renovation. Also, as Kim mentioned, she has a contract for a picture book documenting the renovation and the history of the house. The ghosts will make a great addition to the story."

In order to be considered for the prestigious American Institute of Architects award, the renovation would have to be well documented every step of the way.

"Are you working with a photographer?" I asked.

"We were, but ... a few things happened...." Kim glanced at her husband. "She wasn't comfortable working around spirits. Some people are *so* sensitive. You wouldn't happen to know a good local photographer, would you?"

"As a matter of fact, I do have a friend who might be available." Checking the directory on my phone, I jotted down Zach Malinski's name and number and handed the note to Kim. Calling Zach a "friend" was a bit of a stretch considering he had once sort of kidnapped me. But I still liked him.

"To go back to the overnight visit: You want potential contractors to spend the night in this presumably haunted house in order to win the renovation contract?"

Kim and Marty nodded eagerly.

What they were proposing sounded like a plot for a B movie featuring scantily clad teenagers and psychopaths wielding chain saws. I glanced around the room looking for cameras, half hoping this was a new reality show for the do-it-yourself crowd: *Punk the Contractor*.

All I saw was the pleasant countenance of Mrs. Bernini, the excited smile of Kim-the-Doris-Day-look-alike, the earnest gaze of Marty Propak, and a house that really, really needed me.

Still, no way would I participate in a stunt like this. It was . . . undignified.

On the other hand . . . I could almost taste that AIA award. It was something I had coveted for years, steadily working toward it, and this would be the closest I had ever come.

And yet . . . surely I hadn't fallen so low.

"I thought it might be fun," said Mrs. Bernini, noting my hesitancy. "You could bring a friend or two, and I would be here, and it would be like a slumber party. We could order pizza!"

As she spoke, Mrs. Bernini's eyes lit up and she looked, for a moment, like a young woman. I couldn't help but return her smile. But still . . .

Spending the night in a haunted house to win a renovation contract?

Nope. Nuh-uh. No way.

I have my pride.

Chapter Three

Who was I kidding? I have no pride.

My best friend, Luz, drove me to the Bernini estate the following Saturday evening. Luz was originally from East LA, had clawed her way through college and grad school through sheer grit and determination, and was now a professor of social work at San Francisco State University. She wasn't daunted by much of anything ... except ghosts. And clowns.

"Sure you won't join us?" I teased. "It'll be fun. We're going to order pizza."

"Tempting as that offer is," she said, "it's not sufficient incentive to risk being eaten by ghosts."

"I think you're mixing up ghosts and zombies."

"Whatever. I still don't understand why you're doing this."

"This is the way to get the job. Besides, getting away

from Dad's House of Testosterone isn't the worst idea in the world."

Through a quirk of fate, I live in a big old farmhouse in Oakland with my father, an old family friend named Stan Tomassi, and a former stray dog—male, of course— that has yet to be named. Lately my stepson, Caleb, has been spending a lot of time with us, hanging out with the boys.

I love them all, but this had not been the plan. After my divorce a few years ago, all I wanted was to move to Paris and hide away from the world for a decade or two. I had a vision of myself as a romantic, hauntingly thin woman of mystery who occasionally emerged from her Left Bank atelier only to wander the Champs-Élysées, eat a soupçon of *glace à la cerise*, and entrance a few handsome Frenchmen before disappearing into the Parisian fog to return to her exquisitely solo pity party. *That* had been the plan.

Instead, my mother passed away suddenly, my stunned and grieving father fell apart, and before I quite knew what was happening, I had taken over the reins of the family business, had moved into my father's house, and was living, working, and breathing in the male-dominated world of construction. And if anything, I'd *gained* ten pounds over the last couple of years.

At times I was a little grumpy about it all.

"I understand wanting to take a break from the boys," Luz continued. "But if you ask me, a 'break' should involve mai tais on a foreign beach somewhere, not spending the night in an alleged haunted house."

"It's more than 'alleged,'" I said as we pulled up to find my friends Stephen and Claire leaning against her red Toyota truck, whose magnetic door panels read CLAIRE'S LIVING THINGS. "From what I witnessed the other day, I think it's pretty much fact. This is one genuine haunted house."

As soon as we'd parked and joined them, Claire took a bright orange Tootsie Pop out of her mouth and gestured with it. "Cool house. Didn't know they grew 'em this big in this part of town."

"What's with the candy?"

"Want one? I've got plenty."

"No thanks."

"Oral fixation."

Stephen shot her a questioning look.

"I'm trying to quit smoking," she explained in a scratchy, deep voice that sounded as though she'd gone through a pack a day since puberty. "And just for the record, New Year's resolutions blow."

Claire was petite and flat-chested, tattooed, and wore "steampunk"-inspired clothing, which, she explained, was sort of a mix of punk, Goth, and Victoriana. Her straight dark hair and slightly almond eyes hinted at a mixed Asian heritage, but she'd never volunteered the information and I hadn't had the guts to ask. Despite— or perhaps because of—her diminutive size, she drank and swore like a sailor on shore leave after six months at sea. Claire was also a gifted landscape architect, and surprisingly good at intuiting clients' needs and coping with their sometimes unreasonable whims. I'd invited her to come along tonight in part so she could check out the gorgeous gardens of the Bernini estate, but also because of all my friends Claire seemed brash enough not to be put off by the undead. I imagined she could kick butt if riled. She was already edgy, and nicotine withdrawal is not pretty.

Stephen was here only because I had made the mistake of telling him about the sleepover, and he had begged to come along. I didn't have the heart to say no. Stephen was tall, pale, and so slender that I feared he would be knocked over by a strong gust of wind. He reminded me of a consumptive poet from the nineteenth century, an impression enhanced tonight by his sage green velvet waistcoat with tails.

I was wearing one of Stephen's designs, as well. A fairly tame one: a wine-colored shift with spaghetti straps and a spray of silk roses at the hemline. Over it I wore a long black and purple knit sweater that fell past my knees. My feet were clad in my steel-toed work boots because, well, I *always* wear my steel-toed work boots.

"I gotta tell you, you three look like refugees from a community theater production of *Peer Gynt*," Luz said as she joined us on the porch. Her eyes raked over the facade and she raised an eyebrow in my direction. "*This* is the house you're so in love with?"

"It needs me."

"Huh," she said, clearly unconvinced.

Just then a shiny black full-sized truck with "Avery Builders" painted in scrolled letters pulled into the drive. From the cab emerged a well-built man in his thirties. Tall, broad-shouldered, and blond, he was a Viking in work boots and plaid shirt. He had a sleeping bag tucked under one brawny arm, and a duffel bag slung over his shoulder like an Eagle Scout. Or maybe a Navy SEAL.

Josh must take after his mother's side of the family. I

had known Tom Avery for years; he was an excellent contractor, but he was also short, blustery, and overweight, and had a drinking problem.

Luz glanced over at me, raising her eyebrows and sticking out her chin as if to say, *Not bad. Not bad at all.*

I widened my eyes at her in reply: *Zip it.*

She flashed a big grin. "I tell you what, girlfriend, you do land yourself in some interesting situations. All right, all you intrepid ghost busters, listen up. Have fun tonight, and be careful. If you find yourself in need of rescue, whatever you do, *do not* call me. Upon the morrow, should you decide it's time for a mental health assessment, I'm your gal. And the offer of bail for misdemeanor offenses stands."

Luz climbed into her car and took off as Josh made a beeline for Stephen.

"Hello there. You must be Mel Turner," he said, holding his hand out to shake. "I'm Josh, Thomas Avery's nephew."

"Nice to meet you, but I'm Stephen. *This*" — Stephen put his arm around my shoulders — "is Mel, short for Melanie."

I elbowed him in the ribs for outing my real name.

Josh blinked. My gender was a surprise, no doubt, but I imagined this evening's getup wasn't helping him envision me as his cutthroat competition.

We shook hands and exchanged business cards.

"I didn't realize we were supposed to bring backup," said Josh, looking at my companions.

I hadn't realized tonight's sleepover was going to include my rival. I had assumed we'd be here on different nights.

"They're my . . . assistants," I said, unwilling to admit

that I was afraid to spend the night by myself. "Claire Allen and Stephen Nikolai."

"Ghost-hunting assistants," explained Claire, looking about twelve years old with that sucker in her mouth. At the mention of ghosts, Stephen's Adam's apple bobbed up and down and he wrung his hands, as skittish as a kite at the marina. It occurred to me our colorful trio might not make the best impression on my potential clients. Especially standing next to the overgrown Eagle Scout with the big-boy truck.

It was a little late to indulge in that kind of thinking, so I pushed the thought aside and knocked loudly on the door. I half expected little Anabelle to answer.

"Speaking of ghosts—," Josh began, but stopped when the door opened.

"Welcome, *welcome*," Kim Propak practically squealed as Marty, next to her, smiled. "Isn't this *exciting*?"

"Very," I said.

"Oh, come in, come in. And these must be your friends," said Kim as her blue eyes raked over us. She seemed to hesitate, but her smile remained intact.

"I hope it's okay I brought a couple of—"

"Ghost-busting assistants," interrupted Claire, putting her hand out to shake. "Nice to meet you."

"Oh, of course. Assistants! Isn't that nice? I'm going to put you three in the east wing, and Josh in the west."

"I'll show you to your room," said Marty to Josh.

"And the rest of you, follow me," said Kim as she headed for the stairs.

Claire and Stephen fell silent, looking about the place with wide eyes. We climbed to the second floor and took a right at the landing. At the very end of the hall sat a towering old grandfather clock.

"Beautiful clock," I said. "Does it work?"

"Sadly, no. Mrs. Bernini told me she tried to have it fixed, but no matter what they do, it stops at twelve after one, every time. Here we are!" said Kim as she flung open a door with a flourish. "I would give you all separate rooms, but although there are plenty of chambers, several are used for storage, and only a few have decent furniture."

The room was large, and set up with five twin beds. Intricate crown moldings and an inset tray ceiling gave the room character, but the furniture was a mishmash of chests of drawers, bureaus, and cheap plastic cubbies. Three big guillotine windows overlooked the courtyard garden, subtly lit by the moon and low path lights.

"Would you all like to share this room? Or, Stephen, would you like your own accommodations?"

"I think we should all stay together," I said.

"No worries, he's our gay best friend," Claire told Kim.

"That's right," said Stephen with a glare. "Except that I'm not gay."

"Who's not gay?" said Marty as he joined Kim at the door.

"Stephen, it seems," answered Kim. "Well, to each their own, is what I say. Marty and I have, well, what you'd call a more traditional marriage. But we're just fine with all the . . . 'alternative' ways of life. You know, we're not from here."

"You could have fooled me," Stephen said.

I shot him a look.

"Aren't you just a *dear*?" Kim said. "We knew the Castro's reputation before we got here, of course, but we're still getting used to the neighborhood. I do adore it, though. Don't you, honey?"

Marty nodded. "It's very . . . vibrant."

"Over the Christmas holidays we saw naked Santas! Right out on the street! Not that there's anything wrong with it, of course. But we didn't have this sort of thing back in Fort Wayne, if you know what I mean."

"I *do*," Stephen said. "I know *exactly* what you mean."

"This room will be fine. Thank you, Kim," I said, hoping to bring this little chat to an end.

"Marty and I are staying just down the street, at the Lincoln B&B." She handed me a piece of scratch paper with a phone number. "Don't tell anyone, but we're checking out the competition. Plus, we don't want to mess up the signals or anything." She leaned toward me and said in a conspiratorial voice, "I'm very *sensitive*. You know what that's like, Mel."

"Sure do," I said, relieved to learn they were leaving. "But Mrs. Bernini's staying, right?"

"Oh yes. Her bedroom's on the first floor, on the other side of the kitchen. She's very attached to this place."

"I imagine she'll enjoy having guests in when the inn is up and running."

"Oh, I doubt she'll last that long," Kim said. She slapped her hand across her mouth. "Oh! That sounded just *awful*! I simply meant that, well, she's elderly, and we all know how long these remodels can drag on. . . ."

"She's welcome here as long as she wants, of course," Marty hastened to reassure us.

"Of course!" Kim said brightly.

"Of course," I said, though it seemed clear that Kim and Marty wanted Mrs. Bernini out of the house as soon as possible. I felt a twinge of doubt: Did I really want to work for these people?

"Anyway," Kim said, "why don't you all leave your things here? The bathroom's the second door on your right. The central heater's out of commission, but the space heater warms things up quickly. Mrs. Bernini insists on keeping that big fridge chock-full of food, so help yourself to anything you'd like in the kitchen. And by all means, feel free to look around, explore. That's what you're here for."

"Thank you, we'll be fine."

"Don't forget, if you need anything, anything at all, call us at the Lincoln. It's a darling place, run by a *charming* gay couple."

"Sweetheart," said Marty. "You don't have to point out that they're gay every time."

"I don't mean anything by it. Did it sound like I meant something by it?" she asked Stephen. He gave her a reassuring wink.

Marty shook his head and smiled. "Let's go, dear."

"Buh-bye," said Stephen.

"We'll see you all in the morning!" said Kim. Then she waggled her eyebrows. "Or *not*, if you're scared right out into the night."

Chapter Four

I closed the door, leaned back against it, and breathed a sigh of relief.

Claire made a "whoa" face, eyebrows raised, eyes wide.

Stephen just smiled and shook his head. "I think she means well. But . . . lots of energy there. Maybe she'll calm down when she has the whole inn to run." He took a few items out of his backpack and started to fold them neatly into a bureau drawer.

"You moving in?" asked Claire.

"Just getting settled. My mother always used to say, 'No matter how short the stay, no one should live out of a suitcase.'"

Claire rolled her eyes. "*My* mother used to say, 'Stop crying or I'll smack you.'"

Stephen and I stared at her.

"What?" She stuck a piece of licorice in her mouth.

"It was sort of a tough-love situation. Seven brothers and sisters."

"Still, sounds a little . . . harsh."

"So, I've got issues." She shrugged. "Whatever."

"Hey, gang, I want to go find Mrs. Bernini and say hi."

"And order food? Didn't you lure me here with the promise of pizza?" Stephen asked, conveniently forgetting that he'd lobbied to come with me. "I'm starved."

"Feel free to raid my stash." Claire held out a bag that looked as though she had just returned with her Halloween haul. She peered down into the depths. "I've got Red Vines, Twizzlers, standard lollies, jawbreakers, bubble gum, lots of stuff. Help yourself."

Fortified with sour apple Jolly Ranchers and Fireballs, we started down the hall.

The sound of water dripping in a steady *tick-tick-tick* led us to a spacious but outdated bathroom.

The leaking faucet had left a rust mark on the scratched porcelain sink. I tightened the tarnished brass grip, and the dripping stopped. All the fixtures—other than the toilet—appeared to be original to the house, which was rare. Even the humblest homeowners typically redid their bathrooms and kitchens at some point, and those inexpensive remodels were almost always to the detriment of a historic building.

Tatty and in need of a good scrubbing, the lavatory was otherwise charming. I took in the hexagonal tiles on the floor, subway tile on the walls, two pedestal sinks, and huge claw-footed tub. Though the fixtures would need to be removed, resurfaced, and reinstalled, they would make it simple to recapture the bath's original design. I noticed there were no electrical outlets. Back when they were installing electricity in this home, blow-dryers and electric curlers hadn't been invented.

I caught a whiff of mildew, and noticed the small ventilation window appeared to have been painted shut. There was no exhaust fan, either, which was common in old homes where ventilation was primarily passive, achieved through windows or air vents running through the walls. It was good for the environment—in fact, a lot of "green" builders were returning to such traditional methods—but such vents had to be designed and installed properly in order to draw the air effectively. I made a mental note to check that out.

In the corridor, the threadbare runner covered scratched hardwood floors. I opened a couple of doors, revealing bedrooms that were empty or crammed with junk—from furniture to magazines to stacks of cardboard boxes.

A set of double doors led to the master bedroom, which had a few boxes piled in one corner but looked, by and large, inhabitable. A water-stained but intricately painted floral frieze ran between the tall crown molding and a picture rail. There was a matching bureau and highboy set, an old-fashioned vanity, and a queen-sized iron bed sitting slightly askew from the wall.

Could this be the bed that moved, from time to time? Stephen and Claire waited in the hall while I sat on the edge of the mattress, bouncing up and down lightly.

"Just checking," I said in response to their questioning looks. "There's been some . . . activity with this bed. Or so they say."

"I don't want to hear about it," said Stephen, blushing.

"I *meant* paranormal-type activity. Seems normal at the moment."

Directly across the hall from the master was another set of double doors. Claire tried the glass knob, but it was locked.

"I'll bet Mrs. Bernini has the key," I said.

"I'll bet there's a *reason* it's locked," said Stephen, eyes wide.

"*I'll* bet I could open it in two minutes with a bobby pin," said Claire, bending over to inspect the old-fashioned keyhole. "Or any skeleton key should open it."

"Let's refrain from referring to skeletons, shall we?" said Stephen.

Claire cast a disgusted look his way. "At this rate you're not going to make it through dinner, pal."

Then came a far-off sound: *clank, shuffle, scrape.*

Claire grabbed Stephen's arm. They both stopped in their tracks, wide-eyed. At this rate, *neither* of them was going to make it through the dinner hour.

"That's just Mrs. Bernini," I said. "She uses a walker. Let's find Josh, and we can all go down and meet her."

From the upstairs windows I could see long white fingers of coastal fog creeping down over nearby Twin Peaks, and it was starting to drizzle. It seemed a perfect night for a haunting.

We finally found Josh's sleeping bag and duffel in an innocuous-looking bedroom in the wing opposite ours, but he was nowhere to be found.

"Must be exploring," I said.

"Just so he's not been eaten," said Stephen.

Claire blew a gargantuan bubble with her gum, popped it, and said, "Zombies. Or werewolves."

"Excuse me?"

"Don't you ever go to the movies? Only zombies or

werewolves actually *eat* you. Vampires suck your blood. But ghosts mostly scare the crap out of you."

"Thank you," I said. "You see, Stephen? Independent verification."

We descended the stairs and found Mrs. Bernini in the kitchen.

"Mrs. Bernini, I'd like you to meet my friends, Claire and Stephen. Claire is a gifted landscape architect. I told her about your gardens."

"You'll have to meet my friend Gerald. He calls himself Mountain, since he's a big boy. You'll look like a hobbit next to him!"

Claire smiled gamely. She wasn't wild about anyone— even a harmless old woman—teasing her about her size.

"And Stephen, what do you do, a handsome young fellow like you?"

"I'm a barista."

"A what, dear?"

He smiled. "I work at a café, making specialty coffees. But my real love is costume design."

Mrs. Bernini looked puzzled, but gave him a vague smile.

"Have you seen Josh?" I asked. "Big, tall, blond . . ."

"Gorgeous," Claire added.

The elderly woman shook her head. "Only you. Is there someone else here? I swear, there could be a small army in this house and I wouldn't know it. That's why we needed foster children, just to fill it up."

I glanced at my watch—it was almost eight. "Let's go ahead and order—he'll turn up."

"Sylven's has wonderful pizza. I like just about any- thing except anchovies. Sometimes they make me up a special pie, custom-made just for me. Isn't that sweet?"

We agreed to take our chances with a custom pizza that might include just about anything except anchovies.

"Young man, will you bring me that magnet off the refrigerator?"

Stephen obliged, and Mrs. Bernini dialed Sylven's Pizza. From her side of the conversation, it was clear she was a regular customer.

After hanging up, Mrs. Bernini opened an enormous pocketbook and handed me a crumpled twenty-dollar bill. "Here, for the pizza."

"It's on me," I said.

"Nonsense. Take the money. I'm glad for your company. And tip the delivery fellow well. He's a good boy, takes care of his mother."

For the next half hour Mrs. Bernini kept us entertained with stories about her foster children and the evolving flavor of the neighborhood over the past several decades. But then she was interrupted by something that sounded like the hollow clops of horses' hooves on cobblestone streets. We heard the clink and clank of a carriage, a whinny, and the jangle of a harness.

"What is *that*?" Stephen asked in a loud whisper.

Mrs. Bernini said, "Pizza's here."

"Well, that's something different," I said as I headed for the door. "But doesn't horse and carriage seem a bit much in the city?"

"This *is* the Castro," Claire said.

We opened the front door to find a young man in a Giants baseball jacket and an Oakland A's cap covering his long, dark hair. "Oh, hey . . . ," he said. "Where's Mrs. Bernini? She all right?"

I peered beyond him to find a beat-up yellow Volkswagen Rabbit with an illuminated Sylven's Pizza sign on the roof. It seemed awfully pedestrian when one expected a horse and carriage.

"Hello, Raj, sweetheart," Mrs. Bernini called out, as she slowly made her way across the foyer. "How's your mother?"

He shrugged. "Not so good. How you doin', Mrs. B.?"

"Fine, thank you," she said. "I'd like you to meet my young friends. They're here to redo the house."

"You're redoing the house?"

"Oh, that's right; we're supposed to be keeping it quiet. Don't mention anything, will you? Those boys at the shop—I adore them, but they're *such* gossips. Now, you keep the change on that twenty."

He nodded and mumbled, "Thanks," as he turned back into the chilly night.

I followed Raj out onto the porch and tried to tip him a couple more dollars. It was raining, after all.

"Naw, that's okay," he said. "Mrs. B.'s special. 'Preciate it, though. Oh, hey, with all this rain you should check for water in the basement. There's, like, a stream running through there."

"Thanks. I'll check."

After calling in vain for Josh one more time, we set ourselves up on the big old linoleum table in the dining room and grabbed a roll of paper towels and plates, family-style. There were two pizzas, one with a white sauce and one with a red. Either this was one cheap pizza joint, or they cut Mrs. Bernini a special deal.

"So, I have to ask, do you hear the sounds of horses every time someone comes to the door?"

"Occasionally. And only at night. Some say the sound dates back to when this place operated as a maternity hospital, and patients used to be brought here by carriage at all hours of the night. I've gotten rather used to such sounds, so I don't give them much thought anymore."

Stephen set down his slice of pizza—pea pods and shrimp on a white garlic sauce—as though he had lost his appetite.

"I've been trying to convince my friends that while ghosts can be frightening, they can't hurt you."

"That's right," she said with a thoughtful nod. "Although ... I'd just ... perhaps stay out of the nursery."

"The nursery?" I asked.

"It's across from the master bedroom. It ... well, we used to let the children play there, but it made them feel odd. And Homer swore he saw ghosts there. And then there are those darned marbles."

"I admit, I'm curious. Do you have the key to that room?"

"You don't need one."

"The door was locked."

"It will open tonight."

We all stared at her.

"What did you all think when you came to spend the night in a haunted house? The place has its own way of doing things. I just stay out of the way."

I wondered whether I would ever become so sanguine about living full-time with such oddities. On the other hand, if you came to expect such things, and they never harmed you, I suppose one might become inured. I couldn't help but notice that at the moment there were no ghostly figures walking by, no scraping sounds, nothing out of the ordinary beyond the horses' hooves. The home felt warm and welcoming, just as a bed-and-breakfast should.

"I wanted to mention that I have a friend who hauls things," I said. "He's very good at helping to clean out homes. I've noticed that some of the rooms are full of odds and ends."

Mrs. Bernini nodded. "It's too easy to close the doors and forget what you have. But now I've got Portia helping me to figure out what's here that's worth something. Every time she visits, she hauls some of this stuff out of here."

"That's a good approach," I said around a garlicky bite of pizza. "Go slowly so it doesn't seem overwhelming. And it's easier with another person, to help you make some decisions about what to keep or sell or give away." I thought about how to bring up the next subject tactfully. "You do understand that when we start converting the house into a bed-and-breakfast, there will be some major changes."

Her eyes dimmed and she played with her pizza, carefully peeling off a piece of pepperoni. She nodded vaguely but didn't say anything.

"Anybody want tea?" Claire suggested, standing up. "Come on, Stephen, let's go figure out the electric kettle."

They left to give us some privacy.

"Mrs. Bernini, are you comfortable with all the work the Propaks plan to do here?"

"Of course. I signed the agreement."

"I know that. But I'm sure if you've changed your mind . . . no one wants to force you to do something you're not ready for."

She shook her head. "No, that wouldn't be right. I just . . . I might have made some promises to people, and I hope they won't be upset. . . ." She waved a blue-veined hand across her face. "Oh, I don't even know what I'm saying, for heaven's sake. Don't mind the ramblings of an old woman. I'm ready to go any day now. So whatever happens here doesn't bother me. Really."

I wasn't convinced, but figured I'd butted into her business as much as I decently could for one evening. Stephen and Claire returned from the kitchen with four chipped mugs and a steaming teapot, but Mrs. Bernini stood to leave.

"It's past my bedtime," she said. "I'm going to take my evening constitutional in the garden, then head to bed. Good night, all. Sleep well."

"Could I give you a hand?" Stephen offered. "Or get you an umbrella, maybe?"

"No, I'm not helpless. You sit right down and enjoy your tea."

She clanked her slow, steady way through the foyer and out the French doors to the garden, heedless of the wind and rain.

Chapter Five

"You think she's okay?" Stephen whispered.

I nodded. "I think growing old takes courage."

"She reminds me of my gam-gam."

Claire cracked up. "Your *'gam-gam'*? That sounds so . . . preverbal."

Stephen lobbed a pizza crust at her. "Hey! I *love* my gam-gam. What do you call *your* grandmother?"

"The Nasty Old Broad."

Stephen and I gaped at her and she laughed some more. "Kidding! We called her Nana, of course. Like normal people."

"Nana? Seriously? Sounds like that dog from *Mary Poppins*—"

"It was *Peter Pan*," Claire said. "Get your stories straight."

"As fascinating as this discussion is, I suggest we explore the house before it gets too late," I interrupted. I was worried about Mrs. Bernini, and their bickering was beginning to get on my nerves.

"At your service, ma'am," Claire said. "You suppose Josh has been looking around, all this time?"

"Good question." I hoped he wasn't getting the jump on me. We would have to make up for lost time now. I had brought my backpack down earlier, so I extracted a heavy-duty flashlight for each of my ersatz ghost-hunting assistants, as well as extra batteries.

"Well, aren't you the proper Girl Scout? Very prepared," Stephen said.

"What's with all the batteries?" Claire asked. "Are you expecting to find underground caverns beneath this house?"

"We might take a gander at the basement, at most. But they say ghosts sometimes siphon off the energy from electrical things like flashlights, necessitating new batteries."

They stared at me.

"Look, I don't really know how it works, but Olivier—"

"That French ghost-busting guy?" Claire asked.

"Right. Olivier, the French ghost-busting guy, says to always carry extra batteries. So I'm carrying extra batteries." I could feel my face flame. Though I was "out" with my abilities to see—and sometimes communicate with—ghosts, the nitty-gritty of hunting for spirits still made me feel foolish. "So there you have it."

"We're not really expecting to see *actual* ghosts, though, right?" said Stephen.

Claire turned to him, incredulous. "What part of 'spend the night in a haunted house' did you not understand?"

Stephen shrugged. "I didn't really focus on that. I wanted to hang out with Mel. I never get to see her anymore since she's so busy working. Plus, I was promised pizza."

"It *was* pretty good pizza," Claire conceded, sticking her flashlight in her belt like a gun. "Come on, let's go stir up some ghosts."

"This place is such an eclectic mix of styles. It's so much fun," I said as we wandered down halls, peeking in through half-closed doors to parlors, antechambers, and bathrooms. "There are columns reminiscent of the Greek, but the verticality is sheer Italianate—also the bracketed cornices, of course."

"Oh, really?" said Stephen, in a tone that indicated polite attention rather than real caring. Not everyone shared my fascination with architecture.

"Shame about the floors," said Claire, noting the patches of warped and discolored wood.

"The strange thing is that you usually see that kind of damage in front of doors or windows, where water blows in. But here, it looks like damage from a leaky roof, coming all the way down through the ceilings." I opened the door and inspected the edging. "In fact, all the windows, and now this door, have weather stripping. And it looks ancient. It's really rare for an old building to have been sealed up this tight. Graham will be impressed."

Graham Donovan was a green construction consultant. A really sexy green consultant. I had a hard time keeping him off my mind.

"I thought you said you wanted to keep Graham away from this place," Stephen said, "so he wouldn't '*muck things up by installing every freaking green tech-nology he can think of.*' "

I glared at him.

"Something like that," Stephen backpedaled with a shrug. "I might have gotten the wording wrong."

"No," I conceded. "I think that's just about what I said. He can be a real pain in the—"

"Hey," Claire interrupted. She was kneeling on a built-in window seat, looking out the bay window to the court-yard garden. "The rain stopped. And it's a full moon. Look—Mrs. Bernini looks almost like a ghost herself."

Stephen and I joined her at the window. Mrs. Bernini did, in fact, look like a spirit shuffling down the garden path, illuminated in a soft, silvery light.

Overhead, there was a loud scraping sound and the rumble of something heavy.

It stopped. But then it was replaced by the sound of someone singing.

We all froze and looked at one another.

"Maybe Josh?" Stephen suggested.

"The scraping sound, maybe," Claire said. "But the singing? It sounds like a child."

"With garlands of roses, and whispers of pearls . . ."

"It's Anabelle."

I headed for the staircase and was halfway up when I realized I had lost my entourage. Stephen and Claire re-mained at the base of the stairs, eyes wide and mouths agape.

"Don't be scared," I assured them. "She really was very sweet."

Neither moved. I stifled a smile and reminded myself what I was asking of them.

"Tell you what: Why don't you two wait for me down here. Just try not to freak out if you see anything, okay?"

They looked at each other; then Claire started up the stairs. "Don't know about you, Stephen, but I'm gonna stick with the ghost professional."

Stephen was hot on her heels. "No way I'm staying down here by myself. The guy who stays behind is always the first to be eaten."

"No one's going to *eat* you," I said as I resumed climbing the stairs. "I've never heard of a single case of a carnivorous ghost."

"Maybe that's because no one ever survived to tell the tale," Stephen said, his voice low.

We reached the hall at the top of the stairs, and I stopped to listen, a finger to my lips. Claire and Stephen, who were compulsively looking over their shoulders, bumped into me. There was some flailing and swearing.

I said a quick, fervent prayer that we weren't all being secretly taped, that this really *wasn't* an episode of *Punk the Contractor*. I wasn't easily cowed by public ridicule, but our trio's antics would be pretty tough to overcome. With my luck the footage would go viral on the Web. Even if not, funny stories were passed around—and elaborated upon—endlessly on jobsites. There was nothing construction workers savored more than the opportunity to make fun of others in the business.

The scraping sound was coming from down the hall. And though Anabelle's singing had stopped, there was tinkling carousel music emanating from the nursery.

The previously locked door now stood ajar, spilling light into the hall.

I paused.

"Let me do the macho guy thing and go first," said Stephen, moving to stand between me and the nursery door.

"In principle I am offended," Claire said, standing right behind me. "In reality, I am grateful. Knock yourself out, you manly man, you."

We huddled together, one big ghost-busting sandwich.

The floorboards creaked underfoot as we progressed, en masse, down the hall.

Stephen took a deep breath, reached out very slowly, and pushed open the nursery door.

Chapter Six

The carousel music stopped. As did the scraping noise. Silence wrapped around us, leaving only the harsh sounds of our nervous breathing.

As I looked around, I saw that a rocking horse was moving, as though someone had just alighted. And the toy carousel's brightly painted horses were still swaying. Marionettes in a puppet theater stirred slightly.

Plus, it was so cold in the room we could see our own breath.

Deep shelves held dusty old dolls with corkscrew curls, flouncy dresses, and wide, staring glass eyes. There was a mechanical monkey with cymbals in its paws, scads of lead soldiers, and several antique teddy bears. Not all the toys were old-fashioned: I recognized several Fisher-Price trucks and a garage I remembered Caleb playing with, along with some *Star Wars* and *Power Rangers* dolls. A big leather-bound toy chest doubled as a bench under the large sash windows overlooking the garden.

The overhead lamp flickered out.

"Bad sign," said Stephen.

"Could be a bad bulb. Or old wiring. Or both," I responded.

We all turned on our flashlights and waved the beams around the room.

Claire chewed nervously on a Red Vines. "Creepy."

"They had a lot of foster children. It's just a playroom."

"Playrooms are *creepy*. Haven't you ever seen horror movies? This is where the you-know-what goes down."

"The you-know-what?"

"Another New Year's resolution: Stop swearing. Those are the two biggies: Stop smoking, stop swearing. But by God, I'm gonna keep on drinking."

"Atta girl," murmured Stephen.

"Let's go get the equipment Olivier lent me and set it up in here," I said. "It seems a likely spot for . . . activity."

On the way out we noticed something on the hallway floor, passing from the master bedroom through the door of the nursery. Gouge marks.

I crouched down to inspect them. They felt rough under my fingertips, and looked fresh. I lifted the carpet runner and sure enough, the scratch went all the way under the rug.

"Could they be claw marks?" asked Claire.

"*Please* don't bring werewolves into this. It's more like something heavy was dragged along here. But I can't see what."

"Dragged *under* the carpet?"

I had no answer for that. We hurried to set up the ghost-detecting equipment. The needle of the EMF detector was fluctuating crazily. Claire and Stephen kept their flashlights trained on me so I could see to set up a tripod with a night camera. I placed a sensitive recorder and a baby monitor on a bureau. Then I clipped the baby monitor receiver to my belt and slipped the EMF reader into my pocket.

When I finished, we searched the room one more time with the strong beams of our flashlights.

Scrawled on the opposite wall with bloodred crayon were childish letters, spelling out, *STAY AWAY. DANGER.*

"Okay," said Claire, biting off a hunk of licorice. "I'm getting really creeped out. I feel sort of . . . funky. Dizzy."

I was feeling pretty disoriented myself.

"Let's get out of here."

As we were leaving, a mechanical voice rang out: *I drive a dump truck!*

We all jumped, then huddled together, looking down at a nearby towel-covered basket as though it were filled with snakes.

Stephen reached out, snatching the towel off the top to reveal yet another bundle of toys. He dug down and pulled out a bright yellow dump truck with a driver. When you pushed down on the back, the driver declared his profession: *I drive a dump truck.*

Stephen smiled. "We must have set it off when we walked by."

Claire and I let out a mutual sigh of relief and turned toward the door.

And there was the silhouette of a man.

We screamed. Stephen flung himself in front of us, crouching slightly with arms splayed out to the sides, for all appearances ready to die first. Since I probably had a good twenty pounds or so on the guy, I had to hand it to him.

"Sorry," said a man's voice, filled with amusement. He stepped into the room, his face still obscured with the hall light backlighting him. But we recognized him: Josh Avery.

"You missed pizza," said Claire in a shaky voice.

"I ate earlier, thanks." He passed his flashlight beam around the playroom. "Wow, talk about scary. In the movies the nurseries like this are always bad news."

"That's what *I* said," said Claire.

His beam alighted on the scrawled message on the wall. *"Huh."*

"We were just leaving," I said, pushing past him to stand in the hallway. No doubt about it, there was something off-putting about that room.

"Where have you been?" I asked Josh as he joined us in the corridor, closing the playroom door behind him.

"Just exploring, checking out the garden, and the basement. So how do we want to go about this?" Josh asked.

"Go about what?"

"To tell the truth, I was so flabbergasted by the idea that I was supposed to spend the night in a haunted house that I didn't ask for a lot of extra detail. Like, for example, am I supposed to stay in my wing and ignore you all?" He grinned, showing white even teeth. Again I was struck by how this guy could be featured on a World War II poster, sort of a cross between an all-American boy and a Nazi ideal. "I'm here all by myself, just chicken feed for the ghosts."

Just then, I caught sight of Anabelle. She was standing right behind him at the end of the hall, looking just as she had appeared the other day, long dark hair, purple dress. This time, though, she wasn't smiling. In fact, she seemed to be softly crying.

I tried to ignore the pounding of my heart. Josh noted my gaze and followed it, looking over his shoulder.

"What is it? You're trying to freak me out, right?"

"No, I . . ." I glanced at Stephen and Claire. Neither of them appeared to be seeing anything out of the ordinary. "Nothing."

Anabelle opened her mouth as if to say something. I couldn't concentrate on both of them at once, and I really didn't like the idea of chatting with Anabelle with Josh at my side. I didn't even know if anyone but me could see her.

"Look, I might as well put my cards on the table," Josh began. "I—"

"Um, do you mind if we go downstairs to the kitchen and discuss this over a drink?"

He shrugged. "Sure, I could use a drink. Why not?"

There was no sign of Mrs. Bernini as we all took seats around a small wood-block table in the brightly lit kitchen, a room so big it was clear it had been built for a cook and her staff. As I reached for some small juice glasses I found on an open shelf, I noticed my hands were shaking from the aftereffects of our close encounter.

"Here's the deal," said Josh, leaning his muscular forearms on the wood block. "This project could make my name. How can I get you to back off?"

Apparently Josh didn't believe in small talk.

"Um . . . you can't?"

"You're pretending you can see these ghosts? Kim mentioned something about a little girl? Don't you think it's a little low, cashing in on a family tragedy?"

"Mel's the real deal," said loyal Stephen. "If she says she saw the girl, she saw her."

"I know it sounds far-fetched," I said, "but the truth is that I've had some experience with the, um, departed."

"She even has ghost-hunting equipment," said Claire as she brought the leftover pizza out of the industrial-sized refrigerator. At Stephen's look, she responded, "What? I'm stressed."

"What kind of equipment?"

"An electromagnetic-field detector, a night camera, a baby monitor. That sort of thing. I've got the EMF reader with me, but we set the rest of the stuff up in the nursery."

"You're pulling my—"

At that moment, the receiver started to crackle. We heard crying, and the clicking of the camera. And then a mechanical voice: *I drive a dump truck.*

Claire dropped her pizza. We all looked at one another for a moment, frozen, cartoonlike.

"What the . . . ?" Josh said.

"Is that clicking, whirring sound . . . the camera going off?" whispered Stephen.

Next we heard the carousel start up, cranking out its tinny tune. And then the sound of cymbals crashing, and more *I drive a dump truck, I drive a dump truck* . . . over and over.

I headed for the stairs.

"Wait," said Josh, then louder as I started to mount the steps, "Mel, *wait*!"

"What?"

Josh looked white as, well, a ghost. "I'm not going up there."

"That's fine. Stay here. I'll be right back." I wasn't going to let Anabelle scare me. As for any other spirits . . . well, I had been okay before. Plus, I was getting aggravated. I'd noticed that always seemed to make me brave, perhaps beyond reason.

"I'm going with you," said Stephen. "Come on, Claire, Josh, we should all stick together."

But when I turned to proceed up the stairs, I heard something rolling across the wood floor.

It was a marble, falling down the stairs. It tapped my foot.

I climbed another tread, but several more small glass balls fell down the stairs toward me.

"Careful of the marbles," I said as I climbed another step. Freezing cold air enveloped me.

Once again I heard a loud scraping noise as though something was being dragged. But this time it sounded like it was headed for the top of the stairs.

I stopped. Josh, Claire, and Stephen followed suit, several steps below me.

And then something appeared at the top of the stairs. One of those glassy-eyed dolls, walking along as though propelled by invisible hands. And then the monkey with its cymbals crashing. And the dump truck.

As though the whole nursery was coming after us.

My heart pounded. My bluster was gone. Anabelle's

ghost was one thing, possessed toys something else entirely. This had turned seriously creepy.

I turned and rushed down the stairs. My entourage beat me to it, running straight out the front door and into the wet night. A dozen more marbles poured down the steps, their clackety sounds seeming to mock us as we ran.

Out on the portico, we tried to catch our breath. The air outside was damp and chill, but no colder than the stairs had been.

"Look, this might be a little more complicated than I first thought," I said as soon as I was able to speak. I *really* wanted a shot at that AIA award, and getting this job was contingent on staying the whole night. Plus, I had an undeniable link to ghostly spirits. But Stephen and Claire were in this only for friendship. "If you guys want to leave—"

"Hey, where'd Josh go?" Claire said.

"Maybe he went screaming into the night," muttered Stephen. "Maybe he's smarter than he looks."

"Well, I guess that would mean I've got the job," I said. "Seriously, I shouldn't have asked you guys here. It's too much—"

"I'm staying if you are," Stephen said, cutting me off.

"Me too," said Claire. "This is beginning to piss me off."

"If you're sure ... look, from what I've read, ghosts can't actually hurt you." I said this as much to myself as to them. "They might freak you out enough so that you hurt yourself, though, so we should try to remain calm. If you can resolve not to be afraid, it seems to be a much easier interaction."

Claire smiled and lifted her eyebrows.

"I know, I know. I should take my own advice. What can I say? I lost it."

I squared my shoulders, took a deep breath, and walked back into the haunted house.

The French doors leading to the backyard blew open with a gust of wind, picking up and scattering paper clippings around the foyer.

Solar path lights subtly illuminated the yard. Stone pathways meandered through and around planting beds, while in the center of the garden a circle of plants surrounded an old fountain. The stone was cracked, but still beautiful: a spritely young Pan playing his pipes.

Clank, shuffle, clank.

Mrs. Bernini was still outside, shuffling down the garden path.

"She shouldn't be out there so long in this kind of weather," I said under my breath, then called out: *"Mrs. Bernini."*

She didn't pause or look up.

"Mel?" Claire said. "Who are you talking to?"

"Mrs. Bernini."

"Where?"

"In the garden."

Claire and Stephen exchanged glances.

"She's walking down the garden path." I pointed to her. "Right there."

"No one's there, Mel," Stephen said softly.

But I saw Mrs. Bernini, clear as day. She wasn't transparent, wasn't appearing only in my peripheral vision, wasn't levitating off the ground.

As I ran out the French doors, I was hit by a frigid

blast of air. A chill ran through me, to my core. I spun around, but I could no longer see the elderly woman.

The flashlight in my hand wavered, flickered, went out.

It couldn't be what I was thinking. *Surely* it wasn't that.

Please don't let it be that.

Chapter Seven

Something glinted dully on the path . . . Mrs. Bernini's aluminum walker. On its side, lying on the wet pavers near the fountain.

And Anabelle stood over the round stone wall of an old well, looking down into the hole. I could hear her high-pitched singing: *"With garlands of roses, and whispers of pearls, a garden of posies for all little girls, la la la la la . . ."*

She threw a flower into the well and walked away, the path lights extinguishing one by one as she passed. Then she faded, and disappeared altogether.

I rushed to the well and leaned over the stone wall, wishing my flashlight still worked. Stephen hurried up next to me, and after him Claire. They shone their lights into the inky black of the well's interior.

There was a flash of something, some sort of fabric. Orange. Crocheted.

Mrs. Bernini's shawl.

Our eyes met over the well.

"Mrs. Bernini?" I called into the pit, saying a little prayer under my breath. Part of me harbored a tiny flame of hope that Mrs. Bernini was still alive, perhaps just hurt or unconscious. "Can you hear me? Betty?"

My voice echoed eerily, sending my words back to me: *"etty ... etty ... etty ..."*

I brought my cell phone out of my pocket to call 911. It was dead.

"Check your cell phones," I said. "Are they working? We need to call for help!"

Stephen started punching buttons on his phone, then held it up against the night sky as though he could catch an errant sound wave floating along on the soft breeze. Claire held hers to her ear, trying several keys before shaking her head.

"This is so bizarre," said Claire. "I just charged it this morning."

"Mrs. Bernini used a landline to call for pizza earlier," said Stephen.

"You're right."

I ran toward the house, Stephen and Claire hot on my heels. There, on a marble-topped sideboard, sat a beige phone, an old-fashioned landline with the handset connected to the base with a coiled cord, the kind my father insisted on keeping in his house in case of earthquake. *When the towers go down, these phone lines are underground,* he would growl. *You mark my words, that cell phone won't be worth the metal it's made of.*

I picked up the receiver.

No dial tone.

I clicked it several times, the way they did in old movies.

"Okay, let's not panic," said Stephen, clearly on the verge of panicking. He grabbed a brown paper bag and held it in one hand, as though warding off hyperventilation just by having it near. "This isn't a horror movie, and we aren't stuck out in the woods somewhere. We're in a crowded urban area. Surely someone has a phone that works, somewhere."

"*No* one goes *anywhere* alone," I said.

"That's what I like about her," said Claire. "Real leadership qualities. I'm sticking to you two, no matter what."

"What about Josh?" Stephen said. "Do we leave him here all alone? What if . . . I dunno, what if they go after him?"

"'They,' who?" I asked.

"The ghosts? Whoever did that to Mrs. Bernini?"

"What if *he* was involved in this?" Claire said in a loud stage whisper. "Maybe he threw her down the well!"

"Oh *Lord*, let's go find a phone. What if she's . . . still alive? If she's hurt, she needs the paramedics."

"I thought you saw her ghost," Claire said after me as I rushed toward the front door.

Anxiety seized my heart; what I'd seen tonight jumbled my logic. I didn't know what to think. All I could concentrate on was getting help.

Out on the street everything was quiet. We raced to the neighbor's house across the street and rang the doorbell. No answer. We tried the next house and the next, but though all had lights on, no one answered their door. Of course, it was late at night in an urban area.

"Doesn't anybody *trust* anybody anymore?" I groused, fighting an unreasonable urge to kick the door we stood in front of.

"Maybe they're just not home," said Claire. "It's Saturday night, after all. Folks go out."

That's right. I forgot things like that.

"Listen," said Stephen. "Now that we're outside, I'm thinking a little more clearly. How about I jump in the car and run to the Castro? It's all of five blocks away—there are always lights and people . . . and phones."

"Good idea." I turned to Claire. "Want to go with him?"

"Yes. But I think I should stay here with you."

"I'll be okay," I said.

"Wait, wait, *wait*," said Stephen. "Geesh, it's like I couldn't even think back there. The night air feels good. None of you is staying here! Someone just shoved that sweet old woman down a well! Get in the car. Both of you. *Right now.*"

Claire and I shared a look. Stephen was right.

We all hopped in. The closer we got to the lights and action of the Castro, the more the tragic turn of events at the Bernini house seemed less about a haunting and more about a very real crime: Someone had attacked Mrs. Bernini. And the worst part was that we had been somewhere nearby, yet unaware she needed help. Sadness and guilt flowed over me. Dear, sweet woman, who'd raised foster children and loved her husband and who was good to her neighbors.

And for whose death Kim and Marty were waiting eagerly.

"Hey, that's the pizza place we called earlier," said Claire as she spied the sign for Sylven's Pizza, one of the first establishments we saw at the intersection with Castro Street. Stephen pulled up, double-parking on the crowded street.

The restaurant was informal but crowded, with several people eating at the half-dozen green, white, and red linoleum-topped tables, and three in line waiting for slices.

"Excuse me," I asked the man behind the register, "could I use your phone to call nine-one-one? It's an emergency."

"Of *course*. Are you okay?"

"I'm fine, but someone's been hurt and our phones aren't working."

I spoke to the dispatcher and gave her the street address and a very short version of a woman down a well. She told me to go back to the scene and wait for emergency crews. Before handing the phone back, I wondered if there was anyone else I should call. . . . The Propaks? No, I decided I should let the police handle all that.

My hands were shaking as I returned the phone. "Thanks."

"I'm sorry. . . . I overheard part of what you were saying." The fellow behind the counter was a smallish man in his fifties, his gray hair buzzed close to the scalp, but with a prominent salt-and-pepper mustache. "Isn't that Mrs. Bernini's address?"

"You know her?"

"*Everybody* knows her. My neighbor across the street

is cataloging her antiques for her. George!" he yelled over his shoulder, to a muscular man shoving a raw pizza into a wood-fired oven. "George, honey, this woman says something happened to Mrs. Bernini!"

George was a strapping fellow, at least six feet and with a gym rat's bulky physique. "What's up?" he said, wiping his hands on his apron as he came over.

"I'm J.D.," the mustachioed man introduced himself. "And this is my husband, George."

"As in Clooney."

"You *wish*," J.D. said with a gentle slap on George's chest. "But tell us, what's going on? Can we help?"

"I don't think so—the paramedics are on their way. I'm sorry, but I really have to get back to the house and see if there's anything more we can do."

Just as I turned to leave, Raj walked in through the front doors, carrying an empty thermal bag.

"Something the matter with the pizza?" he asked.

"No, it was great. I . . . um . . ."

"Something's happened to Mrs. Bernini," J.D. said, shaking his head. "How awful."

"*What?* What happened?"

"I don't know, I think she was . . . hurt," I said. "I'm sorry, I don't have time to explain; we're going back now to meet the police."

"Good heavens," I heard J.D. say as I left, "and we had to break up fisticuffs here in the shop earlier. I swear I don't know *what's* happening to this neighborhood."

"Raj," said George, "take over the cooking for a while. I'm gonna go over there, see what's up."

"Me too," said a young man at one of the tables as he wrapped up the remnants of a huge slice of pepperoni.

I rushed back to the car just in time to see Claire bumming a cigarette from a young man dressed in metal-studded black leather pants and matching motorcycle jacket.

"I thought you quit," Stephen commented as she and I got back in the car.

"Extenuating circumstances," Claire said.

"Let's get back to the house," I said. "Police are on their way."

"Mel, you really should consider carrying a gun," said Stephen, speeding down the residential streets. "In Nevada everybody carries a gun."

"You're right—the only thing that would have improved this evening would have been me shooting at people. And if they shot back, even better."

"I'm just saying if you're going to go around getting involved in murders all the time, you might give some thought to carrying some heat."

"I think the term is 'packing some heat,'" said Claire, lighting up her cigarette and lowering the window to exhale. "Some meanie you are."

Stephen glared at Claire's reflection in the rearview mirror. "I said I was born and raised in Vegas, not that I was with the *mob*. And just so you know, blowing smoke out the window doesn't really help." Stephen waved his hand in front of his face in a theatrical gesture. "Smokers damage their noses so they can't smell it, but the rest of us know perfectly well when there's smoke in the air."

Claire glowered at him, raised her window, and blew a puff of smoke at the back of his head.

"I think we all need to calm down," I said, my dread increasing as we approached the house.

"*I* think we need a freakin' drink," muttered Claire.

"I'm relieved to see that, at the very least, the smut mouth is still on mute," said Stephen.

"One habit at a time, as they say," said Claire, blowing another cloud of smoke toward his sensitive nose.

Next time, I promised myself, I was *so* bringing a different ghost-busting crew.

Chapter Eight

"This blows," said Claire, smoking yet another bummed cigarette as we stood by and watched the gruesome rescue scene.

"You can say that again," muttered Stephen.

I mostly concentrated on breathing.

The rain had ceased, but clouds hid the moon, making the night black and foreboding. There was an otherworldly feeling enveloping the courtyard, all search lamps focused on that too-black hole of the well. It was late by now, but as Claire would point out, on Saturday night in the Castro the real action didn't begin until ten at the earliest. Passersby, intrigued by the lights and sounds of the emergency vehicles, had started to peek through the garden gate in ghoulish curiosity. I recognized a few faces: one of Mrs. Bernini's immediate neighbors, plus George and the other young man from the pizza shop.

But I wasn't feeling social; all I could do was stare at the rescue workers, hoping against hope.

The paramedics had arrived at the house first, then the hook and ladder and the police. We showed them to the well, and after shouting down but receiving no answer, they sent down a walkie-talkie. When that produced no response, the fire department began setting up a hoisting device over the hole so they could lower a rescue worker down into the pit.

His boots slipped on the damp, slick stones as he was painstakingly lowered down the well in a safety harness. Once he reached his goal, he radioed up. His tone was unemotional, matter-of-fact:

"No pulse. Looks like a head injury. Probably dead before she was thrown down here."

Though part of me had known it, my heart lurched to my throat. I heard a muffled cry from Claire; Stephen hugged her to his chest.

Meanwhile, a group of officers crouched down near the central fountain. They called for a floodlight and the photographer, and started setting out evidence tags. Mrs. Bernini's aluminum walker was still lying on its side on the stone path. And there was something else that looked like a splash of dark paint on the edge of the fountain. Was that . . . blood?

I didn't have a chance to find out. The uniformed officer who had been first on the scene escorted us out of the garden and into the front yard, where all the emergency vehicles were crowded in the drive and along the street. He called in a suspicious death on his police radio, then started taking down our stories. I gave him the contact info for Kim and Marty Propak at the Lincoln Inn down the street.

As I listened to Claire's and Stephen's versions of events, I realized it was too bad we hadn't come to some agreement as to what we were going to tell of ghostly goings-on. It was clear from the man's eyes that he thought we were high, or crazy, or both.

More onlookers gathered around the emergency vehicles, standing with umbrellas and rain jackets, a few in bathrobes. After the police officer took our statements, Claire, Stephen, and I sat silently, huddled together under a blue blanket provided by the paramedics. Since they couldn't help Mrs. Bernini, they had nothing to do but make sure we weren't in shock.

After a long wait—I think I fell asleep at some point, suffering from an adrenaline crash—I was awakened by a hand on my shoulder. It was the responding officer.

"Inspector needs to speak with you," he said. "You two wait here for your turns," he said to Claire and Stephen.

I followed him to the driveway, where I was both relieved and disturbed to realize I knew the lead homicide inspector who had caught the call: Annette Crawford.

"Inspector," I said with a nod. "It's, um . . ." It seemed odd to say "nice to see you again," under the circumstances. "Hello."

"Ms. . . . ?"

"Turner. Mel Turner."

"Right. Union Street homicide, upholstery shop."

I nodded. Curious to think that Crawford's world was organized as a series of murder scenes. It made me wonder how a person remained mentally stable as a homicide inspector in a busy urban area. I'd been exposed to just a taste, and was already doubting my sanity.

But those thoughts were soon taken over by other, more self-serving ones: Unless things had changed dramatically since last we spoke, Inspector Crawford did not hold with any of this "ghost stuff." Which might make it difficult to describe to her the night we'd just experienced at the Bernini house.

"You want to tell me what you're doing on another one of my crime scenes?"

"I was spending the night here. I had a rather unusual arrangement with the soon-to-be owners, Kim and Marty Propak."

"They were going to buy the place?"

I nodded. "They had signed a purchase agreement with Mrs. Bernini."

"So they're the new owners of the house?"

"As far as I—"

There was a rustle in the crowd of onlookers.

"But there *must* be some mistake. She left this house to me!"

A woman had broken through the imaginary line everyone else was observing. She wore a polo shirt and khaki pants, but no coat, and she hugged herself against the wintry chill. She looked like she was in her late thirties or early forties but took great care of herself: a French manicure, an expensive haircut, perfect makeup despite the late hour. She reminded me of my ex-husband's new wife: a beautiful, high-maintenance woman.

A man ran up beside her. He was about her height,

and with broad workingman features. Not unattractive, just rather ordinary. He placed a coat over her shoulders, then left his hands resting there.

A police officer tried to shoo them back.

"It's important I speak to the officer in charge," the woman said. "Mrs. Bernini left this house to me. She couldn't have *sold* it to anyone!"

"Come on, lady, back it up," said the uniformed officer. "Right now we're investigating a crime."

"He's right, honey," said her companion, though he flashed a challenging glare at the cop. "Let's go home and we'll figure this all out later."

A murmur arose from the crowd, and onlookers started voicing their opinions. I heard people grumbling loudly: *"It was her house; she could do anything she wanted with it."*

"She was nuts."

"Don't speak ill of the dead."

Inspector Crawford straightened, fixed the crowd with her take-no-prisoners gaze, and then lowered— rather than raised— her voice. It had the effect of gaining everyone's attention.

"Right *now*, if you don't mind, I'd like to figure out who would have thrown a little old lady down a well. Let's keep our focus, people."

Chastened, everyone hushed.

She turned back to me, muttering, "In all my born days . . ." under her breath. Shaking her head, she led me to the front door, where we were clear of the crowd overhearing. "And you spent the night here, why?"

"The Propaks had planned to remodel the house to

be a bed-and-breakfast. They were trying to decide which of two contractors to hire, Turner Construction or Avery Builders. So they asked me and Josh Avery to spend the night at the house."

She quirked her head. "Is that normal behavior in the process of submitting a construction bid?"

"Normal, in terms of ... ?"

"Is it typical? Have you ever done so before?"

"No, not exactly."

"I'd rather not play twenty questions with you, Ms. Turner. Tell me what you were doing here."

I took a deep breath and dove in. "The Propaks—and Mrs. Bernini, for that matter—believed this house was haunted. Kim Propak mentioned that other contractors had fled the building, scared, and she proposed that we try making it through a night here. If we failed, we would lose the bid."

"It's all coming flooding back to me now. You were the one working on the old Cheshire Inn on Union, and you thought it was haunted."

"I believe what I told you at the time was that the *owner* thought it was haunted."

The inspector raised one eyebrow and looked down her nose at me, in an incredulous, "you're a nutcase and/or a liar" move that reminded me of my friend Luz's natural suspicion. "You're saying that you've been involved in two allegedly haunted houses now, by coincidence?"

"There are people who think I have certain ... abilities. When it comes to ghosts."

"And do you? I mean, is this part of your whole shtick?" She made a circular gesture with her hand. "I hire you to put in a new window and you drive my ghosts out of the attic at the same time? For a small fee, of course."

I felt a surge of anger, and my cheeks burned. "I don't have a *shtick*, no. And I've never accepted money for . . . for this sort of 'ghost' thing. But the fact is . . . well, I do seem to have some ability with the beyond. That is, sometimes I, well, hear things. And see things."

Clearly I was going to have to work on my patter if I was going to stand up, open and proud, and embrace my ghost-talking abilities. But it still felt new to me. After the first incident several months ago, I had come clean to certain important people in my life: my dad; our house-mate, Stan; my stepson, Caleb; Luz; even my maybe-sort-of boyfriend, Graham. And of course, now that it was splashed all over *Haunted House Quarterly*, which had been picked up by any number of Internet sites, my name was circulating in cyberspace. But all of that was nothing compared with fessing up to this no-nonsense woman, a woman who dealt with dead bodies—and the folks who made them dead—all the time.

Inspector Crawford was studying me with a cold stare that made me feel not only jumpy but unaccountably guilty. I got the feeling she was one of those human lie detectors, probably trained at Quantico. I told myself not to fidget, desperately trying to remember whether it was looking up, or glancing down, that indicated the suspect was a liar. Indecisive, I swiveled my eyes up, then down, then up again, in a repetitive motion that probably marked me not only as a liar but as an insane liar.

Finally, I forced myself to meet the inspector's dark, skeptical gaze.

"So," she said, "I guess all this leads us to the question: Did you see any ghosts?"

I nodded. "I saw Mrs. Bernini walking in the garden. But neither of my friends, Claire or Stephen, could see her. That's when we realized she was . . . in the well."

"What time was this?"

"It must have been, I don't know, about ten? Maybe a little after."

"What happened next?"

"All of us, Stephen, Claire, and I, looked in the well. But our phones didn't work, and neither did the landline in the house."

She nodded. "Line was cut. What made you look in the well in the first place? Did you hear something?"

"I thought I saw a . . . spirit standing over the well."

"Uh-huh. The deceased, or a brand-new ghost?"

"A little girl. She lived here a long time ago. Named Anabelle; Anabelle Bowles. I had seen her in the house previously."

Inspector Crawford studied me for a long moment, then looked down at her notepad and cleared her throat before speaking again.

"And before you found the body? Any other ghostly activity?"

"In the second-floor playroom, there were some strange interactions . . . with toys," I said.

"Interactions?"

"Unusual behavior: moving by themselves, that sort of thing. And there's a threatening message written on the wall."

"Okay . . ." She pinched the bridge of her nose, as

though fighting off a headache. "Let's go over the whole evening, chronologically."

I told her about arriving with Josh, getting settled in our room, exploring the house, sending out for pizza and eating with Mrs. Bernini, and then the strange noises emanating from the nursery. She asked me numerous pointed questions about the wine at dinner.

"I wasn't *drunk*," I insisted. "I happen to have a very high tolerance. And I didn't drink that much to begin with."

"Uh-huh," she grunted. "And where is this Josh Avery person now?"

"I haven't seen him since we were scared off by toys at the top of the stairs."

She gave me the stink-eye again.

"It was worse than it sounds. You sort of had to be there. We heard noises in the playroom, but as we went upstairs to investigate . . . well, we all wound up running outside." I noticed the curb was now full of emergency vehicles, Josh's fancy truck nowhere in sight. "His truck's gone. He must have gone home."

"Make and model?"

"Big and black." I'm not what you'd call a car person. "It looks like your average truck at a construction site, but new and shiny. With 'Avery Builders' written on the doors."

The inspector wrote down the information, called an underling over to her, and handed it to him, instructing him to put out a call for the truck and its owner.

"According to your agreement with the owners, if Josh Avery fled the house first," she said, looking back over her notes, "you win the contract?"

"Frankly, I hadn't thought about it. Maybe, but since what happened . . . somehow I doubt the original agreement holds. The whole project is up in the air now, right?"

"At least until forensics clears out," she said, taking a deep breath in through her nose and exhaling slowly. "Well, as always, interesting talking with you, Mel Turner. I've got your information here, and I'd appreciate you not leaving town for a few days. I have the feeling we'll need to talk again."

"May I go?" I asked. I had no idea what time it was, but I felt dead on my feet.

"I'm going to go ask your friends some questions, and I might have some more for you. Have a seat and stick around a while. These things take time. Lots of time."

I nodded. As she walked away, she turned back and asked me, "How's your father doing?"

She hadn't remembered me, but she remembered my dad. Story of my life. "He's great. Thank you for asking."

"Give him my regards. He was a nice fellow."

"I will."

Chapter Nine

Inspector Crawford didn't lie. These things did, indeed, take time. Lots of time.

It was several more hours before we were allowed to leave. The inspector, and another officer, returned now and again to ask the same questions, in different ways, over and over. I kept falling asleep and waking again, so things took on a surreal, timeless cast. My eyelids had that scratchy, heavy feeling that comes with sheer exhaustion. And my heart ached for a sweet, elderly woman who had been brutally attacked—while we were somewhere nearby.

If only we had heard a struggle, or looked out to the garden at the right time, and been able to intervene.

"So what's the deal? Now we're all suspects?" asked Claire, smoking again as we waited for a police officer to move the cruiser blocking her truck in the driveway.

"I don't think so, not really," I said. "As my dad would

point out, the police have a job to do and need to rule out all suspects. We were in the house when the crime occurred, so naturally they need to get the full story from each of us."

"Wow. I've never been a suspect in a crime before. It's kind of awesome, in a weird way."

"A woman was killed tonight."

"Okay, yeah, you're totally right. That part is terrible. But other than *that*, it was quite a night. Ghosts, chasing around that old house, and getting interrogated. And here I thought it was going to be all about pizza."

I gave a humorless laugh.

"C'mon, I'll take you home," Stephen said to me after Claire drove off.

"You don't have to do that. You live in the opposite direction."

"It's four in the morning. What are you going to do, take the bus?"

As he had pointed out earlier, I wasn't even packing heat.

"You're right. Thanks, I'd love a lift."

At this hour, it took only twenty minutes to reach my dad's place in Oakland. Every other house on the street was a small stucco bungalow, but several years ago my parents bought the original large farmhouse dating from back when acres of orchards gave the neighborhood of Fruitvale its name. Even at this hour of night, even looming large in the silvery moonlight, the house looked warm and comforting. This was due, in large part, to the mellow glow of the porch light and the distinct, shaggy outline of a dog's head in the front window. He must have awakened to check out who was parking outside his house.

As he pulled up to the curb, Stephen asked for the fourth time: "You sure you're okay?"

I nodded. "How about you? Wasn't this your first run-in with such things?"

"Oh, you know. There are ghosts of brokenhearted gamblers wandering the streets of Vegas, so it's no big deal." He gave me a crooked smile. "But yeah. It's a lot to process. Poor Mrs. Bernini. And that it happened while we were right there. I wish we could have . . ." He shook his head. I could see a sheen of tears in his eyes.

The green glow of the clock on the dashboard indicated four thirty in the morning.

"Why don't you come in?" I suggested. "My dad will cook us a huge breakfast."

"It's the middle of the night."

"Dad might well be up by now. He never got over early construction hours, and as he ages, it seems to be getting worse. Falls asleep in front of the TV by seven. Soon he'll start to wake up before *The Late Show* comes on."

"I really couldn't."

"Don't be ridiculous. The man loves nothing more than to force-feed people huge traditional American breakfasts. He's like a stereotypical Jewish grandmother, except with a five-o'clock shadow and a bad attitude. And he's not Jewish. But other than that . . ."

"You really don't think he'd mind? I actually . . . I think I could use some company. Not sure I'm ready to go home yet."

"Great," I said, patting him on the knee. "Let's go."

Stephen followed me in through the back door of the house, where we were greeted by a very sleepy brown mutt who snuffled and snorted while frantically wagging his tail. His whiskers stuck straight up on one side: doggy bedhead.

"Hey there, Dog," I said, ruffling his coat and giving him a squeeze. The veterinarian's best guess was that Dog was "some sort of lab mix." Several months ago I had found him hanging around a construction site, miserable and starving. I tried to get rid of him, but after he helped save my life—and spent the night here at the house—he became part of the family. But we still hadn't decided on a name for him, so for the moment he just went by the profoundly uninspired moniker of "Dog," or "Brown Dog" when we got fancy.

Stephen was an animal lover, so he greeted the canine with some vigorous petting. After receiving his fill of attention, Dog turned tail and ran, woofing loudly, into the living room. Barking his fool head off was his canine way of saying hello.

Unfortunately, it was ear-piercing and well-nigh indistinguishable from his manner of going after intruders, or murderers for that matter.

"That ought to rouse the old man," I muttered.

Sure enough, moments later Dad hustled halfway down the stairs. He was clad in his typical worn blue jeans, with a white T-shirt straining slightly over a small potbelly. His thinning gray hair was disheveled and his five-o'clock shadow was so heavy it was nearly a beard.

He held a Smith & Wesson in one hand, and looked mighty annoyed.

"It's me, Dad," I said in a hurry. His eyesight wasn't as sharp as it used to be.

"What the hell? Who's *that*?" He gestured vaguely with his gun.

"You remember my friend Stephen." The aforementioned was looking like he wished he were safe at home right about now. His Adam's apple bobbed up and down, and he appeared to be speechless. "You've met."

"Where the hell's Graham?"

"Home in bed, like a sane person, I would guess." Graham Donovan was a very sexy green builder, who used to work construction with my dad. Dad liked him. A lot. In particular, Dad liked the idea that Graham might "make an honest woman" out of me, which, in his mind, my ex, Daniel, had never managed to do. Maybe it was my cynicism talking, but it seemed ironic to imagine I might be made "honest" by virtue of a romantic association with a man. Seemed to me as if quite the opposite would be more likely.

I checked myself. Yep, pretty sure that was the cynicism talking.

"What are you two dressed like that for?" Dad asked, looking us up and down.

"We were in a community theater production," I said, just to be snarky. *"Peer Gynt."*

"Huh. You eat yet?" Ah, the real issue.

"No, but we're starved."

"Well, come on in." He scooted us back into the kitchen. Stephen and I perched on stools at the counter while Dad started rummaging through the ample contents of the refrigerator, extracting a dozen eggs, bacon, and milk.

He set a bag of potatoes and a grater on the counter in front of me. "Make yourself useful. Wash those and shred 'em up fine for hash browns."

I did as I was told. My father had raised me and my two sisters with the sort of undisputed military authority he'd honed during two tours of Vietnam. I had rebelled by the time I hit adolescence, so he and I had butted heads through much of my youth. But since I had come back to stay with him after Mom died and I divorced Daniel, we'd worked out a sort of détente: I avoided talking about politics, he avoided talking about when he was going to start back in running Turner Construction, and we dealt with each other's quirks with as much patience as we could muster.

As he whisked eggs to make an omelet, I asked him about Thomas Avery and his nephew Josh.

"Old Tom's all right . . ." He hesitated. Dad wasn't the kind of guy who said negative things behind other people's backs—he was more the sort who didn't say anything if he couldn't say something nice.

"But . . . ?"

"Well, as you know, we were competitors. And truth is . . . he was a fierce competitor."

"Would you say he was underhanded at all?"

He stuck out his chin, then frowned. "No, nah. Nothing like that. Didn't adhere to Turner Construction standards of cleanliness on the jobsite, things like that. But then, who could?" he asked with pride. "Tom had a nice old German shepherd. Good dog."

Upon hearing the word "dog," our brown mutt scampered across the kitchen to beg at Dad's feet. Now that he was fed regularly, his brown coat had taken on a shiny deep chocolate hue and was silky to the touch—he was so pretty that strangers stopped us on the street to ask what breed he was. But unlike almost all the mutts I've known in my life, Dog wasn't smart. At all. He was sweet, but dim. Very dim.

His English vocabulary consisted of maybe three words: "Dog," "cookie," "walk." That was about it. He didn't know how to play ball, or Frisbee. He didn't fetch sticks, much less bring a person her slippers at night. And to top it all off, he got carsick. As dogs went, he was less than ideal. We all adored him.

"And Tom's nephew Josh, have you ever met him?"

"Never heard of him," he said as he turned the bacon that was sizzling and popping in the huge old iron skillet, filling the house with enticing aromas. "But Tom's kids all left the area, so I'm not surprised he'd bring someone else in."

"They're not all lucky enough to have a daughter like you," said Stan Tomassi as he wheeled himself into the kitchen. Stan had been one of my dad's best friends for twenty years. They used to work together until a construction accident landed Stan in a wheelchair. Now he lived here, and the two men were like an old married couple, bickering over the TV and cooking together.

Stan was also the one who had roped me into taking over the construction business "for a couple of months" after my mother's sudden death, when my father fell apart. Two years later, I was still waiting for my dad to step back in.

I think Stan felt a little guilty about it, and I wasn't above letting him wallow in the sentiment. Still, he was a huge help to me by running Turner Construction's home office, charming customers with his homespun wisdom.

"Good morning, Stan." I got up and gave him a kiss on the cheek. "Did we wake you?"

"Nah, you know how it is. Back hurts after five or six hours in bed. Besides, I must be getting old like your father —I can't sleep past five anymore." Stan rolled over to the refrigerator and pulled out a blue plastic pitcher. "Orange juice? Squeezed it fresh yesterday."

A few scraggly trees in the yard still gave twice-yearly citrus harvests.

"Get a load of that," muttered Dad. "Stan Tomassi, aka Martha Stewart."

"I'll take some, thanks. Hey, Stan, we were just talking about Thomas Avery, Avery Builders?" I said. "You remember him?"

"Sure. Tom was one tough old bird. Beat your dad out of more than one juicy contract, if I remember correctly."

Dad snorted. "He underbid, then ran over on change orders. Not professional in my book."

"You just told me he was a decent guy," I said.

"All's fair in love and business, Mel," said Stan with a smile. "Just not for Turner Construction. We hold ourselves to a different standard—says so right on our business cards."

"And his nephew Josh?"

"Never heard of him. But it seems to me Tom mentioned a couple of sisters, so it wouldn't be too surprising."

Could Josh have killed Mrs. Bernini? But why? He had disappeared, true ... but why would he have killed Mrs. Bernini while Stephen, Claire, and I were looking around the house, then come back to join us, then run away after the toys attacked? It made no sense.

Speaking of Martha Stewart, as we talked, my father had been frying up delicious-smelling hash browns, bacon, and omelets. I'm not a breakfast person in general, but I make an exception for bacon and hash browns. Besides, something about being up all night gives a person an early-morning appetite.

Though he made it a point to be surly, I could tell Dad was inordinately pleased to have me at the table. It was a source of daily disappointment to him that I grabbed only coffee for breakfast.

When the food was ready, we all sat around our scarred pine kitchen table and dug in. We chatted, and I described the architectural details of the Bernini house but kept things vague with regards to our evening, and ghosts. I sidestepped the subject of murder altogether.

Dad stared at me as I ate bacon and hash browns but avoided the eggs.

"You want waffles, babe?"

"No thank you."

"Different kind of omelet?"

"Nope. I'm great. Thanks."

He stared some more. "Cream of Wheat?"

"Dad, I'm the daughter who doesn't like breakfast foods. Remember?"

"I thought you liked pancakes."

I shook my head. "Different daughter."

"*I* like pancakes," Stephen said.

"Good man." My dad slapped him on the back.

I was beginning to think Dad was getting the wrong idea about Stephen and me. He hopped up and down bringing salt and pepper, and butter, and refills of juice to the table. You'd think this breakfast was my dowry for all the attention he was giving it.

Probably he figured if I couldn't land Graham, he might as well welcome the second string. The man was developing a morbid fear of me dying an "old maid." No amount of argument would convince him that in the modern world, there really *was* no such thing as an old maid; on the contrary, a woman who chose to remain single might be fulfilled, or even happier than someone married. *Especially* than someone in a miserable marriage.

For a few blessed minutes we ate in companionable silence. And then Stephen opened his big mouth.

"Mel's leaving out just one little aspect of the evening. The homeowner where we were spending the night . . . she died. Was killed."

"Your client was killed?" Stan looked startled. "Again?"

"It's not my *fault*." I'd been up all night, seen ghosts, practically witnessed Mrs. Bernini's death, and dealt with cops. Now that I had warm food in my belly, I felt like I'd hit a wall. "Why does everybody think it's *me*?"

Dad gave me a Look.

I was cornered, so I gave them an abbreviated version of our evening. ". . . and then the cops took statements from all of us and were collecting evidence. I think that's the end of it, as far as we're concerned."

"Good," said Dad.

"So what does this mean for the job?" asked Stan.

"She doesn't need any more fool jobs where she thinks she's seeing ghosts, for crissakes," interjected Dad. He jabbed his fork in my direction. "Move on to that Piedmont remodel. That'll keep you busy, and it's half the commute anyway."

My father telling me what to do with the business— the business that he had practically foisted upon me, the business I had managed to keep in the black despite the economic downturn, the business that was keeping me from disappearing among Parisians—riled me like no other subject.

"Wow," I blurted out before I lost my temper. I faked a huge yawn and stretched my arms out, like cartoon characters always did when they were sleepy. "Gee, I'm beat. Stephen, would you like to stay over? You're welcome to Caleb's room if you like."

"Thank you, no. I'd better get on home and get some sleep and a change of clothes. Got to be at work by noon."

"What kind of work do you do, there, Steve?" asked my dad.

"I'm a barista."

"A 'barista'?" He reared back and looked at Stan, who shrugged. "What the hell's a *barista*?"

"I make coffee. Lattes, cappuccinos, that sort of thing. I used to work for an evil national chain, whose name I'll no longer mention, but now I work at a little place on Columbus. My *real* love is costume design, but as you can imagine, that doesn't pay the rent."

Unblinking, Dad looked at Stephen for a long moment; then he stared at me. Shaking his head and muttering under his breath, he started clearing the table.

Chapter Ten

I slept until one in the afternoon. Actually, that was an exaggeration—I stayed in bed until one, but I slept only fitfully. I couldn't stop thinking of Mrs. Bernini, couldn't get her sweet face out of my mind. I dreamt of her shuffling down the hallway, the smile that lingered on her lips as she told her stories, the overly eager expression on the Propaks' faces, and then the woman who came to the crime scene and claimed Mrs. Bernini had left the house to her. . . .

I hadn't warmed to the Propaks when I first met them, but could they really have wanted Mrs. Bernini out of the way so badly that they would resort to murder?

And if those thoughts weren't enough to chase sleep from my grasp, my cell phone rang repeatedly. I ignored it and pulled a pillow over my head. I imagined it was either work or the police; I wasn't in the mood for either.

With the supreme self-serving logic of the sleep-deprived, I figured Sunday was supposed to be a day of rest, even for general contractors. And I had told the police everything I knew.

Finally I heard the house phone ringing, and the muffled sounds of my dad answering, then his footsteps on the stairs, and a light knocking at the door.

"*Mmmff,*" I answered.

"Sorry, kiddo. Your ex, Caleb's dad, is on the phone."

"Daniel?"

"Caleb's in the emergency room."

I sat bolt upright in bed. My dad handed me the portable phone.

"Daniel? What happened?"

"Sorry about this," said Daniel. "But Caleb insisted on me calling you. He'll be fine, but he's got to have stitches."

Without so much as stopping for coffee, I pulled on yesterday's clothes and ran out the door. Dog had been in the yard and, assuming my running was an invitation to play, chased me out to the car. Not wanting to take the time to put him back in the house, I let him come along for the ride. Unfortunately, I forgot about his carsickness pills, so by the time we crossed the Bay Bridge, the poor canine was sitting down in the footwell, dry-heaving. I comforted him as best I could.

I rushed to the San Francisco Medical Center, let Dog out to sniff the edges of the parking lot for a few minutes until he felt better, gave him a little water, put him back in the car, cracked the windows, and then made my way to the emergency room.

There, I found Caleb looking reassuringly healthy against the snowy white of the bedsheets. His dark hair was overlong and ruffled; his near-black eyes looked tired. He even had the beginnings of a dark mustache, which always surprised me; I still thought of him as a child.

Speaking of children . . . Caleb was being tended by a doctor who looked almost as young as he. At least the attending nurse looked reassuringly grown-up.

"Hey there, Goose," I said, wincing at my inadvertent public use of the nickname I had dubbed him with, no idea why, when he was just five. "Wow, *this* is exciting. What do you say, Doctor? Will he live?"

"Nothing much to worry about long-term," said the physician, who had finished cleaning the wound on Caleb's arm and was about to begin stitching. "It's deep, but it missed bone and tendon, just sliced through flesh."

"He'll have a big scar," Daniel said.

"Well, girls love scars," I said, feeling inane chatting like this, but unable to stop. The alternative was to start crying. Or yelling. My heart was pounding. "We'll come up with a good story for you, a knife fight in a bar in Hanoi, something like that."

"You okay, Mel?" Caleb asked.

"Sure. Why?"

He and Daniel shared a smile. "Thanks for coming and everything, but, like, did we get you out of bed or something? Your hair's kind of like . . . messed up."

I tried to smooth it, knowing it was no use. I have impossible hair, thick and curly and with a mind of its own. The only way it looks decent is if I wet it every day and use heaps of conditioner. Rising from bed I could easily be mistaken for Medusa's frizzy-haired doppelgänger. Nor was I wearing any makeup. I had thrown on yesterday's outfit because it was at the foot of my bed, and had run out of the house without so much as looking in the mirror.

"Ingrate. I was a little too anxious to be with you to attend to my usually rigorous beauty regimen."

Caleb managed a half smile in response, keeping his eyes on me but wincing each time the doctor passed the needle through his skin.

Across the bed, I saw Daniel turn white as the sheets Caleb sat on. He was a loving father, but he'd never been strong in the face of blood. I, on the other hand, had dealt with my fair share of sliced appendages and broken bones on the jobsite, so that part didn't faze me. The idea of my baby being hurt, however . . . that was a different story.

"Maybe you should wait outside for this part," I told Daniel. "I'll stay with Caleb."

Daniel blew out a breath and seemed like he was about to lose it. He was looking anywhere but at his son.

"It's cool, Dad," said Caleb. "Mel'll stay with me."

"I'll be right outside," Daniel said, and fled.

As soon as his father left, Caleb whispered to me, "Mel, listen. I think it might have been a ghost."

"What ghost?"

Caleb's reaction to my ability to see spirits had been patient yet patronizing, rather like Stan's. They weren't overtly hostile to the idea like my father, but neither were they what one might call supportive, much less believers.

"Um, Dad and Valerie are having some work done at the house, or whatever? Like, the kitchen, and now the bathroom that's attached to their bedroom . . ."

"The master bath?" Back when I was married to Daniel and lived in that house, I had gutted that bath and painstakingly replaced all its fixtures and finishes with vintage items.

"Yeah. Anyway, there's been some stuff, like, happening?" He grimaced as the doctor continued to work on the wound.

"What kinds of things? Can you be specific?"

"Weird stuff, like things left out of place, or found scattered around, stuff going wrong . . . and all the plumbing keeps backing up. Valerie ruined her favorite pair of shoes. Ah, man, she was *so* pissed."

Call me petty, but the visual of Valerie standing in her own toilet water in her Manolo Blahniks brought a little sunshine into my heart. Caleb and I shared a wicked smile until he winced again at the stitches, and I remembered that he could have been seriously hurt.

"So this morning, I got up early for basketball practice. I was going downstairs and I thought I heard something, so I looked up, but then something fell from the top of the landing."

"What was it?"

"A broken toilet thingee. You know, the part that, like, goes on the back?"

"Sorry, little man, we're going to have to go with the knife-in-the-bar story. A toilet tank lid just isn't going to cut it with the ladies," I said. "Pardon the pun."

Caleb smiled and nodded. "Right? I was thinking that myself. But listen, do you think it could, like, really be a ghost? Valerie thinks so. . . ."

"Have you mentioned this to your dad?"

"I wanted to talk to you first to see if you'd come over and check it out. You don't have to—I mean, I know

Valerie's there, and you and Dad, well, you're like, whatever. When I think about it . . . I mean, you don't have any actual real connection. You don't have to if you don't want."

I tried to ignore the pang deep in my gut. *You don't have any real connection.* True. An ex-stepmother might have only a tenuous connection, at best, to her stepson. But I had lived with Caleb from ages five to twelve and without exactly meaning to, I wound up doing the mom thing: Besides sword fighting, I kissed a hundred boo-boos and packed a thousand lunches and stayed awake through too many interminable school plays. I left his father in high dudgeon and without a second thought, but Caleb was a different matter altogether.

I would lay my life down for the boy without a moment's hesitation. That gave me sort-of-Mom status, right?

"Sixteen stitches," said the doctor, as she finished up. She patted Caleb awkwardly on the shoulder as the nurse stepped in and started dressing the wound. "Good job."

"I'll see what I can do," I said to Caleb. "I'll talk to your dad about it."

"'Kay," Caleb grunted in that teenage way that made it hard to believe there was a keen mind behind the grunting. "Mom's already freaking out, so I didn't want to tell her."

"She'll be back tomorrow?"

He nodded. "But she's putting together a big conference, so she's hecka busy. I told her not to worry, it's totally not a big deal."

As the bandage grew larger, I thought she might have

a different response when she saw the actual damage. I knew I would.

I stepped outside and found Daniel on his phone in the waiting room.

"Caleb thinks there might be something suspicious about what happened," I said after he hung up.

Daniel nodded, his lips pressed together in annoyance. "Let me guess: Valerie's got him convinced it's a ghost."

"I take it you don't agree?"

Daniel gave me the look I remembered too well: disbelief mixed with downright disgust, topped by a patronizing smirk.

"I'm not saying she's right," I said, "but why not let me snoop around the construction a little? I could let you know what I think of the job they're doing. You know I'd be able to see things you can't. And if Caleb's safety is at stake . . ."

"Caleb's perfectly safe."

"Which is why we're in the emergency room?"

He jangled his keys in his pocket, as if to imply he had places to be, people to see. About my height, he appeared taller with his sense of authority and the demeanor of a university professor who could teach you a thing or two. And he could. Of all the things I could fault Daniel with, his smarts weren't one of them. He was one of the most intelligent men I knew, able to make logical leaps and disparate connections in a way that never ceased to fascinate me, even in the deepest despair of our divorce. The fact that those smarts didn't translate into making good choices about his personal life, much

less his personal development . . . well, that was a different story altogether.

Daniel had been dashing when I'd married him. But
his dark hair had gone from sophisticated gray at the
temples to an all-over salt, and was thinning. In addition, he'd cut it very short and shaved his trim beard,
so that now he appeared jowly and middle-aged. Which
he was. He was twelve years my senior, and I was pushing forty.

"All right," Daniel said finally. "Actually, I think we
could use your help. Valerie . . . well, she might be out of
her depth on this one."

"Who's the general on the remodel?"

"Valerie's overseeing everything."

"*Valerie?* Valerie's directing all the subcontractors
and managing her own project? That sounds like a recipe
for disaster."

I saw by the look on Daniel's face that I'd overstepped.

"I meant to say it would be difficult for any homeowner," I lied. We both knew what I *really* meant to say
was, how could you leave *Valerie* in charge? But this was
one situation where diplomacy really was the best policy.
"I was practically raised on a construction site, but even
I had a lot to learn. It's a tough gig."

Daniel nodded, accepting my explanation at face
value. "It really has been tough. I'd appreciate it if you'd
take a look, thank you. I'll talk to Valerie and figure out
a good time."

"How about I swing by tomorrow, noonish," I said,
just to be in charge. "My schedule's pretty full."

He nodded curtly, and we both went back in to be
with Caleb.

*   *   *

I put Dog on a leash and took him for a short walk while I made some phone calls: to let Dad know Caleb was okay; to reassure Caleb's mother; and while I was on the phone, I returned a call to a stained-glass artist who was restoring the intricate windows of a Queen Anne Victorian called Cheshire House, over on Union Street. That was where I'd met Inspector Crawford, not even a month ago, at the site of yet another murder.

Dog had regained his naturally happy disposition and wagged his tail as he sniffed at a sad patch of weeds, lifted his leg on a fireplug, and then tried to eat some unidentifiable bit of ickiness he found on the sidewalk.

I yanked him away and headed back to the car, feeling at loose ends. It was Sunday, so my crews weren't working, but it wouldn't hurt to get a jump on things for Monday by checking on the progress over at my friend Matt's house, which was still undergoing a protracted renovation. Or . . . My mind wandered back to last night.

What was going on with the Bernini house? Had the police contacted the Propaks, and were they considered suspects? They might have wanted Mrs. Bernini out of the house so they could step up progress on the B&B, it's true, but she was allowing them to line up contractors and do all the preliminary work, so it wasn't as though she was standing in their way . . . at least not at this point.

And what about Josh Avery? His disappearance seemed very odd. But what possible motive could he have to harm Mrs. Bernini? Did he have a prior relationship to her? And if so, wouldn't there be a better way to off the pour soul? Why risk it with us around as witnesses—unless he wanted us there as suspects, or to confuse matters? But besides all of that, there couldn't have been enough time between when Josh disappeared and when we found Mrs. Bernini for him to have killed her, could there? Unless he had an accomplice, someone who had set up a supposed haunting with the dolls and marbles while we were in the kitchen, then killed Mrs. Bernini while we were fleeing, distracted by the haunting. That seemed pretty convoluted to my mind.

Or could it have been a crime of opportunity? Had Mrs. Bernini been wandering her garden at night, just enjoying the evening ... and what? Someone jumped the fence and thought she was carrying a wad of cash under her shawl? Besides, she'd mentioned she strolled in the gardens every night, and had never run into trouble.

And what about the woman who came forward at the scene, saying she was supposed to inherit the house? That was bizarre. I wondered what Inspector Crawford had found out, and whether she would share any information with me. Or whether she might consider letting me back in the house to see if I could speak to the ghosts.

Maybe Anabelle could tell me what had happened, who had killed Mrs. Bernini.

Or could I find a way to communicate with Mrs. Bernini's spirit? She hadn't responded to me at all when I saw her spirit in the garden, but I once communicated with a newly minted ghost. Then again, I'd had a close interaction with him just before he died. I wished I knew more about how this sort of thing worked, but in all the research I'd done, I hadn't found a lot of agreement. I guess that's one reason the field of supernatural research was considered less than scientific. Still, it couldn't hurt to try.

I put Dog back in the car and started driving.

The phone rang. I checked the readout and my heart sped up.

Graham.

I switched to the hands-free Bluetooth. "Hello?"

"How are you?" he asked.

"Oh, fine. Fine."

He chuckled. " 'Fine'? I take it Caleb's okay?"

"Yes, he'll have a scar, but we're coming up with a good story so he can get all the girls."

"I would expect nothing less. And you're okay? Not thrown by your night of murder and mayhem?"

"Let me guess: My dad called you?"

"Just hung up. He doesn't like the idea of you hanging out with your ex-husband, especially after the night you just had. You sure you're all right?"

"I'm not 'hanging out' with Daniel. And as for last night, nothing happened to *me*. It's not even as though we witnessed anything. . . . It was just that the woman who owned the house, Mrs. Bernini, went missing, and then we found . . ." There was a little hitch in my voice. I swallowed, hard. ". . . found her in the garden, in the . . . uh . . . well."

I thought I heard him swearing. "And you weren't threatened?"

"We had no idea what was happening. That's the part I can't get over, actually. If only we could have helped her . . ."

"If you'd tried, you might have been hurt yourself," he said, his voice gruff. When he spoke again, he sounded more upbeat, almost teasing. "Your father also said something about you bringing home another man."

"It wasn't another man. It was Stephen."

"And you're saying Stephen's not a man?"

"Stephen's my gay best friend."

"That would be a comfort except for the fact that he's not gay." I heard Graham chuckling again, and realized I was grinning like a fool, myself. I forgot what we were talking about for a moment, just enjoying the sound of his voice, having him on the other end of the line.

"Where are you now?" he asked.

"Near UCSF Medical Center, on Parnassus near Irving."

"How about I meet you at the Mucky Duck? We could have a beer, and it looks like the rain has passed.... Maybe take a walk on the beach?"

"A walk on the beach? Seriously? Sounds like a personals ad."

"That's why I suggested it. I thought we could check out all those folks from the ads who claim to love romantic walks on the beach. I'm sure they'll all be there."

"I, um, just got up," I said, stalling. A glance in the rearview mirror confirmed my worst fears: Caleb had been right to laugh. And despite Luz's frequent admonitions that grown-up women carry around makeup bags with them for such instances as these, I had nothing with me. Not even a comb.

I heard a strange noise and looked over at Dog, who was back in the footwell, rocking slightly and grunting, as though ready to hurl. Poor pooch.

Dog and I were quite the glamorous pair. I blew out a frustrated breath. I felt sure this sort of thing wouldn't happen if I were living in Paris.

"Okay," said Graham, "how about I take you to a place that serves Sunday brunch late?"

"I don't like breakfast."

"Lunch, then."

"I . . ."

"Mel, if you'd rather not get together, just say so. But I'd like to see you, and knowing you, if no one intervenes, you'll check on your jobs while you're in the city."

"I don't suppose . . . I mean, you wouldn't be interested in going over to the Bernini house with me, would you?"

"The haunted house you ran screaming into the night to escape? The one where a little old lady was killed last night?"

"That would be the one."

"You're not going back there."

"I didn't realize you were my boss." Graham might be adorable, but I'm not great at taking orders.

"It's not safe."

There was a long pause. Graham and I had been dancing around this romance thing, and this ghost thing, for a bit. The romance had begun with a few toe-curling kisses right before Christmas, but then the craziness of the holidays hit, relatives visited . . . and our nascent affair was put on hold, enticing but not quite attainable; a glittery, leftover present still under the tree.

More, my nervousness and—dare I say it?—*bitterness* about male-female relationships didn't help. I was gun-shy, to say the least.

But as for the ghosts, at least Graham didn't think I was a lunatic. He'd witnessed enough to realize there are dimensions we don't fully understand. But he was protective of me, and if I admitted the truth, that tendency made me warm somewhere deep in the pit of my stomach. Still, I wasn't about to curtail my activities to please anyone, no matter how well he kissed.

"Let me rephrase," said Graham. "*Please* tell me you're not going back there."

I didn't say anything.

After another long moment, he grumbled: "Give me the address, and I'll meet you there."

Chapter Eleven

There were a couple of workers outside as I pulled up, a plumber's van and a furnace/air-conditioning truck blocking the drive, so I parked out in the street behind Graham's pickup.

"Do I have to tell you I think this is a bad idea?" Graham asked, leaning down to greet Dog.

In his faded jeans, worn leather work boots, black T-shirt topped with a plaid work shirt jacket, Graham cut a fine figure of a man. He'd been something of a rebel as a youth, roaring around on a motorcycle, but he worked his way through school by working on my dad's construction crew, and grew up fast. And in the last decade or so . . . he'd mellowed. In a really good, alluring way.

"Thanks for coming."

"Only thing worse than letting you go is letting you go alone. Your father would kill me. And I've seen the man's arsenal." He gave me a smile and pushed an unruly lock of hair out of my eyes.

After a long moment, I realized I was staring. This happened far too often when I was around Graham. It was embarrassing. Almost as mortifying as the fact that I had made a quick stop at a drugstore to buy eyeliner, mascara, bobby pins, and a comb, then done the best mini-makeover I could manage in the rear-view mirror.

It's the character that counts, I know. I stand by that principle. But sometimes bad hair makes character hard to spot.

Just as a reality check I reminded myself that Graham was the reason I had to cope with the hassle of installing rooftop solar panels on the historic Victorian I was finishing up across town. Graham was a certified "green" consultant; he was smart about construction, and had great, innovative ideas. But like most environmentalists— and I include myself in that number—he could be a real pain in the butt. Certain energy-saving features were difficult, if not impossible, to gracefully mesh with historic restoration.

Only now did I remember that I meant to keep him far away from the Bernini estate lest he screw up any chance I might have to qualify for the AIA award.

But I was getting ahead of myself: Who knew where the B&B project stood, at this juncture?

I had harbored a vague hope that Anabelle might answer the door again. I had a few questions prepared for the specter. But I didn't even get a chance to knock— Kim Propak was out on the porch, finishing up with the workers who were getting back in their trucks and pulling out of the drive.

"Everything okay?" I asked Kim.

"Oh, the taps drip, incessantly. Also, we're trying to get that old heater working. We're freezing," she said, wrapping her arms around her torso and hiking her shoulders in illustration. She looked pale, with circles under her eyes. "Who knew *plumbers* could install new gas lines, but the heating man deals with the furnace hookup? Oh, *Mel*," she breathed. "Can you believe it?"

"Kim, this is my friend Graham Donovan," I said. "Graham, Kim Propak."

"Oh my, another friend. And a *dog*."

"I just let him out for a second. I'll put him back in the car."

"Oh no, no. He can come in and look around. He's a sweetie." She rubbed his silky brown hair and he leaned into her leg, gazing up at her with impossibly big eyes. She started speaking in a baby voice: "Aren't you a sweetie widdle baby? You want a widdle snack? Scooby snack? Cookie?"

At the sound of a word he knew, Dog's ears perked up and he wagged and wiggled, slapping Kim's legs with his extravagant plume of a tail.

She laughed. "Come on in, let me see what I can find in the fridge. Suppose he'd like some leftover pizza?"

"I'm sure he would, but I'd appreciate something a little plainer. A cracker or a piece of bread would be fine; he's not picky. At all. Only thing he doesn't like is tofu." Which gave me pause, too, frankly.

We followed her into the front room. I peered down

each hallway off the main foyer, hoping for a glimpse of Anabelle or Mrs. Bernini. No luck.

Graham and I sat on the beige brocade couch, and Dog lay at my feet.

"I just can't believe it," Kim said again, perching on the edge of an upholstered chair. "Poor Mrs. Bernini! They say she was . . . incognizant . . . before she was tossed in the well, so that's good, at least. They found the spot she was . . . killed . . . in the garden, near the fountain. They think the killer was interrupted and panicked, put her body down the well to hide it. I just can't bear to think of her . . . to think of . . ."

"I think it's best not to think about it too much," I said. Though, as usual, it was easier to give advice than to follow it oneself. I couldn't get the visual out of my mind, either.

"Mel, I'm sorry to say that since Josh outlasted you here at the house, strictly speaking he won the contract."

"Oh, that's . . . fine," I said, stunned that we were talking about renovating Mrs. Bernini's home so soon, and so coldly. Besides . . . I thought *I* had outlasted Josh, strictly speaking. But I wasn't about to quibble over the construction contract at this point. "Speaking of Josh, do you happen to know where he went last night? We didn't see him after we found Mrs. Bernini, and then we went to call the police. . . ."

"That's right, I heard your cell phones didn't work? That happens to us here, as well. Do you think we're in a dead zone?" She frowned. "I wonder if it would help to switch carriers?"

"It's not that our phones didn't pick up a signal. Their

batteries were drained. Have you experienced that here?"

She shook her head, her pageboy still unmoving. "Sometimes they don't pick up reception. Maybe your phones were searching for service, so they used up their batteries."

"Maybe so. Anyway . . . Josh?"

"I really don't know. The police tracked us down at the Lincoln Inn this morning, so we came straight over. I'm so sleepy I can't stand it. Why, we've been up since before dawn."

If Kim was planning on running a bed-and-breakfast worth its salt, I thought, she'd better get used to rising at five every morning to put fresh muffins and coffee on the table. I was beginning to wonder whether she had any inkling of the day-to-day reality of running one's own hospitality business. From what I'd heard, it was a never-ending, difficult job—fun, but more about endurance than glamour.

"So you don't know if the police spoke with Josh?"

"Not really. I'm sure he'll be in touch, though. He was very determined to win this bid."

"Do you know . . ." I searched for the right words. "Is this place a crime scene now? And are you able to continue living here in the interim, and continue with the renovation plans?"

"Oh, I don't see why not," she said, as though the thought had never occurred to her.

"Is the house in dispute at all? The ownership?"

"Well, the Berninis didn't have any legal children, just foster children. I don't think any of them normally inherit, do they?"

"I really don't know. Is there a will?"

"Let's not worry about any of that at this juncture," said Marty from the doorway.

Dog's head lolled over toward the newcomer; then he thumped his tail a couple of times before going back to sleep.

"Hello . . . ," I said, standing up to greet him but not sure what else to say. It didn't seem like condolences were appropriate, but then, what was? "I'm so sorry about what happened."

"Thank you. Me too. Very traumatic."

"This is my friend Graham," I said. "He's in construction, as well."

"Hello," said Graham, holding out his hand to shake.

"Good to meet you," said Marty. "A competitor?"

"Not at all," answered Graham. "I work with Mel all the time. I'm a green building consultant."

"Is that right? A green builder? I'd love to pick your brain for ideas. Do you have a card?"

Darn it. I *knew* I shouldn't have let Graham know about this place.

"I was just informing Mel that while we appreciate her continued interest in the project," Kim said, "Josh technically stayed in the house longer than she, so he wins the contract."

I opened my mouth to respond, but Marty beat me to it.

"I wouldn't be so sure," Marty said. "There were extenuating circumstances. Maybe we should get all this behind us, let the dust settle, and then try again."

From the way they were talking, it didn't sound like Marty and Kim were letting the little hiccup of Mrs. Bernini's death slow down their renovation plans. I've been accused of being hypersensitive, so maybe I was over-reacting . . . but it dawned on me that the gruesome tale of an old lady down the well might not be the worst thing for a haunted bed-and-breakfast.

"There was a woman here last night who said that she was supposed to inherit the house."

"You mean Mountain? He's not a woman. . . ." Her eyes widened and she looked at her husband. "*Is* he?"

Marty shook his head.

"No," I said. "It certainly wasn't Mountain. . . . Are you saying that *Mountain* might think he was inheriting the house?"

"As I understood it," said Kim, "Mr. Mountain was working on bringing the gardens back from the brink with the understanding that he would inherit the home. He worked for free for Mrs. Bernini."

"Really. So, what does that do to your purchase agreement?"

"That still holds," said Marty. "I guess the money just goes to a different source."

"Does Mountain know that?" I asked. It always amazed me when people talked about houses as money, rather than as objects of love. If Mountain was sentimental about the Castro neighborhood, he might well be counting on the house itself, to love and fix up and take care of. If I had my heart set on a house, no amount of money would sway me.

The two shared a look. I was guessing not. "You didn't mention it to him?"

"It was Mrs. Bernini's idea," said Marty. "She didn't want him to stop working—the place was looking so fabulous. She told him we were relatives who just wanted to fix the place up. She thought, really quite reasonably, that he would be more than compensated by the money."

That seemed rather manipulative. Maybe Mrs. Bernini wasn't quite the sweet old woman I'd thought she was. Presuming these two were telling me the truth.

"And so the woman who claimed she was inheriting — you have no idea who she is?"

"Mmm . . ." Kim trailed off with a quick shake of her head and a little shrug, her blue eyes widening just a tad as she looked at a spot over my shoulder. I wasn't trained at Quantico, but I was guessing she was lying. "Oh, by the way, I contacted the photographer whose name you gave me, Zach Malinski? What a sweetheart. He's *darling*."

Graham let out an exasperated, mirthless chuckle.

"Oh, good," I said, hoping neither of them noticed Graham's reaction. "I'm glad that worked out."

Dog suddenly lifted his head, looking out into the hallway. He glanced up at me, big dark brown eyes questioning. When I petted him, he laid his head back down, but after a few seconds he lifted it again. A low rumble sounded in his chest.

Dog might be a dim bulb, but like a lot of animals he seemed able to sense spirits better than even the most sensitive human.

"You know," I said, "the other night I left some things in the room where we stayed. Would you mind if I take a quick look upstairs?"

The smile on Kim's face froze, but she shook her head and said, "I'll take you up," as she rose. Graham followed suit.

Darn it. I was hoping to walk through the house alone.

Dog trotted along beside us, but when we got to the bottom of the stairs, he started barking, then ran the rest of the way up.

Kim gazed at me, wide-eyed.

"He does that," I said. "It could be nothing."

That was true. Dog occasionally seemed to remember he was on guard duty, at which point he would run around as though on the track of something real, hackles raised, and barking like a wild thing. Soon enough he would forget what he was doing and get interested in food. It was the way it went.

But right then, I heard humming, and then the song: *"A garden of posies for all little girls. . . ."*

I looked all around us as we climbed the stairs but saw nothing. Neither Kim nor Graham gave any indication of hearing anything amiss. At the second-floor landing, though, there was a different kind of music—not Anabelle's off-key singing, but the tinny notes of the toy carousel.

This, my companions heard. Kim stopped short and stared down the hall, mouth slack.

Dog crouched in the hallway, barking and snarling at the partially opened door of the playroom.

Chapter Twelve

"I . . . uh . . ." Kim looked ashen. Again, I couldn't help but wonder. . . . This was the woman who wanted to run a haunted bed-and-breakfast? "Where is that *sound* coming from?"

"I think it's the toy carousel in the nursery," I said. "We heard it the other night when we stayed here."

"I've never gone in there. Mrs. Bernini told us . . . she said it was best not to. We let Portia go in there and take a few things out, but I've never gone in."

"How about I go check it out?" I offered.

She bobbed her head, eagerly turning back toward the stairs.

"I'm right behind you," Graham told me.

"You really don't have to. In fact, it might be best if I go in alone."

"Not happening. Am I the only one who remembers there was a murder here last night?"

I proceeded down the corridor, toward the door that stood ajar. I hesitated a moment, then pushed it, slowly, all the way open.

The carousel stopped abruptly, its little horses still swaying. The nursery had been trashed, with dolls, trucks, and assorted playthings tossed everywhere. The rocking horse was on its side, the marionettes tangled on the small theater stage.

"Anabelle?" I called.

No response.

Graham picked his way carefully through the toys strewn on the floor, not touching anything as he walked the perimeter of the room. He noted the words scrawled on the wall in red crayon and looked at me, his eyebrows raised in question. I shrugged.

Dog, I noticed, hadn't set a paw inside the playroom. He whimpered and growled but stayed out in the hall.

"Anabelle, I need to talk to you," I said. "I want to ask you about the other night—can you help me find out what happened?"

Nothing. The silence began to fold in on me. I started to feel strange, not myself.

The ghost-hunting equipment I had borrowed from Olivier was scattered on the floor. I knelt to gather it.

The temperature of the room dropped precipitously.

A marble rolled across the wood floor toward me. The sound of its rolling rang out in the quiet. It tapped lightly against my knee.

I could hear the jingle of Dog's tags as he took off down the hall.

Clank, scrape, shuffle. I heard the noise first, then

caught a glimpse of Mrs. Bernini shuffling by the open doorway as she made her laborious way down the hall.

"Wait!"

I ran out of the room, but stopped short when I saw Anabelle standing in the middle of the hallway, arms folded over her little chest. She looked angry.

I put my hand up to my pounding heart. "You scared me!"

"Mrs. Bernini can't hear you."

"Why not?"

Anabelle cocked her head and gave me a quizzical look that seemed much older than her years, reminding me of when I first met her at the door and asked whether Mrs. Bernini was her grandmother. "It takes a while to learn how."

"How to what?"

"Speak. Or at least speak so people can hear you. Most can't. Why are you so odd?"

"Born that way, I guess. Can you tell me what happened to Mrs. Bernini?"

Tears pooled in her big eyes and her bottom lip started to tremble. But she just shook her head.

"I don't know. I don't *know*," she cried. "It's like before. . . . I just can't remember. I want to find out what happened. . . ."

"You don't know how you . . . died?"

She shook her head. "For a long time, I didn't even realize . . . things were different, but the same. It's hard to explain. Can you tell me what happened?"

"I don't know, but I'll try to find out. But . . . are you angry we're here? Did you write that note on the wall of the nursery?"

"Of course not," she said with a soft hiccup. She sniffed loudly. "*I* don't write on walls. That was Ezekiel."

"Did he toss everything around in there?"

"*No*. He's not *that* bad."

"Is Ezekiel here with you now?"

She shook her head. "He's looking for our puppy. Besides, he doesn't like you."

"Why not?"

"He says you've brought death to this house. We think you should *GO AWAY*!" She shrieked that last part, rushing at me, then disappearing right in front of me.

I collapsed against the wall.

"Mel, are you all right?" Graham rushed over and helped steady me. He was looking around, searching both directions of the hall.

"Did you see her?"

"I didn't see anything. I could hear your side of a conversation, but no one else was here. It was—"

"What's going on? Who are you talking to?" asked Marty, who had materialized at the top of the stairs. He looked at me with concern, then addressed Graham. "Has she been seeing ghosts? The little girl?"

"Yes," I answered for myself. "And Mrs. Bernini."

"Is she . . . you're saying Mrs. Bernini's ghost is here? She's inhabiting this house now?"

"I think so."

Marty seemed startled. "Can she tell you anything about what happened last night?"

"She doesn't seem to hear me, or even acknowledge my presence. But maybe if I spent a little more time . . ." At the moment I wasn't feeling particularly upbeat about spirits, or my abilities to communicate with them.

Much less the idea that these particular ghosties were supposed to charm a bunch of bed-and-breakfast guests. I wondered quite how to phrase this to Kim and Marty.

But then again, no one but me seemed able to see Anabelle, and if we'd stayed out of the nursery—like Mrs. Bernini had warned us—my companions last night wouldn't have witnessed anything at all. Heard a few noises, at most. Perhaps the spirits came after only a few of us.

Still, the idea of child ghosts running these halls made my blood go cold. Most likely they had died of disease; those were the days when a flu bug could sweep through and decimate the child population of a city. But then, wouldn't Anabelle remember being sick? She couldn't remember what had happened to her, much less tell me who killed Mrs. Bernini. Was that what she wanted from me? To help her figure it out?

Marty turned to Graham: "Did you see the ghosts, too?"

Graham held his hands up in front of him, palms out, as though helpless. "I can't see a thing unless Mel kisses me."

"What?"

"He's kidding," I said to Marty, shooting Graham a quelling look. "Reference to a long-ago event."

Graham smiled.

Marty, for his part, still looked shaken and uneasy.

He opened his mouth to speak, but Kim's voice floated up the stairs. "*Sweetheart? We really need to go if we're going to make our appointment.*"

"*Be right down,*" Marty called. He turned his attention back to me. "Look, we're in something of a limbo right now. I'm not sure, legally, where we stand. Whether we can even maintain our residence here, whether the purchase agreement is still valid . . . or what. Kim doesn't really grasp all the ins and outs—she's more the style guru."

"Unless you've been ordered to leave the premises, it would probably be best for everyone if you stayed on, just to look after the place until things are settled. Empty houses have a way of inviting all kinds of problems," I replied.

"That's a good point. In fact, Kim and I are scheduled to go back to Fort Wayne for a few days. . . . It's terrible timing, what with, well, everything. People are snooping, peeking into the garden and all."

"If you'd like, I could stay here while you're gone." I could feel Graham's eyes boring into me. "I could keep an eye on the place, and it would give me a chance to work up a detailed bid for you."

"I'm not sure how Josh Avery would feel about that."

"I'd be happy to share all my measurements and findings with him. It wouldn't give me any unfair advantage." All right, now I was lying through my teeth. But this was no longer just about a construction contract; I wanted to have time alone in this house, with these ghosts.

"Let me talk to Kim, and I'll get back to you on that. And"—Marty gestured to the mess in the playroom—"any idea what happened in here? Was it . . . ghostly antics of some sort from last night?"

"It wasn't like this last time I saw it," I said as I picked up the rest of the broken equipment—the baby monitor and voice recorder. "But there was definitely some . . . activity. On the other hand, maybe the police were searching for something?"

"I don't think so," Marty said as he escorted us down the hall so Graham and I could retrieve the overnight bags that Stephen, Claire, and I had left in the bedroom. The police had had the chance to look through them last night, if they'd needed to. "They did a walk-through of the house, but they've been concentrating on the garden."

We carried the bags outside, where we met up with an anxious Kim, who had her coat on, her purse in hand, and urged her husband to hurry for their appointment.

"One more question, Marty: Do you know what happened to the family that lived here? I've heard references to a family tragedy?"

He shook his head and sighed, looking defeated. "Somehow I thought it happened so long ago that it wouldn't affect us. After all, Mrs. Bernini lived here for so many years and never seemed to be bothered by it. . . . Or . . . one of the neighbors suggested maybe this place has a curse, and that's why she died a violent death, too?"

Marty studied my face, as though I should know the answer. I realized he was thinking of me as a knowledgeable paranormal professional. There was more to this ghost-busting stuff than first appeared.

"I . . . I don't think it's anything like that."

He shrugged. "As to how the original family died, I really don't think that anyone knows for sure. All I heard was that the parents and the two children were found by the servants one morning. The whole family was huddled together in the same bed. Dead."

Graham and I watched as Kim and Marty took off in their massive gas-guzzling Escalade. Vaguely, I wondered how long that vehicle would last in this parking-challenged, environmentally conscious city. Before the year was out, I'd wager, they'd be driving a compact hybrid.

"What a mess," I said as we tossed the broken equipment and overnight bags in the back of my Scion. "On top of everything else, I sure hope that roof can hold it together for another season. What with the inheritance questions, I imagine the building will be in limbo for some time."

"Good," said Graham. "So there's no need for you to be dealing with this place, for a while at least."

"Mmm," I said while absentmindedly petting Dog.

"I don't like the sound of that. 'Mmm . . .' means that you're planning something you don't want to admit to."

"Not necessarily. It's just a sound, you know, a kind of nonresponse response."

"Uh-huh. *Please* tell me you weren't serious about house-sitting while the Propaks are gone. A murder took place here, Mel, and if word gets around that you can talk to ghosts, and presumably to the recently deceased Mrs. Bernini, you're practically begging the killer to come back and take you out of commission, as well."

"The thing is, Graham, I did see a ghost. Or two. In the house."

"I realize that. I just witnessed you talking to the wall, remember?"

"Hey! We really are making progress in our relationship. There was a time you would have thought I was nuts after witnessing such behavior."

"When it comes to ghosts, I've always believed you," he said in a quiet voice, watching me carefully. Graham made me nervous when he got serious.

"So." I cleared my throat. "I'm thinking there must be a way for the spirits to tell me what happened. And then I could tell the police. . . ."

"And the police could go catch themselves a killer."

"Something like that." Dog started barking at nothing and whirling around, excited. I hushed him.

"And how would you explain knowing how the murder occurred, and who was responsible?"

"Um . . ." That hadn't occurred to me.

"If you know enough detail about the crime, *and* you were here that night, wouldn't that cast you in a suspicious light?"

"But I didn't do it, so I don't have to worry, right?"

"Because innocent parties are never accused and convicted of crimes." Dog kept barking; this time Graham hushed him.

"I know they are sometimes, but . . . okay. Good point. So I'll be judicious about what to share with the police."

"Mel." He seemed to be searching for the right words. "I know you have a passion for justice, and for stepping in when someone needs help—"

I snorted, reminding myself of my father. On my worst days I feared I was going to morph into a female version of him: an old curmudgeon who watched an enormous TV and harangued any poor sod who would listen about the wretched state of the world. Still, he had his lovable side.

"That's not true," I said. "I'm a misanthrope."

One corner of his mouth kicked up. "Oh, that's right. I forgot that. You're a misanthrope, except for the fact that you stick your neck out for people all the time, no matter the consequences. Like when your friend Matt was in trouble, or when you were worried about the family on Union Street, or when your dad needed you to step in and take over the business."

I felt myself blushing, studied the paint job on the car door, and shrugged.

"I'm a patsy. Not the same thing. And besides, when I'm trying to figure something out, well, I'm sort of like ..."

"A dog with a bone."

"I was thinking more like determined. Indomitable. Unwavering," I insisted, not pleased with his analogy.

"Stubborn as sin."

"I thought you *liked* me."

"I *do* like you. But, Mel, if you're really seeing what you think you are, and you can really speak with them ... don't you see? You're putting yourself in danger. If someone thinks you'll be able to lead the police to them, they could come after you. And remember, we're talking about someone cold-blooded enough to toss an old woman down a well."

At that moment there was a loud crashing noise as something was thrown through an upstairs window.

Graham pushed me down behind the Scion, sheltering me with his body. Dog ran after us, tail between his legs.

Shattered glass rained down upon the drive.

We looked up but couldn't see anyone at the window.

Anyone *alive*, that is. I caught a quick glimpse of Anabelle, and another face beside hers—presumably Ezekiel. Both were rosy-cheeked and so real-looking it was hard to fathom they had been dead for almost a century.

"Stay here," Graham said. Warily, he hurried into the

drive, his eyes on the upstairs windows of the house, silent and foreboding as they reflected the afternoon sun. He picked up something and brought it back to me.

It was a brick, wrapped in a note. I smoothed out the piece of paper. On it, a message was written in pretty, florid handwriting, almost like a scroll.

Stay out! There's room in the well for you all.

The next morning I hit the road early, answering incessant phone calls and doing my usual check-in with all my crews. There was solace in the rote everydayness of my Monday routine.

In Pacific Heights I checked in with the foreman at a great Beaux Arts building on Vallejo. This project had been nearly completed when the quirky owner—my friend Matt—decided he wanted to raise the roof. The new drawings were now up for review by the permit office, and I'd spent more time than I ever wanted down at city hall.

This was the problem with being a small-business owner: I rarely got to do any actual hands-on work, since most of my time and energy was spent on administration and client relations. Stan was my right arm, completing paperwork, dealing with payroll, and fielding phone calls, but there was no getting around the fact that someone had to run around from jobsite to city hall and back again, checking on progress schedules, getting clients to sign off on agreements, and shepherding paperwork through San Francisco's bureaucratic morass.

Next, I stopped in at Cheshire House. Not so long ago this building had been the site of a serious haunting, but now that its unhappy specters had been laid to rest, the place felt different: peaceful, serene, and strikingly beautiful. It would soon be a warm home for the young family who was ready to move into the house.

I stood outside for a moment, looking up at the facade of the splendid Queen Anne Victorian. It featured two turrets and curlicue woodwork known as "gingerbread" along every window and ledge, and under the roofline. This was the kind of house that put San Francisco on the architectural map. Unfortunately the pattern of decorative shingles on the roof would be marred by the solar panels Graham was having installed for the owners, but sometimes historical accuracy had to make way for the future of our planet.

I spent half an hour developing a punch list, or a tally of final details to attend to, with the owners, Jim and Katenka Daley. Their young son was walking now, drooling and happy as ever. We went over some paint colors and gilt ideas for the exterior details, and I ran some suggestions for the interior decorative touches past them—Queen Anne was not a subtle architectural style. The home's tall ceilings called for plenty of embellishment, and some of the original had been stripped or damaged during the years the building operated as a boardinghouse.

Finally, I spoke with the refinisher and confirmed arrangements for the wood floors to be sanded, stained, and sealed. The floor guys would be among the last workers in; after the final coat of polyurethane was laid down and thoroughly dried, Katenka and Jim could start moving into their beautiful new old house.

I couldn't decide who was more excited: them or me. I adore seeing a project like this coming to fruition, a historic home reclaiming its grandeur with the help of appreciative owners. Before I left, I presented the Daleys with a scrapbook filled with before-and-after photos, progress pictures, and ephemera from the project, as well as a group portrait of everyone who had worked on the house. There were blank pages in the back, to be filled with photos when the furniture was in place and the house was ready to live in. These mementos were a Turner Construction tradition my mother had started for our clients years ago, and I always felt like she was with me as I pasted and stamped and jotted down notes.

As I left I noticed a small pile of mossy bricks in the still-undone front yard. They put me in mind of yesterday's incident: the brick sailing out of a window of the Bernini house, straight for us.

More to the point, I thought about the threatening message: *There's room in the well for you all.*

What a wretched thing to write. Who could have done such a thing?

After reading the note off the brick yesterday, I had called Inspector Crawford. She retrieved the evidence from us, but seemed underwhelmed at the idea that this "clue" might crack the case wide open. She appeared more interested in why I had returned to her crime scene, and then suggested I stay away from the Bernini house altogether.

"Do you think you'll get any evidence from the brick, or the note?" I asked.

"I'll send it to forensics," she said. "But I don't expect much."

"You think it was the killer who threw it?" I asked. "The threat about the well and all?"

She shrugged. "It's a talkative neighborhood. By early this morning I imagine everyone from the pizza guy to the heater repairman had been weighing in with details about the crime and the crime scene. It would be easy enough to break into this old place, and it's so big I imagine you could be in there for some time without being noticed. For all we know, it could have been a local kid who thought it was funny."

Or a spirit? I wondered. The handwriting was unusual. Could it have been written by the ghosts? And would that mean that *they* had harmed Mrs. Bernini? I didn't think ghosts did such things, but could I be sure? In any case, I knew better than to share my suspicions with the skeptical inspector.

After meeting with Inspector Crawford, Graham and I took the proverbial walk on the beach to get my mind off things. Then, to *really* get my mind off things we made out a little—enough to steam up all the truck's windows and send me into some kind of hormonally charged needfest—but when I started to feel out of control, I pulled back, and he didn't push. I think he was waiting for me to feel comfortable, and to make the first move.

That was probably a mistake. Graham might have the patience of Job, but I was a tough case.

Enough of such thoughts. I was supposed to be working, so I headed across town to one of my favorite supply stores, Victoriana, which made ornamental plaster castings from original pieces, as well as wood moldings, carved wood pieces, newel posts, and turned balusters. On my way there I noticed a sign that I had seen many times before: HOMER'S DELI. Mrs. Bernini had mentioned that one of her foster sons, Homer, had a deli in this neighborhood. It must be his place. How many Homer's Delis could there possibly be?

I continued on to my destination, and spent the next hour studying the store's inventory, making notes on the fat catalog. Finally, I asked for some small samples of several antique wallpaper borders. I'm not sure where Victoriana had stumbled across this stash, but these were a rare find, heavily embossed and painted by hand. They would look great in Jim and Katenka's master bedroom.

For that matter, one of them would be perfect to replace the damaged frieze in Mrs. Bernini's old master bedroom, presuming the faux finishers were unable to perform their magic and repair it convincingly.

It's not my job, I reminded myself. At least not yet.

My mind went from thinking of the Bernini house, to Mrs. Bernini's death, to a school photo of a Howdy Doody–looking boy with freckles, long neck, and big ears. How would someone like that have aged? I wondered. And more to the point, what might he be able to tell me about the hauntings at the Bernini house? I was very curious to meet this Homer.

I checked my phone for the time: eleven twenty. Nearly lunchtime. A deli sandwich was sounding good right about now.

Chapter Thirteen

I assumed by the loading dock out front that Homer's Deli did a lot of wholesale business, but right inside the no-frills front door were a counter and a chalkboard listing today's special sandwiches. Opposite the deli case were huge freezers full of lasagna, tortellini, ravioli, picrogi, and a variety of sauces and ragùs.

At the back was a doorway with KITCHEN written on the door.

The line for sandwiches was long, the workers harried. I tried to catch someone's eye to ask for Homer, assuming that neither of the young men working behind the counter was old enough to be him, but they were too busy to be bothered.

Instead, I snooped. I poked my head through the plastic flaps over a side doorway, keeping the warm air in. Out in the loading dock area were several more freezers, refrigerated trucks, and tall stacks of boxes printed with the Homer's Deli logo: a man with an exaggerated mustache and a tall chef's hat. I headed for a small glassed-in office in one corner.

"I'm looking for ... ?" I said to the woman at the front desk, though I needn't have bothered. My eyes alighted on the man in the interior office. He was lanky, with strawberry blond hair shot through with silver, freckles, and rosy cheeks.

Howdy Doody, all grown up.

He was holding up two phones, one to each ear. His desk looked a lot like mine: covered in tall, loose piles of paper. It dawned on me that not only was I catching him at a bad time, but he might not yet have been informed of Mrs. Bernini's death. Who was I to break this kind of news to him?

"May I help you?" asked the receptionist.

"No, my mistake," I said, deciding discretion was the better part of valor.

I was about to scurry away when Homer's eyes met mine. We stared at each other for a moment through the doorway.

"Wait!" I heard from behind me as I turned back toward the door. "Are you ... you wouldn't be Mrs. Bernini's new friend, by any chance? The, uh ... ghost whisperer?"

"Um, yes, I think I am. How did you know?"

"The way you were hovering there ... Mrs. Bernini told me all about you the other day, and described you to a tee. You and your ... outfits."

Today I was wearing a bright pink, rather low-cut T-shirt Stephen had given me that read: "Rome wasn't built in a day." I had matched it with a jeans skirt and tights, and wore a leather jacket over the whole ensemble to ward off the city's foggy chill. Oh, and my work boots, of course.

"Come on in, please. Have a seat. This whole thing . . . it's been such a shock."

I felt a wave of relief that he had already been notified of her death. "I'm so sorry for your loss."

"Thank you." He ran a pale, freckled hand through his hair. "I'm not sure it's really sunk in yet. It's so . . . sudden. And I just feel, well, guilty that I didn't get over there more. We Skyped every Saturday morning, but that's hardly a substitute for visits. It's just . . . I hate that place."

"Which place?"

"That old house."

"Why?"

"There were always weird things happening, and it was freezing. And that damned radio always came on, and . . ." He stopped suddenly, wiping his palms on his trousers. "Well, you're in the business, so I'll just say it: I think there are ghosts in that house. They . . . they used to run us out of the playroom. I've never seen anything like that before or since, thank goodness. But those . . . whatever they were . . . sure didn't want us playing in that nursery. Mrs. Bernini would send us up there to play, and they would chase us out. She didn't believe us at first, but she finally let us play downstairs instead."

"What sorts of things did you see?"

He shook his head and let out a long breath. "Mostly the toys . . . they would move of their own accord. There was a puppet theater and the marionettes would move by themselves. And a toy carousel that played creepy music. Once . . . once or twice I thought I saw a little girl. The first time I thought she was a new foster child, but then I realized she was something else altogether."

"Did she say anything to you?"

He shook his head. "No. Thank goodness. I think that might have done me in."

"Could you tell me anything about the other foster kids?"

"There was a passel of them. Kids from all over. A lot of them were short-term; I was one of the longer ones."

"Could you . . . I'm sure the police have probably talked with you already, but I was just wondering . . . can you think of anyone who would want to harm Mrs. Bernini?"

He looked at me askance. "I thought you were there for the ghosts. . . . Are you looking into the murder, as well?"

"Not really," I hastened to assure him. "I guess I'm just trying to make sense of it all."

His desk phone started to ring and Homer stared at it as though it had never before done such a thing. Then he shook his head. "I don't really know. I can't imagine, except . . . my foster mother had a way of getting what she wanted. She was wonderful, don't get me wrong. But sometimes she made promises she couldn't keep. I gathered from what the police said that there might be a couple of different wills floating around, which doesn't surprise me. Knowing her, there might be half a dozen. And that place must be worth a fortune. . . ."

He trailed off, leaving me to come to my own conclusion. I wanted to ask whether Homer had expected to inherit something, as well, but couldn't think how without sounding a whole lot like someone poking her nose in where it didn't belong.

"Mrs. Bernini spoke fondly of you," I said. "She mentioned that a lot of the foster children came back for a memorial service when Angelo died. Do you suppose you'll want to arrange something for her, and let the others know?"

His freckles stood out against his pale skin, and there was a sheen of tears in his pale eyes.

"Yes, definitely. I'll take care of it."

I pondered my conversation with Homer as I stood in line to buy a sandwich. Did this whole mystery boil down to who held the authentic will? That sounded like more of a challenge for the lawyers than for me: sifting through the paperwork to find the legitimate heir. Period.

On the other hand, that still didn't determine who killed Mrs. Bernini, and why.

While the man behind the counter was piling prosciutto, roasted red peppers, provolone, and tapenade on a fresh sourdough roll, my stomach growled and my mind turned toward more prosaic issues. I decided to buy a platter of frozen ravioli and a tub of ragù to take home for dinner. I figured it could defrost in the car. It would last in the January chill.

The sandwich was massive. It made me think of my perpetually hungry friend Luz.

"I have food," I said over the phone as I tried to convince her to join me. I was supposed to go over to Daniel's house. The house where his current wife was remodeling my careful renovation, where I was sure to have to bite my tongue when I saw what they'd torn out, and where my stepson, Caleb, had been hurt, perhaps by ghosts. I felt sleep-deprived, scared, and in desperate need of moral support. "Aren't you off early on Mondays?"

"Yes, but as I've told you, I don't know how many times: I don't like ghosts."

"I doubt there really *are* any this time. For real. Plus, it's the middle of the day, for heaven's sake." This didn't stop ghosts from appearing, in my experience, but there was no doubt that confronting a specter at night was more disconcerting than in broad daylight. "Plus, we'll be seeing Valerie."

Her tone perked up. "Valerie?"

"Mmm-hmm."

"And I get to torture her just as much as I want? What about the Worm? Will he be there?"

"I'm not sure." The Worm was her nickname for Daniel.

"But if he is, I get to do a number on him?" Luz was a loyal friend, which in her mind meant that Daniel and Valerie were evil, pure and simple. As was the case with most human relationships, things were slightly more complicated than that. Still, there was an undeniable beauty to having a pal act out one's basest impulses.

I stopped by her place, an old 1920s art deco apartment building that had been converted to condos. We ate our sandwich for fortification, then headed toward my former residence.

"*Mel*, so glad you could make it." Valerie met us at the door. Her long, silky hair hung dark and sinuous down past her shoulders, and her creamy complexion was set off by the crisp wool designer outfit she was wearing.

The ensemble was tasteful but boring. Rather like the woman herself.

Don't be mean, Mel. I forced myself to smile in greeting.

Valerie's eyes flickered over my getup, a flash of distaste registering on her face before she managed a polite smile. Since I'd just done the same thing to her, I was in no position to throw stones.

It didn't escape my notice that Valerie and I treated each other rather like wary competitors, which was strange in that I had no desire, in any part of my being, to have Daniel back. What I wanted was to get him out of my head entirely. But I wasn't willing to give up my stepson.

"Hi, I'm Luz. Rhymes with 'juice,'" said Luz as she thrust out her hand, almost aggressively, toward Valerie.

"Nice to meet you," said Valerie with a tight smile.

"The pleasure's all mine," Luz said as she pumped Valerie's hand enthusiastically. "Really. Can't get enough of it."

Valerie and Luz had met several times, but Valerie never seemed to remember. This resulted in Luz making a big deal out of introducing herself, each and every time.

Luz cracked me up.

The building was a classic San Francisco Victorian town house, not particularly grand, but charming. A long flight of exterior stairs led to the entrance on what was called the first floor, containing the living room, dining room, entry, and kitchen. Above this was the second floor, with three bedrooms. And below, on the ground floor, were the garage, a couple of guest bedrooms, and Daniel's study, which led out onto the garden. The house stood in an exclusive neighborhood, near the corner of Presidio and Clay, so it was worth a small fortune despite its lack of ostentation.

When I first moved in with Daniel, I set about renovating it—it was my very first attempt, back when I was still pretending to be an anthropologist. I made a lot of beginner's mistakes, but I brought this place back from an unfortunate 1970s remodel with the sweat of my brow in a misguided attempt to make a beautiful home for me, my husband, and his son.

Turns out my time would have been better spent on, say, doing my nails. Or just about anything. Still, I learned a lot.

Valerie stepped back and gestured us into the front hall. I steeled myself to see exactly what direction Valerie had taken with the renovations; I hadn't set foot in here since I liberated my things when the divorce became final a year and a half ago. The furniture she'd chosen was understated and expensive, covered primarily in shades of ecru and beige. The walls had been changed from the historically accurate colors I had chosen—deep wines and ochers, sap greens and robin's egg blue—to various shades of white. It wasn't ugly, just lackluster. It didn't suit my house.

Her house. Hers and Daniels.

Once again I felt a fervent desire to escape to Paris.

"Is Daniel here?" As much as I disliked my ex-husband, I would rather deal with him than with Valerie.

"No, he's on campus today," Valerie said as she led the way across the foyer. "He told me you would be stopping by."

"And Caleb?" Luz asked. "How's he feeling?"

She shrugged. "Seems fine. He emerges for food every once in a while, but goes back downstairs to play video games or God knows what. What else is new?"

Caleb spent most of his time at his mom Angelica's house, but stayed part-time with his dad. He had an official bedroom on the second floor, but preferred a room down on the ground level, which led directly into the garage and had its own entrance. To my mind, providing a teenage boy with his own entrance—which also served as an *exit*—seemed like a bad idea. Amazingly enough, no one had asked my opinion.

"It sounds quiet," I said, noting the lack of any activity indicating construction work being done in the house. But plastic sheeting covered the stairs and the foyer floor, and drop cloths protected the carpet.

"Daniel shut things down, temporarily, after Caleb's accident. Sent everyone away for a few days. He's pretty upset."

"Could you run me through what happened?"

"Well, what started this whole thing was that the toilet lid broke. One of the workers got sloppy, I guess, but no one would admit to it. Anyway, I reminded them that these things cost money, and money doesn't exactly grow on trees."

"Uh-huh. And then?"

"Then yesterday, Caleb went up for his basketball shoes and was coming back down. He was on the lower part of the stairs, right there." She gestured to the short flight of steps off the entry. The balustrade, I noticed, had so far escaped alteration; it was made of intricately carved and turned newel posts, putting me in mind of the Bernini house. "He heard something, turned to look up, and luckily stepped up a stair right before the broken toilet lid fell down on him. When he looked up"—she paused for dramatic effect—"there was *no one* there."

"No." Luz gasped and put a hand to her cheek. I thought she was overdoing it a tad, but Valerie seemed to take it seriously. She nodded solemnly.

I climbed a few steps, peering upward. "You can't see anything beyond the railing from here," I said. "Someone might have knocked it accidentally, then jumped back, out of sight. Scared of what had happened."

But why would a toilet bowl lid have been balanced to drop from the landing above?

Rage and fear coursed through me. I couldn't keep from thinking what might have happened if the heavy porcelain had hit Caleb on the head, rather than simply scraping his arm. I made a silent promise to the universe: If someone had done this on purpose, they would pay.

"Or," Valerie said, her dark eyes imperious, "there could be ghostly activity here. . . . Maybe the men were telling the truth when they denied doing it. This isn't the only thing that's happened."

"Really?" gasped Luz. "What else? Do tell."

"Tools turn on by themselves—just last week a jigsaw took a chunk out of the new dining room table. It's a total loss. *Look* at this." She showed us the table, with, indeed, a chunk taken out of it. "Things have gone missing, and then someone—or some*thing*—took my clothes out of the closet, all of them, and spilled on them."

"Awesome." I heard Luz chuckling under her breath.

"Spilled what?" I asked, ignoring Luz.

"*I* don't know," Valerie said impatiently. "Something . . . icky."

"Ectoplasm, maybe," Luz suggested. "That's *super* icky."

Valerie's big eyes gazed at Luz, as though she was unsure how to respond.

"Could there be a disgruntled worker on the crew?" I asked.

"Of course not. They should be thrilled to have work in this economy."

So said the woman with no visible means of support, other than her husband.

"Daniel mentioned you're acting as your own general. That's a tough job, under any circumstances. Has anything happened between you and the crew? Any heated words exchanged, anything like that?"

She shook her head vehemently.

"Mind if I look around? Where are they working mostly, upstairs?"

She nodded. "We had a bit of a fiasco with some of the kitchen cabinets—they have to redo the ones to the far side of the stove. But other than that, they're pretty much done down here, so they're concentrating on the bathroom upstairs, the master. But while they're here, we're having them do a few other odds and ends—a door in Daniel's office to open onto the garden, retiling the downstairs baths, that sort of thing."

I nodded. This happened all the time—a small, contained job expanded. Once homeowners realized they had skilled labor on the premises, they remembered all sorts of odd jobs and wish-list items that had been adding up over the years. Often this was fine, as contractors charged for the added jobs. But some contractors failed to factor in extra time for such change orders, so they were under pressure to finish up jobs in order to move on. If a client wasn't a great listener, for example, she might inadvertently step on toes.

On the other hand, disgruntled workers were more likely to be angry at their immediate employer, the owner of the construction company. They screwed things up on the job to make the company look bad. I should follow up with whoever was providing the workers . . . unless they were freelance, which I doubted. I couldn't imagine Valerie pulling up in front of a home-improvement store parking lot and picking up day workers. Among other things, she didn't speak a word of Spanish, which was pretty much a requirement for general contractors in the Bay Area.

Valerie led the way up the stairs to the second floor. Daniel and Valerie must be spending their time in another bedroom, I thought, as the master bath job had spilled out into the majority of the bedroom.

I noticed old coffee cups, sawdust collecting in crevices, even a few cigarette butts. This wasn't unusual, but I would never allow my jobsites to look this messy. My dad had trained me from childhood: *Things look sloppy enough on building sites, by necessity. No need to exaggerate things. If it's sloppy in public, imagine what it looks like behind the walls.*

The tub had been torn out of the bathroom. The old cast-iron slipper tub that I'd found at the Sink Factory in Berkeley, the one I'd scrubbed with a wire brush and repainted on the outside with noxious oil-based enamel. The one with feet that looked like claws holding balls.

I had adored that tub. I presumed the still plastic-wrapped fiberglass Jacuzzi sitting in the bedroom had been brought in to replace it.

"Do you still have the old bathtub?" I asked.

"I told the guys they could take that and the pedestal sink to Urban Ore or wherever, just to get them out of our hair."

I literally bit my tongue to keep from saying something nasty. No sense getting upset. I could probably still track it down at the salvage yard if I really wanted it back.

Next I studied the plumbing that was being done inside the wall: They were using copper piping, which was excellent, but some of the joints were poorly soldered. A couple of the framing two-by-fours were out of plumb, and they had used particleboard in the cabinet under the sink, a definite no-no in wet locations. Still, I kept my mouth shut. *Never* did contractors say anything nice about the work done on a structure before their arrival. It was ubiquitous. I always wondered whether it was so we could have someone to blame if something went wrong later, or so we looked good by comparison. Though often tempted, unless it was a health and safety violation, I tried to refrain from jumping on the critical bandwagon, since it made the clients feel unsure about the quality of their home and put in doubt their decision making about previous workers.

Still, I might mention the particleboard no-no to Daniel. But by and large, I wasn't here to inspect the quality of work. I was looking for ghosts.

And so far there were no signs of the kinds of ghostly pranks I'd seen elsewhere: footprints and marks in unlikely places, cold spots, knocking in walls, doors opening and closing, that sort of thing. No whispers or quick moves out of the corners of my eyes. No figures appearing in the mirrors, other than me, Valerie, and Luz.

Feeling rather sheepish, I brought out the EMF reader.

"What's that?" Valerie asked, eyes wide.

"It's supposed to note energy changes, if there are any," I said. "Ghosts are said to draw on the energy in the room, and this device measures the fluctuations."

Luz was wandering around the bedroom, picking up one tchotchke after another, frowning and looking off into space, as though she were feeling vibrations.

"We might need to perform a full séance," she said in a portentous voice. "I'm feeling . . . *something*. I can't quite put my finger on it. . . ."

I ignored her and checked through the bathroom, by the master closet, then moved over to stand next to her. The whole time I waved the EMF reader slowly from one side to another in front of me. It wasn't registering so much as a click.

"Luz, back off a little," I said out of the side of my mouth.

"Oh, I'm just getting started," she whispered back. She closed her eyes, held the fingers of one hand to her brow, while making sweeping gestures with the other, mimicking my moves with the EMF detector.

"I feel . . . could it be? Lingering spirits. The unhappy, restless ghost of a cruel stepmother . . ."

Valerie paled.

"Look, Valerie," I interrupted. "I don't see signs of anything paranormal. But in any case, I should talk to the folks you've got working on this, and see what they have to say. Have they complained about anything, any of the guys think there's a ghost of some kind?"

Valerie nodded eagerly. "Several of them have told me about them."

"Really?" I'd like to talk to them directly. "Who's doing the work? Anyone I might know?" There were a thousand general contractors in town, and another thousand or so unlicensed builders, and at least as many carpenters. That didn't even count the folks who were handy and sold their handyman services. Sometimes running small crews, sometimes getting in over their heads.

Valerie brought a slick business card out of her nightstand and handed it to me. "Avery Builders. They come highly recommended."

No *way*.

Chapter Fourteen

L uz looked over my shoulder, and read the name aloud. "Avery Builders ... wasn't that the group you were telling me about? They're the folks who spent the night with you in the Castro?"

"Just Josh," I said, ignoring Valerie's wide eyes. The way Luz described the haunted evening made it sound like a wild orgy in what was, admittedly, one of the most libertine neighborhoods of the city. "And I didn't exactly 'spend the night' with him...."

"Still, 'of all the gin joints in all the towns...,'" intoned Luz.

"Mind if I keep the card?" I asked Valerie.

"Be my guest," she said. She still seemed shaken. "Do you think we should move out, someplace safe?"

"You know," said Luz, "in a situation like this we're often faced with spirits that follow the victims. You can't get away just by moving locales." She tapped, hard, on her temple. "They're *inside* your head."

"Valerie, Luz is kidding." I didn't like Daniel's wife, but that didn't mean I wanted the poor woman to be traumatized. Still, as I tried to placate her I could tell that Luz was mouthing something and making some sort of hand gestures toward Valerie. I didn't look directly at her for fear I would burst out laughing. "In all probability, this was just an accident, a terrible mistake. I'll go talk to Avery Builders and see what I can find out, okay?"

"Thank you, Mel," she said, a delicate hand—sporting a massive diamond and ruby ring—fluttering up to play with the heavy gold chain at her neck.

"Mind if we stick our heads into Caleb's room and say hi before we go?" I asked.

"Be my guest. I have a hair appointment—can you let yourselves out?"

"Of course."

Luz and I descended two flights of stairs to a ground-level hallway. Caleb's door was closed. In response to my knock came a sullen *"I don't want any."*

"It's me, Caleb. Mel, and Luz."

"Oh . . . come in."

He was sitting in a big T-shirt and droopy jeans on an unmade twin bed, in his stocking feet, looking a lot like an oversized, bewhiskered version of the boy I knew back when he wore Batman pajamas and underwear printed with dinosaurs. My heart lurched, once again, at the sight of the bandage on his arm. I couldn't stand the thought that he had been hurt—perhaps on purpose.

"What's up, Goose?" I asked. "How do you feel?"

He shrugged.

"Dude!" said Luz. "Must be hard to play that with only one good hand. Let me try."

She made him move over, sat on the bed, and started playing his video game with him. I envied her easy ability with teenagers. She demanded of him, and he gave in with a kind of grudging good humor. With me he was surlier. Once they hit puberty, making kids happy was a lot harder than simply pulling together a new pirate costume.

"How's the arm?" I tried again. A vial of pain meds sat on his bedside table.

He shrugged again.

"I know your mom's working a lot lately. . . . Want to come over to my dad's house for a few days until you have to go back to school?" I offered. "I could see if it's okay with your folks—that way my dad can coddle you and you guys can watch football on his big screen."

That got a response.

"Really? That'd be hecka chill."

Hecka chill. I was going to assume that was a good thing.

There was spotty cell reception from the basement level of the house, so I stepped outside into the small side alley to place my calls. It reminded me of not being able to use our cell phones at the Bernini house. Amazing how quickly we grow accustomed to new technology, so that when it fails us we are at a loss.

I called Caleb's mother, Angelica, first. She was smart and funny and ambitious; I only wished she spent more time with Caleb and less time at the office. But her high-powered job took her out of town a lot, and even when she was home, she often didn't arrive back from work until late evening, many times leaving again at the crack of dawn. So Caleb was left on his own, or at the mercy of Daniel and Valerie. Daniel loved Caleb, of course, but even though he worked a lot at home, he was mentally absent. And Caleb and Valerie . . . well, that wasn't exactly a meeting of the minds.

I couldn't help but wonder about people who had children when they clearly didn't want to spend time with them. Then again, I reminded myself, I wasn't a "real" parent, so it wasn't my place to judge.

Another late New Year's resolution: Stop *judging* people.

Angelica and Daniel both sounded happy to let Caleb recuperate at my house for a few days. Then I called my dad and gave him the heads-up.

"I better go grocery shopping," he grumbled. I knew him well enough to realize he was secretly thrilled at the prospect. "He'll probably bring a bunch of friends with him, and you know how teenage boys are. Eat you out of house and home."

"Thanks, Dad. You're a good grandpa. Oh, that reminds me, I bought ravioli for dinner tonight."

He grunted in reply.

I signed off and went back into Caleb's room.

"Got the go-ahead," I said. "I'll pick you up tonight after work. I'll call when I'm on my way, but be ready to go, okay?"

He nodded, eyes still fixed on the screen.

I gave him a kiss on his dark, wavy hair, and Luz and I left through the door that led to the narrow alley between houses.

"You think someone did this on purpose?" Luz asked as we climbed into my car. "Why would anyone want to hurt Caleb?"

I shrugged. "No idea."

"Did you feel anything ghostly, at all?"

I shook my head and sat there for a moment more, pondering my next move. A gleaming Lexus wanted my parking spot and tooted its horn. People were impatient in neighborhoods like this one. I started the engine and pulled out.

"Want to go with me to talk to Avery Builders?" I asked.

"Bet your ass I do."

The office was located in San Francisco, in an old converted warehouse not far from the Design Center, which was itself a conglomeration of old warehouses used to display the goods and services of designers catering to the city's high-end customers.

In the lobby of the brick building there was a café, lots of potted plants, and big windows displaying designer furniture and pricey decorative items. Four people had already jammed themselves into the tiny elevator, so I opted for the stairs. Luz trailed me up to the third floor, complaining the whole way. Luz was allergic to exercise, and she ate like a horse. Still, she managed to remain extremely slender. If I didn't like her so much, I would hate her.

A slate gray sign read THOMAS AVERY, ESQ; AVERY BUILDERS. We walked into the entry to find a meticulously decorated room, sporting professional dioramas of buildings and pictures of completed projects. Various objets d'art were spotlit in arched niches. Classical music played softly. Behind a gleaming reception desk sat a handsome young man who beamed at us as though our arrival gave special meaning to his life.

"Wow," I whispered.

"You can say that again," whispered Luz.

My first thought was steeped in feelings of inadequacy: Turner Construction might want to ratchet up the professionalism. My second thought was that clients were the ones who ultimately paid for this kind of high-end locale. Turner Construction spent very little on overhead, and we were known for paying above market to our employees, on the assumption that they would work harder and remain loyal. And we had a trustworthy, steadfast workforce in an industry known for transience.

Still, a real live office like this would make a person feel like a grown-up.

"My name's Braden," said the eager young man. "How can I help you?"

He had light honey brown hair cut short on the sides and tousled, quite purposefully, atop his head in a metrosexual do that, I was pretty sure, probably cost more than my rotary saw. Maybe I should get myself a job as a receptionist.

"Is Thomas Avery available, by any chance? I'm Mel Turner, from Turner Construction."

His mouth puckered in a little moue of disappointment. "I'm so sorry, do you have an appointment? Mr. Avery is—"

"Right here," said the man who had materialized in the doorway to the inner office. Blond, square-jawed . . .

"Josh," I said.

"Mel. Fancy meeting you here. And this is . . . ?"

"My friend Luz. Your paths crossed briefly outside the Bernini house on Saturday."

"Yes, indeed. Good to see you. Welcome to Avery Builders. Braden, would you brew us all coffee, or tea?" He turned to us. "What would you like?"

I noticed a granite-topped wet bar holding a French press, at least a dozen different tea selections, and a few delicate-looking porcelain teapots. No Mr. Coffee for them.

"I . . . uh . . . coffee would be great, thanks. Black."

Josh met my eyes and smiled. "Of course. Strong and black, no doubt."

Was my coffee choice a reflection of my character? I smoothed my skirt, suddenly feeling self-conscious.

Luz asked for green tea, and we all tromped into the inner office and sat around a low coffee table. The love seat and chairs were a bright lipstick red; the walls were painted charcoal gray. Strategically placed lights illuminated a couple of modern paintings and several pre-Columbian-looking artifacts.

But the most impressive feature, to me, was the numerous framed photos and dioramas of jobs completed by Avery Builders. The display was very slick and professional. *Maybe Turner Construction should do something like that,* I thought. But then, we rarely had clients over to our cluttered home office, right down the hall from our decidedly down-home kitchen. Instead, I brought our portfolio to them, or directed them to the Web site Stan maintained.

"Nice place," Luz said.

"Thank you. We just moved in a month ago—my uncle had operated the business out of his warehouse for the past twenty years. But we've decided to dial things up a notch."

"Why?" I asked.

"I'm sorry?"

"I mean, was there a reason you decided to 'dial it up a notch'?" I clarified, realizing that my blurted query sounded rude. "I thought your uncle's business was doing quite well."

The receptionist brought in our drinks and set them on the coffee table before us. We all sipped from our steaming mugs.

"Oh, it was, sure. But I have a background in design, and when I joined the firm, we decided to go after fewer but more exclusive clients."

"Like the Bernini estate?" Though it was intriguing, I wouldn't have pegged the Bernini project as particularly exclusive. San Francisco was the land of old-money families like the Gettys, and new-money celebrities like Danielle Steel—*those* were the truly exclusive, high-profile jobs.

Josh just nodded, then smiled as he gave me a thoughtful look. "I see you survived the night at the Bernini house intact. I wasn't entirely sure."

"I wish we could say the same for everyone," I said.

"Ah, *damn*," he said, shaking his head. "Poor woman. Have the police made any headway on the case, do you know?"

"No idea," I said. "But it's only been a day and a half."

"Don't you assume, Mel, that whoever was responsible for the mayhem in the nursery was most likely distracting us from the atrocity of Mrs. Bernini's death?"

"Maybe." I was no expert—that fact kept being brought back to me—but from what I'd seen and heard, that playroom was honestly haunted. "Where did you disappear to that night?"

He ducked his head, smiled, and shrugged in an adorable gesture. "I'm embarrassed to say I was scared. Crazy, huh?"

"Not so crazy. Encountering spirits is pretty overwhelming, especially if you're not prepared."

He looked genuinely puzzled. "You're not saying you actually think it was ghostly behavior?"

I opened my mouth, but no words came out.

"Mel has a certain sensitivity when it comes to other dimensions," said Luz, blowing on her tea. "She can't help it. Born that way."

That last made me smile. Made it sound like the ability to communicate with ghosts was a congenital condition.

"Well," Josh said finally. "I guess that would come in handy for a renovation like this, where the clients are actually hoping the 'ghosts' will stick around."

"Maybe. But I'm not actually here to talk about the Bernini estate," I said, remembering the cause of my visit. "I understand you're working on a house near the corner of Presidio and Clay, for Daniel Burghart?"

He tilted his head in question. "Are the Burgharts former clients of yours? I have to say, some of the work was pretty shoddy."

I felt myself blush, half with embarrassment, half anger. "Actually, it's my former house. Daniel is my ex-husband."

"Otherwise known as the Worm," Luz muttered.

"Really?" said Josh. "I'm . . . surprised."

"No, seriously," said Luz. "That's his name: the Worm."

Josh smiled. "I meant, I'm surprised that the house used to be Mel's. The work there was . . ." He trailed off with a shrug.

"I did some work on it when I lived there, a long time ago," I said. "Before I ever got into the trades. It was my first . . . well, it was an amateur's attempt. But it was done with love."

"Of course."

"Anyway, the point is I'm sure you know that my stepson was hurt there yesterday. Seriously injured."

"How is he? Your ex is livid, and I don't blame him. But as to how it happened . . ." He trailed off and shook his head. "I really don't see how it could have been any of my men. We adhere to very strict standards of jobsite—"

"Do you maintain a presence on-site, or are you more of a paper guy?" I interrupted. I knew I was being rude, but the thought of what happened to Caleb made me gruff. There was something about Josh and his fancy office that made me pretty sure he wasn't as hands-on as I was, project-wise . . . and given what had happened, that pissed me off. "I know Valerie was acting as her own general, but could I talk to your lead on the project?"

"It's not that big a job," said Josh. "There are only a few—"

"I'd like to talk to whoever's in charge on-site."

There was a bit of a staring contest before he gave me a brief nod. "Of course. I'll make some inquiries, and then let you know."

He didn't even *know*? I knew every one of my foremen, and almost all the workers, on every site under my control.

"Could you check now?"

"I'll have to get back to you on that," he said, glancing down at a gleaming gold watch on his tan wrist and standing. "I'm afraid I'm already late for a meeting."

There wasn't much else to say on the subject.

"About the Bernini house," Josh said as Luz and I stood to leave. "It sounds as though given what happened when we stayed the night, the Propaks will be making a decision based upon a more traditional proposal."

I nodded, not sure what he wanted me to say. But by the quizzical look he fixed on me, I was guessing I was supposed to respond.

"So it seems," was the best I could come up with.

"I don't know quite how to say this . . . but I hope you're not going to include a bunch of ghost hooey in your proposal."

I opened my mouth to respond, but Luz beat me to it.

"Mel makes it a practice not to mix ghost hooey and business," she said.

I nodded sagely as Luz and I walked out of the inner office. As we passed through the antechamber, Braden jumped up from behind his desk and wished us a *fabulous* day.

Luz and I shared the elevator down with a well-coiffed woman in what looked like a mink coat—a highly unusual choice for San Francisco. For one thing, it wasn't cold enough and for another, wearing furs was not popular in an area where almost half the population was some form of vegetarian and the others insisted their soon-to-be dinner be free-range and treated with dignity. The woman held a tiny dog under her arm, and by the time we escaped the confines of the elevator, Luz and I were gasping for breath, overcome by her strong perfume.

We crossed the lobby, exited the building, and stood on the sidewalk for a moment, breathing deeply of the fresh air.

"Is it just me, or was that sort of weird?" I asked.

"Definitely. Who wears White Shoulders perfume under the age of eighty? And a mink coat, in this town? Really?"

"What? No, I didn't mean the woman in the elevator. . . . I was talking about Avery."

"Good tea," she replied. "But otherwise, yeah. I'd say that man has something to hide. Cute, though."

"In a sort of Aryan-supremacy way."

She grinned at me and slung an arm around my neck, leading me down the sidewalk toward our car.

"What *is* it with you and the Nordic peoples? They just happened to be tall and blond and gorgeous. They can't help it, any more than you can keep from seeing ghosts."

Chapter Fifteen

As I drove across town, Luz peered at the car radio in the dash.

"What's with the funky music?" she asked. "Is this a station, or a CD?"

I hadn't noticed at first, but Luz was right: The radio was playing old-timey songs that were scratchy, fading in and out. I didn't remember turning it on.

Luz played with the knobs, but the music continued unabated. Then I heard an unmistakable tune: *"With garlands of roses, and whispers of pearls . . . la la la la la . . ."*

Luz sat back suddenly and stared at me. "It's not on."

"What?"

"The radio would seem to be playing," she said as she crossed her slim arms over her chest and her gaze turned into a glare, "but it is *not* turned on."

I fiddled with the knobs, then hit the dashboard. It wouldn't stop.

"I suppose maybe . . . there's a loose wire?"

"Or . . ."

"Or maybe someone could be sending a message?"

"Mel, is this like exposure therapy? Did you turn this vehicle into some kind of ghost car to try to get me over my perfectly *sane* aversion to ghosts?"

"Of course not. Stop looking at me like that. I have no explanation."

"*I* have an explanation," said Luz. "You're fooling around with some scary stuff."

"The little girl I saw at the Bernini house? She likes music. I mean . . . some of this sounds like old recordings, but every once in a while I can hear her singing that tune: *With garlands of roses, and whispers of pearls . . .*" I gave it my best shot, crooning the phrase. "Do you know that song?"

She stared at me. "As your best friend I feel obligated to tell you that you have a truly wretched singing voice. I'm sure this doesn't come as a surprise to you."

"Do you recognize the song or not?"

"Not. But I'm just saying . . . I'm not sure I would recognize anything under these circumstances."

"I wonder if it has anything to do with . . . well . . ."

"Maybe she just likes music. But why would she be following you around, via your radio?"

"I think she wants me to do something about Mrs. Bernini's death."

"Something like what? She can't tell you who did it, right?"

"I don't think so. I have to get back into that house, preferably alone, so I can speak with her without being interrupted. It's not . . . it's not as simple as dropping in on a person and having a normal conversation, you know. She's . . . a little odd."

"Uh, *yeah*. Maybe because she's *dead*."

"There must be some reason she didn't just tell me what happened, or who did it, or even straight out that Mrs. Bernini had died. I don't think she knows."

"Maybe you need an undead rule book."

"I was thinking the same thing. But I have no idea where—"

"I was *kidding*," Luz interrupted as I came to a stop in front of her condo building. She paused with her hand on the door handle before climbing out. "Listen, Mel, I wish you'd stop poking around into this ghostly murder business, but I know you won't, so I won't push it. But really? Figure out the radio thing, 'cause that's just plain creepy. And from now on, when we go anywhere, we're taking *my* car."

After dropping off Luz, I forced my mind back into work mode. I went back to one of my renovation projects to go over the Victoriana additions with my clients, and to meet with the wood-floor refinishers.

The floor people were magicians in my book. Given the right kind of monetary motivation, they were able to match just about any kind of wood, stain, or pattern. Then they sanded it all to the exact same height, protected it with polyurethane, and it looked as though it had been perfect all along.

In this case, we needed to match a complicated Greek-key motif that was found in several of the bedrooms, but which had been ruined in the main hall because of walls moving and water damage. The cheapest way to do it was to sand and tape the design on the floor, then stain it dark to mimic the look of an inlaid pattern. Happily, the owners had deep pockets and wanted historical authenticity, so the wood was going to be actually inlaid, which was, of course, much more complicated and required more skill and time.

After okaying the staining and inlaid samples with the head floor guy and my clients, I headed outside to check on the landscaping progress.

The front yard was tiny, only large enough to host a little fountain and lush greenery. But the backyard . . . this was where a landscaper could let loose and have some fun.

I found Claire chewing a big wad of bubble gum and directing half a dozen women as they filled in the classic garden with old-fashioned flowers: aster, sage, coreopsis, Shasta daisy, delphinium, and foxglove. In addition, they were lining the main walk with rose trees, and training fuchsia bougainvillea and orange trumpet vines along the new gray-stained fence topped with lattice.

One of the many reasons I liked working with Claire was that she employed so many women. Since I always felt vaguely guilty—and distinctly frustrated—over the lack of women in the building trades, I felt that at least this way we invited some estrogen into the place.

In addition to the plantings, workers were building a fire pit encircled by benches, a play structure for the Daleys' young son, and a small outdoor kitchen near the back door.

"Hey there," I said as I approached, "this place is looking great. If I'm good, could I drive the Bobcat later?"

"Only if you're good. It *is* looking great, though, isn't it?" She blew a huge bubble, popped it, then began chewing again frenetically. "I always love this part."

As was the case for house renovations, garden landscaping had to suffer through plenty of boring but crucial steps: setting the lighting and irrigation systems, piping gas to the fire pit and the barbecue, amending the dirt, bringing in stone or wood for paths or decking. Only then could the fun part begin: putting in the trees and shrubs and flowers and finally flicking that switch on the fire pit.

"So, how you holding up after the other night?" Claire asked. "Did you hear anything further from the cops?"

"Not much." I shook my head, deciding to spare her the tidbit regarding the brick and its threatening note. "I doubt they'll be calling to let us know how the case is coming."

"You know, one thing about that night seemed odd to me. . . ."

"Only one thing?"

"Okay, several things. But that well? The Berninis raised how many kids in that house? Aren't kids, like, forever falling down wells?"

"I think that's mostly wells at ground level, when the opening is hidden by weeds, or the cover has rotted away," I said. "You'd have to make an effort to fall into the well at Mrs. Bernini's place."

"I wonder how far back it dates," Claire mused. "Did you know that back in the day the Castro had a waterworks that provided much of San Francisco with its drinking water?"

"Seriously?"

She nodded. "That was before the area was incorporated into the city. It was like living out in the boonies. Whenever my mom visits, we do a lot of local history stuff, walking tours and things. It's pretty cool."

I love history, myself, so I could understand her enthusiasm. To me, houses are our everyday connection to history. That's why I worked on old buildings rather than, say, the suburban developments from which so many of my competitors made a fortune.

"Seems to me there was some dispute over water rights," Claire continued. "Someone built a waterworks and got a contract with the city. Then somebody else built above him on the hill and stole the water. It was a big deal—a feud with folks taking up one side or the other."

"Over water?"

"Wars will be fought over water, mark my words. Don't let the San Francisco fog fool you: This area's prone to droughts. You can live without electricity, and there are a lot of alternative heating sources. But you can't live without water. Ever tour the old armory, over on Mission?"

"I thought a porn studio was operating out of that place."

"I think they call it 'erotica,'" Claire said with a shrug. "But yeah. Anyway, they give tours."

"Of . . . ?"

"The building," she said, and rolled her eyes. "Okay, some of the sets for the movie studio, too. Those basements, all that old stone, very evocative. *Anyway*, Mom and I went in order to see the *building*."

"You took your mother on a tour of a porn studio?"

"No. I took my mother on a tour of an old *armory*.

The reason I mention it is that in the basement of the old armory building there's a huge room with a creek running through it. Turns out they intentionally built the place on a creek so in case they were ever under siege, the armory would have a water supply."

"Huh. I had no idea."

"History's cool. Oh, and speaking of the Bernini place, I'm supposed to go over and meet with Mountain man," she said with another pop of a bubble.

"You mean Mountain, the gardener?"

She nodded, then directed one of her assistants to move the *Brugmansia* closer to the back door. "The scent of the trumpet flowers will knock 'em out, come spring."

"How do you know Mountain?" I asked.

"I don't. Marty Propak called and asked if I would talk to him about the gardens." She looked at me, perplexed. "I assumed they had mentioned it to you—they want me to come up with some sketches for the garden."

I had given the Propaks Claire's name the first time we met, but it seemed rather cheeky to contact her so soon after Mrs. Bernini's death.

"Do you think there's anything wrong with it? I'm actually super excited to talk to him, 'cause it turns out he's the one restoring that crazy tropical garden not far from the Bernini house."

"What tropical garden?"

"You don't know it? It's pretty well-known in the city, at least among us gardening types. There are specimens that go way back, from when the original owner, Owen Campbell, lived there, like, a century ago."

"When are you meeting him?"

"This afternoon."

"Maybe bring a friend along with you, just to be sure?"

She looked at me with a question in her eyes. "You don't think he had anything to do with . . . what happened, do you?"

"No, of course not. I mean . . . I don't actually know anything other than an old woman was killed, and we were nearby at the time. I just think we should be . . . cautious. Especially around anyone with an interest in the Bernini house."

"Okay . . . I'll bring Stephen with me."

"Don't you have any . . . I don't know, any huge cousins?"

She smiled. "You're really worried about this, aren't you? Tell you what, I'll make like you and bring a whole entourage. And I'll watch my back."

"Good. There's probably no need, but after what's happened . . ." I trailed off with a shrug, not wanting to cast aspersions. "Oh, and could you let me know what he says? And now . . . could I drive the Bobcat?"

That evening I picked up Caleb, called ahead to tell Dad to preheat the oven, and headed over the Bay Bridge toward Oakland. We arrived to find my father making garlic bread from a big boule of sourdough. He put the tray of ravioli in the oven, then set a head of lettuce — iceberg, of course — and a few sad-looking carrots and stalks of celery out on a cutting board.

"Caleb, the salad needs making," he said before we'd even set our stuff down.

"Dad, he's injured. Besides, why do you insist on a

salad no one will eat?" I asked before I could stop myself. "At least let me buy some decent greens at the farmers' market."

"What?" he said, as though he didn't understand. As though this weren't a discussion we had several times a month. "Iceberg's not good enough for you?"

I sighed and reminded myself that I was living in his home, and he was cooking for me and my stepson. I dropped my things at the foot of the stairs and came back into the kitchen to give him a kiss on his stubbly cheek.

"Smells good," I said.

"Nothing fancy," he said with a shrug. "Get yourself a drink and take a load off."

We were both saying we were sorry. This was the way we worked it. Living together as adults wasn't easy; in fact, living with him as a kid hadn't exactly been a picnic, either. Nevertheless, he was a good dad. A great dad.

"Thanks, I think I'll do just that," I said, pouring myself a glass of cheap red wine.

Caleb, meanwhile, was using his good hand to pick the brown spots off the lettuce to make a salad none of us would eat. I thought about telling him he didn't have to—his left arm was in a sling, after all—but he knew that. As long as I didn't impose my expectations that they actually converse, Caleb and my dad got along fine, their interaction consisting primarily of watching sports and doing the occasional chore around the house together, and grunting. Must be a guy thing.

Stan and I met in the home office to go over paperwork, phone calls, and assorted supply issues that had arisen during the day. I also placed a call to Marty

Propak, hoping he would tell me I could get back into the Bernini house to start putting together a project proposal. He told me he and Kim hadn't yet had a chance to decide what to do, given the circumstances. I wondered whether they were finding their dream of a haunted Castro District B&B a little overwhelming, and might be contemplating moving back to Fort Wayne.

Half an hour later Dad called out, *"Dinner's on!"* as though we were at the neighbor's house rather than just down the hall.

I pushed Stan back to the kitchen. He was a pro at getting himself around in his chair, but I assumed it must be tiring. He never complained, but being in a chair brought with it a slew of related physical challenges, from back pain to circulation problems.

"Oh, I made some phone calls," Dad said as we took our places around the kitchen table. "Old Tom Avery's living on his boat down at Jack London Marina. Guess he pretty much stepped out of the day-to-day operations of the company."

"There's a lot of that going around." I glanced at Dad, who was busying himself with putting the hot tray of ravioli on a trivet we'd used ever since I could remember. It had a painting of a woman in traditional Navajo dress, tending to a baby. Mom had told me they bought it in a secondhand shop in New Mexico on their honeymoon, and she considered it magical that it had survived, unbroken, through so many moves and dinners and children.

I missed her with a longing that went straight to my gut. But, as I looked at the thinning gray hair of my dad, I knew he missed my Mom—his Dorothy—in a way I could never fathom. He had always seemed so in charge, but when she passed, it was clear that she had been his compass, his touchstone. I wondered whether it was just wishful thinking on my part, but he seemed to be acting a little more like his old self lately, putting himself out to be more active in the world.

For instance, making a call to check up on Tom Avery on my behalf.

The ravioli were excellent, and the conversation lively. Caleb's presence brought out the blustery best in my dad, and Stan adored my stepson as well. After dinner I brought out the bag of smashed equipment I had recovered from the Bernini house's playroom.

"I don't suppose any of you mechanically inclined guys would know how to recover any of the information from these devices?"

"I don't think you can do anything about the recorder," said Caleb. "But even if the camera was dropped, the memory card should be fine."

"Memory card?" I wasn't what you call high-tech.

Using his one good hand, he opened a tiny door on the camera and told me to pull out the little card.

"You're saying this stuff shows proof of your ghosts?" Dad shook his head and made a beeline for the Barca-lounger in front of his big-screen TV. "I'm watching the game."

Stan, Caleb, and I went to the office and Caleb slid the memory card into a port on the computer. We crowded around the monitor and squinted at the confusing images.

"No offense, Mel, but you suck at photography," said Caleb.

The photos were full of gleaming lights—four, to be

precise. And something that looked like mist. And a big white mound ... what *was* that?

"Looks like a bed, maybe?" said Stan.

I squinted some more, cocked my head, and used my imagination. "I think you might be right. Maybe the playroom used to be a bedroom?"

"Does that tell you anything?" Stan asked.

"Not really."

The only thing it told me was something I already knew: It was high time for me to spend a few hours at the California Historical Society. I needed to see what I could dig up on the history of the house, and try to figure out how the family had died. It was clear they had unfinished business and were causing disturbances in their old home. Unfortunately, due to recent budget cutbacks the society wasn't open tomorrow; I opened my schedule and blocked out some time to visit the archives the following day.

Stan and Caleb eventually got bored cracking jokes about the orbs in my photos and returned to the kitchen to wash the dishes, but I lingered and used the Internet to look up the song that Anabelle kept singing. I didn't know its name, but I put the lyrics I could remember into the search engine and it brought back this info: It was written by Philip Emery in 1949. I found an old recording of the song and listened all the way through:

With garlands of roses, and whispers of pearls ... a garden of posies for all little girls. So come see the fairies, and dance with the sprites, we'll all play together from morning till night.

The lyrics themselves provided no explanation. It was just a sweet, straightforward little ditty.

What was odd was that Anabelle had died decades before the song was written. I looked up the history of radio broadcasting and learned that while radio devices existed in the early 1900s, public broadcasts didn't begin in earnest until the 1920s.

Well after the unfortunate demise of the Bowles family.

Chapter Sixteen

The next morning I was up and out bright and early. I was not, after all, getting paid for my ghost-busting services, and I still had Turner Construction to run. Our subcontractors and full-time staff depended on me to keep the company in the black, and to make payroll every month, despite whatever ghosts I might have seen or murders I might be trying to figure out.

After going over some final drawings with carpenters at Matt's place in Pacific Heights, I headed to Cheshire House to make sure all the subcontractors were on schedule to be out before the floor refinishers started their job, which would render the house uninhabitable for more than a week.

By the time I finished up there, it was almost one in the afternoon. My stomach was growling as I drove down Market to the giant rainbow flag that marked the entrance to the Castro. This area was once home to so many working-class northern European immigrants that it was called Little Scandinavia. Later, Irish families moved in. There were still traces of each, but by the 1970s Harvey Milk, who would become the most famous resident of the neighborhood, opened a camera store and became politically active in the quest for gay civil rights, contributing to the notion of the Castro as a gay-friendly destination. I was very young at the time, but I still remembered the horrifying assassinations of City Supervisor Milk and Mayor Moscone in 1978.

I found a rare two-hour parking spot, and stopped in at Sylven's Pizza. As before, the place was half-full of men eating slices. Other than a young woman taking phone orders, I was the only female in sight.

"Oh my Lord! You poor, poor thing." J.D. came out from behind the register and gave me a hug as though I were a long-lost friend. "*George!* George, look who's here, the poor doll from the other night. You know I had *no idea* how serious it was when you came in that night— I was trying not to listen in as you talked on the phone, so I just assumed the poor doll had been knocked down and broke her hip, or there was a break-in or something. I had *no idea*."

George came over, wiping his hands on his apron. "How are you? I'll bet you're traumatized. You poor thing."

"I'm Mel Turner, by the way." I handed them my business card, feeling overwhelmed but gratified by their reactions. "Mrs. Bernini and the Propaks invited me to spend the night on Saturday. I'm one of the general contractors vying for the job to transform the place into a bed-and-breakfast."

"You know, we heard something about that, just the other day," said J.D. "We were a little surprised—Mrs. Bernini hadn't mentioned anything. And usually we know everything that's going on around here, don't we, George?"

"Just about everything." George nodded.

"Mel, you just sit right there and we will serve you the most delicious pizza you've ever had."

"I tried it the other night," I said as I took the proffered stool at the counter. "With Mrs. Bernini, in fact. It was her favorite."

"Oh, of course. Poor old doll. You know there wasn't a *thing* she didn't like on her pizza, except for anchovies, was there, George?"

"Not a thing but anchovies," George confirmed. He was already back at the ovens, making more pizzas. The phone rang almost constantly, the young woman writing up tags and suspending them on an overhead metal contraption.

"We used to make her up something special, a little different each and every time. Last time we put pea pods and shrimp on a white sauce, didn't we, George? And on the other, what was it?"

"Prosciutto and melon, and pepperoni. She liked pepperoni."

"That's right . . . Oh, but you must know all this, don't you, since you were with her that evening?" J.D. looked off into space for a moment, clicked his tongue, and shook his head. "That poor old doll. I'm glad, at the very least, that she had a scrumptious last meal. Is that wrong of me to say?"

I shook my head and smiled. "I think she was very

happy to have you all in her life—she loved the pizza and spoke of you as her friends. She was worried about Raj's mother, for instance. Clearly she was interested in you all."

"Oh, yes, Raj went over there frequently. He's a good boy, our steadiest worker. Or at least he used to be. . . ."

"Remember before she got her walker," said George, "how she used to walk down here every day?"

"She called it her morning constitutional," said one of the young men sitting at a table by the door.

"And long before that," J.D. said, "she used to take in all those kids. . . . She was a little . . . well, good at getting her way, but let's not speak ill of the dead."

"You guys seem to know a lot about the neighborhood. Do you know anything about the family that used to live in Mrs. Bernini's house? I'm curious about its history."

"Well, I know the *legend*. I have no idea if it's true or not."

"Legend?"

J.D. grabbed a spray bottle and a rag and started cleaning the already gleaming counter as he talked. "It was ages ago, the family that originally built the house. They say the father, Franklin Bowles, who ran a maternity hospital in that place, had been fighting with a neighbor over water rights. And one morning the servants walked in to find the *entire* family dead."

"How were they killed?"

"No one knows. The servant who found them said they were all in one bed, and that they looked 'healthy and pink.' That was why Evil Campbell was never convicted of anything. But some say he dabbled in magic from the islands. He used to live . . . George? Where did Evil Campbell used to live before he came to San Francisco?"

"One of the islands," George answered. "Haiti, maybe?"

"Maybe that's where he got the voodoo?"

"Seriously? Voodoo?"

J.D. waved his rag in the air. "I don't think anyone actually said *voodoo*. But it seemed like some kind of evil magic. Otherwise, how would the family have died like that? Afterwards, the house was empty for some time, since everyone thought it was cursed. I guess that's how the Berninis could afford such a big place, since no one else wanted to live there."

"Huh. And everyone around here knows that story?"

"Sure. Sometimes the local kids—and by kids, I mean adults, too—dress up as Evil Campbell for Halloween."

While we talked, George continued making one pizza after another, taking steaming cooked pies out of the ovens and replacing them with the freshly made raw ones in a continuous cycle. It was mesmerizing to watch.

"Have you heard anything more about what happened with Mrs. Bernini?" J.D. asked, putting away his rag and washing his hands.

"No. They're not exactly keeping me informed."

"I heard she was killed in the garden before . . . well, before she was thrown . . . well, you know," added a young man standing in line for pizza. "They say maybe the killer was interrupted and panicked. . . ."

His eyes grew huge and he fixed me with a look, his mouth making a perfect O.

"Hey, it was probably you people who scared him off!

Man. What does it feel like to have been that close to *a killer*?" His voice dropped on the last couple of words, so he was whispering.

Frankly, I hadn't really thought about it in those terms. I had realized we were nearby when the horrific event occurred, but the thought that we scared the person off . . . that was especially frightening. And once again I felt a wave of sadness and guilt that our presence hadn't averted her death.

"Good *heavens*, J.D.," said George as he placed a plate with two massive pizza slices in front of me. "What a morbid imagination you have. Oh, *my*. Let's not talk of such things any further. We'll just remember her as she was, a fine lady."

"Is Raj around, by any chance?" I wanted to ask him about that night, if there was anything at all he had seen, anything out of the ordinary. I was sure the police had interviewed him already, but it couldn't hurt to hear about it firsthand.

"No, his mother's sick."

"Mrs. Bernini mentioned that. I'm sorry."

"He works a second job to pay for her treatment. I do *love* my country, but the health care . . . ? It's out of control."

Murmurs of commiseration echoed through the restaurant. I nodded in agreement, while taking a huge bite of cheesy, delectable pizza. Health care was one of my biggest expenses as an employer. But in construction good health coverage was critical.

"Do you all know a man who goes by the name of Mountain?"

"Oh, sure."

A few glances were exchanged around the room. "He's had a hard time of it, the last couple of years."

"Did anyone happen to hear . . . that he might inherit the Bernini house?"

More significant glances.

"We heard him say something to that effect, but I guess no one really believed him," said J.D. "George? George, what do you think about Mountain inheriting the Bernini house?"

"Oh, probably not," said George. "I think he probably misunderstood."

"You have to understand how Mrs. Bernini was," J.D. said. "She had a way of telling people they might inherit from her—heck, she once said she liked our pizza enough to leave the place to *us*. And probably to Raj every time he delivered. No one took her seriously. I mean, that place has got to be worth a fortune, despite its checkered past. And Portia from across the way, she was working with Mrs. Bernini, helping her catalog the antiques. I thought she said something about Mrs. Bernini leaving the house to *her*. And frankly, she's a little more credible."

"Across the way?"

He pointed through the window to Kirkbride's Antiques.

"Right across the street. She was unloading more stuff from the Bernini house just yesterday. She uses her husband's truck, and it blocks half the street when she pulls up."

"Thanks," I said as I polished off one of my pizza slices. "I think I'll need to take this second slice with me."

"You just give that right on over and I'll wrap it for you. It'll be your teatime snack."

"How much do I owe you?"

"Oh, you should know your money's no good here! At least, not today," J.D. said with a wink. "In the future, when you come back to see us, I'll let you pay."

"Thanks for everything. For the pizza, and the ... chat."

"Oh, and hey, you find out anything about a memorial service, you be sure to let us know."

"I'll do that."

Talking about Mountain reminded me to check in with Claire. Out on the sidewalk, I dialed her number.

"Thanks for worrying about me, Mel, but everything was just fine. We walked through his garden and talked shop. It's amazing—there are historical specimens from all over. I guess Owen Campbell brought them with him and they're still alive today, or have been propagated. You have no idea how rare a collection like that is."

"He didn't happen to say anything about Campbell's ghost hanging around, maybe?"

She laughed. "Um, no. But I didn't think to ask. Mountain *did* say something interesting about Campbell's wife dying at the Bernini house, back when it was a maternity hospital."

"Really. His wife?"

"I guess Mountain found one of Campbell's old diaries, which was great since it listed all the plant species he brought over. And he wrote about his dispute with his neighbor who used to live in the Bernini house—over water rights; *told* you they were important—and then about his wife's death. Mountain's a talker, couldn't get him to stop once he started. Oh, one more thing: He's trying to expand Campbell's garden, and was hoping to use some of the Bernini land."

"Some of the land?"

"As a community garden, or a park. She had a big lot. I guess they had talked about it—he said she was on board with the idea."

"So you didn't feel anything weird, not threatened at all?"

"Not at all. He's a little, well, odd, but you could say that for a lot of us. Yours truly, for sure."

"You're no odder than any of my other friends."

"Like that's a ringing endorsement. Catch ya later."

I hung up wondering, did I now have an answer to Anabelle's question, about how her family had died? Had they been magically killed by Evil Campbell?

Seemed like a bit much. Ghosts I could handle. I would leave the magic to others.

One glance through the squeaky-clean plate-glass window and I knew: I didn't have the money to shop at Kirkbride's Antique Shoppe. In fact, any store that called itself a "shoppe" wasn't usually my kind of place.

Despite my passion for all things old—or perhaps because of it—I stayed away from the sort of establishment where the owners knew exactly what they had, and were happy to gouge their customers. I preferred back-roads junk stores where you dug under musty piles of worthless magazines and auto parts with the hope that you might uncover a treasure . . . which you then scored for a couple of bucks.

A bell tinkled as I opened the door with "Antiques"

written in gold gilt on the window. Inside, the air was scented with the pleasant fragrance of lemon furniture polish and potpourri. I heard the lilting sounds of 1920s music emanating from an old-fashioned radio on the counter. Tiffany-style lamps and brass and ceramic tchotchkes were displayed upon cherry vanities, walnut highboys, and redwood burl desks that gleamed under stained-glass sconces. The furniture styles ranged from the 1890s on and featured fluid nouveau carvings, deco details, and Greek Revival columns. The walls were lined with oil paintings and sepia-toned photographs in gilt frames.

"Good morning," said Portia Kirkbride from her desk at the rear of the store. A huge calico cat snoozed by the register, noting my entry with a lazy lift of her head. "Feel free to look around at your leisure. Would you like a cup of tea?"

As I'd suspected, Portia was the woman who had come forward the night Mrs. Bernini was killed, saying she was supposed to inherit the house. As she had that night, she wore a cream polo shirt and khaki capris that fit perfectly, her sleek dark hair pulled back and secured with a clip at the base of her skull. She gave no indication of recognizing me.

"No, thank you," I said as I made my way to the back of the shop. "I don't know if you remember me? I was at Mrs. Bernini's the other night. . . ."

Portia's already frozen face seemed to stiffen even more. But she said nothing.

"I'm Mel Turner, with Turner Construction. We do historical renovations. . . ." I held out my card. When she didn't reach for it, I placed it on the counter.

"Oh, yes. Mel Turner . . . you were supposed to be

staying the night with Mrs. Bernini when she ... was ..."
She let out a sigh. "I recognize the name now."

"You've heard about me?"

"They say you're a ghost hunter. It's all over the
neighborhood. I'm . . . about the other night, I'm so
embarrassed. I was just so . . . shocked by the whole
thing."

The cat meowed at me, having roused herself to come
demand some attention. I petted her soft coat and
scratched under her chin, partly because I like animals
and partly in an effort to ingratiate myself with Portia.
From the look on her face, my ploy didn't seem to be
working.

"Watch out," said a man's voice. "She's our guard cat."

"Very fierce, I can see that."

I looked up to the man who had been with Portia that
night, the fellow who'd placed a coat over her shoulders
and shielded her from the cops. He was dressed in worn
jeans, boots, and a sweatshirt—an outfit that stood in
marked contrast to Portia's refined, old-money air.

"Everything okay, darling?" he said as he moved behind the desk and gave Portia a kiss on the forehead.

"Oh . . . yes. I'm sorry. This is Mel Turner. She was just
telling me that she was there the night ... the night of ...
when Mrs. Bernini ... passed away." There was a little
hitch in her throat.

"Oh, baby," the man said, and hugged her to his chest.
He glanced over at me. "I'm sorry, Mel, is it? It was a
great shock to all of us. I'm Edgar."

Such a formal name didn't really suit him. I was willing to bet that down at the corner bar he was known as
Ed or Eddie.

"Nice to meet you. And I'm sorry, yes. I know it must have been a great shock. You knew Mrs. Bernini well, then?"

Portia finally spoke, her voice muffled somewhat as she pushed away from Edgar's chest. "Yes, very well. I was cataloging her antiques for her."

"What was the idea behind cataloging them?"

"You've been in her home; I'm sure you noticed what a jumble it is in there. There's so much junk that I was concerned if . . . when . . . Mrs. Bernini passed away, someone might come in and toss everything just for the sake of expediency. This way there's a record of everything that's valuable. . . ."

"She also agreed to sell some nice pieces on consignment, like those two there." Edgar gestured to a marbletopped walnut sideboard, and a gleaming dining room table with inlaid design. Next to them sat a large chest of tooled leather and wood—it looked like a twin of the toy chest I noticed in the playroom.

"She needed money," Portia said.

"Don't we all," said Edgar with a grunt. His wife gave him an icy look.

"So of course I was donating my services, doing it all for free."

"For free, except that she promised to leave the property to you in return?" I said.

There were tears in her eyes, and she let out a shaky sigh. "Of course, I thought she meant years from now."

I couldn't help but remember that Portia didn't seem nearly so broken up about Mrs. Bernini's death on the night she was killed. But, I reminded myself, we all mourn in our own ways. Unfortunately, I'd had some experience lately with the myriad reactions to sudden death.

"But you do have a will that deeds the property to you?"

She nodded. "A holographic will, but I've been assured it's legal."

"Holographic?" In my mind I pictured a 3-D image of a will.

"That's what it's called when a will is handwritten by the testator. It's just a fancy name for an informal will. But it's still legal, unless someone else can produce a more recent version."

"Do you think she might have changed it?"

Portia shrugged, but her expression remained unchanged. The wonders of Botox. "We argued recently. And she could be peevish when she didn't get what she wanted. Things just aren't selling that well these days, what with the economic situation. Also, we accidentally took the wrong piece out of one room. She didn't like anyone going into the playroom, but our assistant Raj didn't realize."

"Raj, from the pizza place?"

She nodded. "He does some odd jobs for us."

"Speaking of pizza, the fellows there mentioned you brought in some more items from Mrs. Bernini's yesterday?"

"Those items were already agreed to before . . . before Saturday. They were just waiting to be picked up." Portia stood suddenly. "You'll have to excuse me. I have to . . . I have to run out to the bank."

And without further ado she left, the bell ringing as she slammed the door behind her.

"I'm sorry," said Edgar. "She's really upset about what happened. Portia doesn't really . . . it's hard for her to handle her emotions at times. If you're interested in things from the Bernini estate, let me show you this—it's my favorite."

It was a photograph of Anabelle Bowles, dressed as a flower girl, with a basket of petals in her lap and a few strewn on the floor. Her hair hung down in long curls, secured by a ribbon around her head. And on her face was that same straightforward, almost saucy look I had come to know—except the last time I saw her, when she was crying and asking for help.

"Where did you get this?" I asked.

"That . . . ? It was some time ago. I believe I picked it up at an auction, in a lot."

"A lot?"

"At auction you don't always buy specific pieces, but a whole grouping of stuff called a lot. Sometimes it's full of garbage. I also bid on storage units, that sort of thing. It's become a competitive sport around here nowadays. We show out at the Alameda antiques fair, as well. As a matter of fact, tracking down the source of that picture was how I first met Mrs. Bernini."

He showed me a number of other items, as the shop had a whole section dedicated to items from the surrounding neighborhoods. There was one arresting portrait, a formal oil painting, of a woman with dusky skin, full lips, black eyes, her dark hair bound up in a bright cloth.

"She's lovely, isn't she?" said Edgar.

"Very. Who is she?"

"Her name was Tallulah Campbell. She was from the West Indics, married a man who brought her here, and they moved into a place, actually, not far from the Bernini house."

"Campbell—as in Owen Campbell?"

Chapter Seventeen

"Yes." He looked surprised. "You know the story?"

"Just a little. There was a feud between the two families, as I understand it?"

He nodded. "The way I heard it was there was a great animosity. And after Tallulah passed away in childbirth, Owen Campbell became a recluse."

"I heard Campbell was thought to be involved in the death of the other family?"

He shook his head. "Didn't hear that much, but I'm not much of one for gossip. Portia handles that aspect of things. And in a neighborhood like this, there's always plenty of tongues wagging."

"I thought when gossip is about things that happened long ago, it takes on the sheen of 'history.'"

He chuckled. "I guess that's true. And Portia is a devoted amateur historian."

"Have you heard anything about what happened

more recently, to Mrs. Bernini? Is anyone whispering anything?" It was a long shot, but as my mom used to say: in for a penny, in for a pound.

He hesitated, put his hands deep in his pockets, and rocked back on his heels. "Like I said, I don't hear much. But . . . I guess people are wondering whether the Propaks were tired of waiting."

I nodded. I had wondered myself. It seemed the most obvious explanation.

"I'm not saying that they would do any such thing . . . ," Edgar said, a blush rising up his neck and marching across his broad features. "It's just that there was some tension. Mrs. Bernini didn't even want people to start cleaning, really, much less beginning construction."

"Do you know a man who was working on the gardens, goes by Mountain?"

"Oh, sure," he said, but didn't make eye contact.

"Do you think he would have any reason to have done such a thing?"

More blushing. It was attractive, making him seem as though he'd been sitting out too long in the Mediterranean sun. I thought about Anabelle's high color; wasn't it rare for ghosts to be so rosy? Maybe she'd been spending time in the sun, as well. Before she died, that is. But that seemed odd for the time, when wealthy people most often tried to remain pale.

"Mountain is a decent guy, I think. I've certainly never had a problem with him, though he and Portia were sometimes at odds. But now—I can't believe he says Mrs. Bernini left the house to him. Her intent was clear; she and Portia were very close."

"Mountain wasn't the one who told me he was inheriting—it was the Propaks."

"Really? Huh. Maybe it's based on something actual, then. But . . . Mountain's always been a bit . . ." Edgar seemed to search for words. "Well, frankly, odd."

"So you don't think he has any legitimate claim on the house?"

"As I said, we have a will, and as far as I know, he hasn't been able to produce a more recent one." He slipped his smart phone into his pocket and grabbed a clipboard full of what looked like work orders, along with a bright yellow notice. "Anyway, I'm sorry to rush you, but I need to lock up and get back to the office. I'm sure Portia will be back soon, though, if you want to speak to her some more. She just needed to get herself together. You might give her a day or two."

"You don't work here?"

"I wish! *Some*one has to work to pay for this place," he said, his tone jolly but in the classic "gotta keep the spouse happy, but boy they're expensive" vein. "I try my hand at fixing items as they come in, love to work in my woodshop out back, but it doesn't pay the bills. Though lately, with the state of the economy and all, even working a real job barely pays the bills, am I right? You run your own place, though, right? I envy you."

"Sometimes. But since I'm in charge, I feel like I mostly do paperwork and run around from one jobsite to another," I said. There were days my hands literally itched with the desire to make something, fix something. There never seemed to be enough time.

But then I wondered if I was whining. This had been

another one of my New Year's resolutions: Quit *whining*, already.

"So you were actually there at Mrs. Bernini's house the night of the tragedy?" asked Edgar as we walked to the door. The bell tinkled again as we passed through. He turned the sign to CLOSED and locked the door behind him.

"I was, yes."

"You were the last to see her?"

"Among the last. There were several of us there."

He looked down the street, seeming to hesitate to say something.

"I don't know how well you know this neighborhood, but folks here know one another. We're pretty tight."

"So I'm learning."

"There was one piece of gossip I did hear," he said finally.

"What was that?"

"Everybody says you saw a ghost there. Actually *spoke* to a ghost there. Is that true?"

So much for keeping a low profile.

I'd only been in my two-hour parking spot for an hour. I hated wasting things. And I was only blocks away from the Bernini house. I had been warned—by Inspector Crawford, Graham, and a note on a brick—not to go back there, but a little stroll *past* it to get a sense of the neighborhood couldn't hurt, could it? My recent conversations with Mrs. Bernini's neighbors had made me feel like I was getting closer to determining who might have wanted to cause harm to the elderly woman. I would make a few more work-related phone calls, and then I might just walk on by. Real casual-like.

I was about to jaywalk across Castro Street when a beige sedan pulled up to the sidewalk, blocking my way. I glanced inside and saw what looked like a police radio, and a blue light. An unmarked police car? Only then did I notice the driver climbing out.

"You wouldn't be methodically hunting down suspects and interfering in my case, now, would you, Ms. Turner?" Inspector Crawford didn't look at me while she spoke. I followed her gaze to see Edgar Kirkbride crossing the street half a block down.

"Jaywalking is a real problem in these parts," I said, shaking my head. "You get pulled off homicide for the crosswalk beat?"

"Cute," she said, though a slight curl of one lip indicated that she'd been amused by my joke. "I'm surprised I have to tell you this, but here goes: Keep out of my investigation."

"I wasn't . . ." Actually, I supposed I was. "I just wanted to meet Portia Kirkbride, since she was cataloging Mrs. Bernini's antiques."

Crawford nodded, studying me. "I was headed there myself. I take it by the 'closed' sign she's not in?"

"She ran out to the bank. I don't imagine she'll be gone long."

"She tell you anything I should know about?"

"Just that she thinks she's inheriting the house, and so does Mountain, um, Gerald, the gardening guy?"

She nodded.

"But the Kirkbrides claim they have the most recent will. I think that's about it. That, and the fact that everyone in the neighborhood thinks I can speak to ghosts."

"I thought *you* thought you could speak to ghosts."

"Well . . ." I started to avoid her gaze, and began doing some weird twisty thing with my mouth and other facial features, over which I seemed to have no power.

"Nervous?" Inspector Crawford asked, a barely there smile hovering over her lips.

"I, uh." I blew out a breath and my tongue played inside my cheek. What was I *doing*? One thing was becoming increasingly clear to me: No matter how wildly frustrated or righteously angry I might become, a life of crime was not an option for me. If I felt this guilty when I was perfectly innocent, I could only imagine my reaction if I were *guilty* of something. "Yes, I think I am."

"Since you're here, I'd like you to go over what happened that night, one more time, focusing on you thinking you saw Mrs. Bernini in the garden when no one else did."

I repeated my story, hyperconscious of trying to tell it as I did on Saturday night. I reminded myself that since I wasn't guilty of anything, minor discrepancies in the tale wouldn't indict me. But, boy, this woman made me nervous. Especially when she whipped out a small notebook and started to jot down a few items.

"Josh Avery said he wasn't with you early in the evening, but then joined you all for a bit, separating again after the alleged 'haunting' of the toys. And this unusual toy activity would have occurred either right after, or concurrent with, the homicide."

I nodded. "Josh was staying in the other wing. . . . We didn't see him during dinner, and then we split up again after we heard noises in the playroom and things fell down the stairs. I didn't see where he went after that, though he must have told the Propaks he was still there, since he claims to have outlasted me at the house."

"And you didn't hear anything, see anything—no matter how small—happening in the garden?"

"No, nothing. But we were pretty absorbed in what was going on in the house. . . ."

"Right, the 'spirits' and whatnot."

I felt a flash of anger at her dismissive tone. "Whatever was happening in the house was real."

She gazed at me again, for a long time. This time I didn't look away. I stood my ground . . . for a moment, at least. Then I started to wonder, is it even *legal* to be a ghost hunter? Do you have to be licensed by the state . . . or something? Knowing the way things were in California, surely the powers that be had found a way to tax such endeavors?

At Inspector Crawford's continued silence, I asked, "I hear Mrs. Bernini was actually killed in the garden and maybe the killer was interrupted by us, and threw her body down the well. Is that true?"

"Where'd you hear that?"

"Around. It's a talkative neighborhood."

"So I've learned."

She didn't seem like she was going to answer my question, so I posed another. "Do you know anything about the mix-up over the whole inheritance thing?"

"All I know is that the Kirkbrides are making a claim. We're still waiting to see whether another, more recent version turns up." She gave a little shrug, and her pounded copper earrings glinted dully in the winter sun.

"Figuring out the legality of the inheritance, and the status of the Propaks' preexisting purchase agreement, are not my job, happily enough. I'm only interested to the extent that they may or may not serve as motives for this crime. Ms. Turner—"

"Call me Mel, please. This is our second murder, after all."

"Okay, *Mel*, presuming you're telling me the truth and said ghosts are real, why is it they can't just tell you what happened?"

"I'm not sure they can't. Do you think you could arrange for me to go back in, by myself, so I could see if I could communicate with them?"

She raised one eyebrow and fixed me with a look. It occurred to me that she and Luz might well be long-lost sisters.

"Nothing personal, Mel," she muttered, "but the day I start setting up séances is the day I hand over my shiny police badge. And I'm nowhere near retirement age."

After Inspector Crawford took off, I continued walking toward the Bernini estate.

I knew the inspector would rather I stay away from the scene, but it wasn't illegal merely to stroll by, was it? The sidewalk was a public space, wasn't it?

It was cold, but bright and sunny as befitted a San Francisco winter. I wore fingerless gloves that my sister Daphne had knit me for Christmas, and a colorful scarf my other sister, Charlotte, had woven. I was the only one of three girls who managed to skip the crafty gene.

I built stuff. End of story.

Oh, also, I talked to ghosts. And apparently figured out

murders from time to time. Okay, *think*, Mel. Who would want to kill Mrs. Bernini? She was so fragile, it wouldn't have taken much strength to knock her down. I would bet even the slender Portia could have managed it.

The Propaks might have wanted to hurry along her demise, and I suppose they might have wanted us there in order to cast suspicion on one or all of us . . . but surely there were better, more subtle ways. A pillow while she slept, for example. It was horrific to think about, but certainly no worse than throwing someone down a well.

Mountain and Portia both thought they were supposed to inherit the house, at least partially in exchange for services rendered. A house of this size, and a lot of these dimensions, would be worth millions in this city. And that was as is, with no renovations whatsoever. That was generous remuneration, I don't care how many antiques were cataloged or roses pruned. So there was motive, except that Mrs. Bernini was old and frail. Wouldn't it have made sense, if inheritance was the goal, to wait a few years for nature to take its course?

Josh Avery wanted the renovation job, and he seemed to be an ambitious sort. Which would make him likely to kill *me*, maybe, but why Mrs. Bernini? She may have been reluctant, but she gave no sign she would stand in the way of the construction work.

What about Howdy Doody Homer? Might he have expected to inherit, and been angry about the Kirkbrides and/or Mountain?

And what did the ghosts have to do with anything at all?

I stood across the street from the Bernini house, taking it in. The house showed no signs of the other night's events, other than a black bow on the front door, in Victorian style. I appreciate those old-fashioned public ways of signaling grief, the old conventions of loss: wearing black, or an armband, closing the shades, putting a funeral wreath on the door. There was something so ... horrific and shaming about having to inform person after person of a loved one's death, and then to be put in the position of having to comfort them or thank them for their awkward words of condolence.

When my mother died, I remember wishing everyone somehow could have known without me telling them. I wanted to wear my grief on my sleeve and yet not have to engage in discussion with anyone: I didn't want to hear their own stories of sadness, or take their advice on how to move on, or accept their tales of her being in a better place. I wanted to wallow in my sadness, to scream and cry and be left alone with my grief.

But Mrs. Bernini ... who were her loved ones? Did the foster children visit? She certainly had enough portraits around the house.

But then I noticed a shrine had sprung up near the garden gate. Bundles of flowers, votive candles, a teddy bear with a balloon. One thing was for sure: She had fans in the neighborhood. I felt tears prickle the back of my eyes, and suddenly I was back there, that night, peering down into the darkness of the well and seeing that crocheted shawl, knowing, deep down, what had happened. I could still hear the *shuffle, clank, scrape* of her walker.

Trying to shake it off and get my mind back on work, I returned a few phone calls about getting the HVAC—heating, venting, air-conditioning—guy out to the Cheshire House to finish up the venting before the floors were done. There wasn't much need for air-conditioning in a city like San Francisco, but heat, definitely.

While I was on the phone, Kim and Marty came out the front door and headed for their Escalade.

There was a large, leafy hedge at my back and I leaned into it to avoid being seen, but neither Propak was looking across the street. In fact, they appeared to be engrossed in their discussion, or perhaps arguing. They certainly didn't look like murderers ... not that I really knew what a murderer looked like. The past couple of times I'd been involved in homicide investigations, the murderers hadn't come conveniently packaged. It's not as though they wore all black.

Not like me, I realized as I looked down at my nearly monochromatic outfit. Except for the slogan, today's T-shirt from Stephen was black, as were my skirt and tights. I was so funereal today, in fact, that I had thrown on my sister's bright iridescent blue green dragonfly scarf, just to spice things up.

They climbed into their vehicle and took off down the street, as though in a hurry.

Inspector Crawford's words kept ringing in my ears: *Why is it the ghosts can't tell you what happened?*

I really wanted to get into that house and look around, see whether I could talk to Anabelle and/or Mrs. Bernini and figure out exactly what happened. Inspector Crawford had mentioned it was an easy house to break into. . . . Would that be over-the-top? *Yes.* I was pretty sure.

And anyway ... if she knew what was happening, why didn't Anabelle tell me at the time? Were ghosts sworn to secrecy or something? The first time I saw a ghost, he couldn't remember what had happened, and the last time they didn't just come out and tell me what was going on, either. I wish I knew what the afterlife rules were. Luz had been kidding, but she was right: I needed a handbook.

Since I'd started seeing ghosts, I had done a fair amount of reading on the subject. The trouble was, there was a whole lot of hooey thrown in with some semiscientific data. It was sort of like looking on the Internet to figure out whom to vote for—you had millions of hits to sort through, and at least some of them appeared to be posted by nutcases living in Unabomber-style shacks, but with an Internet connection.

The ghost-busting guy I trusted most so far was Olivier Galopin. Sort of. At least I didn't think he was out to spout a whole lot of nonsense for his own gain. He ran ghost tours out of the Eastlake Hotel, and did the occasional gig investigating and documenting hauntings. Still, he maintained a healthy skepticism.

Not long ago he'd invited me to the opening of his new ghost-busting shop, but I hadn't made it over there yet. I was one pathetic excuse for a ghost hunter.

Among other things, I needed to fess up to him about what happened to the equipment he'd lent me. And to ask a question or twenty.

I called him. As soon as he picked up, I asked, "Can ghosts kill people?"

Chapter Eighteen

"And hello to you, too, my house-building friend," he said in a soft French accent. "Is someone trying to kill you? Again?"

"No. Well . . . maybe." Surely not. That brick was just meant to scare us. Probably it was thrown by a neighborhood hooligan, as Inspector Crawford suggested. Who else could have been in the house?

Casting my mind back, I remembered the Propaks had workers in the house that day. Kim said the taps were dripping and they were trying to get the old furnace working. But it was a Sunday. Not even a full day after a murder. I'm accustomed to seeing workers and their vehicles, so I hadn't thought much of it at the time.

Olivier chuckled. "You are such a curious one. Me, if someone wants to kill me, I think I would know this for sure."

"You'd think it would be that easy. I'll admit, I've got a lot on my mind. First things first: the deadliness of ghosts. Can they actually hurt you, even kill a person?"

"This is a very complicated question. And you have not even come yet to my shop. It is the grand opening!"

"Didn't you open a week ago?"

"Yes, but the grand opening will last all month. We are staying open late and offering a little food and drink so people can discover us. You come, have some wine, and we can discuss these new ghosts of yours."

I glanced up the street. Just a couple of blocks away there was a profusion of greenery. Could that be the tropical garden of Owen Campbell? The famous one that Mountain now tended?

"How late are you open?"

"Until nine. But if I know you are coming, I will wait for you."

"I'll come on the early side. Thanks, Olivier."

"*À bientôt.*"

I circled the block to view the Bernini house from the rear, walking past Victorian row houses, a couple walking arm in arm, and a woman pushing a stroller. Everything seemed quiet; the neighborhood appeared to be a peaceful urban oasis.

There were spans of fencing between the two outbuildings at the back of the Bernini property, with a gate in each stretch. I climbed up on some wooden crates piled by one fence to peek over the top. Both gates were padlocked from the inside, but with the proper athleticism or motivation a person could jump the fence.

Which someone apparently had—there were several

flowers strewn upon the stone wall of the well. Or perhaps the Propaks had made the gesture.

Crime tape still cordoned off the well and a section near the fountain. According to the gossip, Mrs. Bernini had been killed before landing in the well. Could it have been a crime of passion, perhaps some argument that escalated . . . an argument over the woman promising the house to more than one person? Maybe someone had gotten angry enough about the multiple wills to push her, not intending to knock her over, not understanding how fragile she was.

It was full light out, the afternoon chilly but bright, not a cloud marring the pure blue of the January sky. It was hard to imagine ghosts on a day like this, but I recalled the scene that night: the rain, the fog, the shadows that might have been hiding a murderer.

Looking toward the well, I remembered that moment of spying the orangey yarn of Mrs. Bernini's crocheted shawl. I squeezed my eyes shut.

Someone goosed me.

I screeched and yanked back, quite literally falling into the arms of none other than Zach Malinski.

I hit him. "You *jerk*!" I hit him again.

He put me on my feet, ducking and holding his hands in front of his face. The effectiveness of his defense was compromised by his laughter.

"Whoa!" He couldn't stop laughing. "Enough! I'm sorry!"

Zach was tall, good-looking, and barely thirty. Young. Way too young for the likes of me. He wasn't exactly what you'd call a friend. . . . He and I met at my first haunted house, and things had gone downhill from there.

But not long ago he'd helped me out, and I had to admit that his blatant flattery and refusal to take no for an answer when asking me out were gratifying. The man was nine years my junior, but he was intriguing and, frankly, fun to be with.

But did I mention he was young?

"Did you forget your key or something? What are you doing snooping around here?"

"Just wanted a new perspective on the place. And you?"

"Wanted photos from all sides." He gazed at me and smiled. "I understand I have you to thank for this gig. I really appreciate the recommendation. I needed the work, and . . . I'm glad you're not holding the whole kidnapping thing against me anymore."

I shrugged. "I saw the Propaks take off a little while ago. Do you have access to the house?"

Zach nodded. "They told me they were going to be out all day, but that I should feel free to poke around and take pictures in the changing light."

"So they didn't tell you what happened the other night?"

He shook his head.

"When did you speak with them last?"

"Yesterday."

Strange they didn't mention it. "There was a . . . murder."

He gave me a disbelieving look and scoffed. "Get the heck out of here."

"I'm serious. Didn't you notice the bow on the door? Or the shrine? I thought photographers were supposed to be observant."

"I just got here. Anyway . . . you're kidding me, right?" he said, searching my face. "That's *terrible*. Who was it? What happened? Wait—are you involved in this somehow?"

"No, I'm not *involved* in it. I mean"—on second thought—"not *involved*, involved. But I was here the night Mrs. Bernini was killed, and I'm trying to get the ghosts to tell me what happened. And I've been looking into the history of the house, and talking to some of the neighbors." Realization was sometimes slow in dawning, but dawn it did. "Yes, I guess you could say I'm involved."

"What happened? Did they catch the guy?"

I shook my head. "The victim was Mrs. Bernini, the elderly woman who owned the house. . . ."

"I never met her."

"She was a sweetheart. It was . . . it's pretty heart-breaking to think someone hurt her. So, Zach, old buddy, do you have a key to the house?"

"Yeees." He drew the word out carefully and took a step back.

"Great. I want to get in there and look around." I started walking toward the front of the house. After a moment I realized Zach was no longer with me. I turned around to see him lingering by the back gate.

"You coming?"

"You just told me there was a homicide here, and ghosts and, you know, a murderer on the loose."

"So?"

"So . . . I'm thinking maybe I should look into that fast-food job, and leave the murder house—and *you*, sorry to say—well enough alone."

"The crime didn't even happen in the house—it was

in the garden. And the police have released the scene already."

"Uh-huh. I'm just saying. You have a way of attracting trouble."

"*I* have a way of attracting trouble? *You're* the criminal."

"Not anymore. And it's not as though I live here."

"Fine time to decide you're a law-abiding citizen. Didn't I meet you during a breaking and entering?"

"I don't understand why you can't just ask the Propaks and go in while they're home. Why were you sneaking around?"

"I wasn't sneaking, exactly . . . ," I said. "It's just . . . look, the Propaks don't actually have any more right to be here than we do, not really. They were Mrs. Bernini's guests, that's all. Anyway, they might have had a motive to get rid of her—they wanted to buy the place, and at least two other people claim Mrs. Bernini had promised to leave the house to them. And then there are foster children who might think they have something coming to them. . . . I really don't know. But a place like this? It's worth a fortune."

"I get all that. What I don't understand is why you're snooping around. Did you become a cop since last time I saw you?"

"There are ghosts in this house, Zach. And I think I might be able to communicate with them, and maybe learn what happened."

"I'm not really a ghost kind of guy, just FYI." He paused. "And if the killer is around here somewhere, and believes you can actually see ghosts, and maybe one of them could tell you who killed Mrs. Bernini . . ."

I nodded. "Then I might be in danger. Which is another reason I need to figure this out, pronto."

He looked at me for a long moment, assessing. "Or you could butt out of it, and not be in danger at all."

"Yeah, no. Doesn't sound like me. Besides, that ghost-talking cat is apparently out of the bag. This is a chatty neighborhood." I put my hand out, palm up. "Hand over the key, Zach."

"Mel . . ."

"Zach."

He sighed, dug in his pocket, and placed the key in my palm. "Just so it's known this is over my objections. If the Propaks find out and ask about it, I'm going to tell them you used your feminine wiles on me. Seduced me, so I didn't even know which end was up."

"And they'll believe you, because I look like such a seductress."

He smiled, reached out, and pulled on a corkscrew curl—one of a half-dozen cowlicks—that had gotten away from today's utilitarian ponytail.

"You ever hear that poem: 'There was a little girl, who had a little curl, right in the middle of her forehead . . .'?" he recited.

I swatted his hand away. "You finish that rhyme, cameraboy, and you'll face the wrath of the contractor."

"That sounds bad."

"You have no idea."

Half an hour later, I was beyond frustrated.

I had been so sure that if I had time in the house, by myself, I would be able to make contact with Anabelle, or Mrs. Bernini, or *somebody*. But the playroom door remained locked, with no sounds emanating from within. The parlors were empty, the hallways silent. No marbles rolled down the stairs, no little-girl ghost hummed in the distance . . . nothing.

Mrs. Bernini's bedroom was bright at this hour, with the afternoon sun streaming through French doors that opened onto the courtyard. But it was a mess: The bed had been stripped; the sheets were on the floor; the mattress was askew. Drawers were pulled open, and a few had their contents spilled on the floor. Could this be the result of a police search for clues?

Among the items strewn about the room were several beautiful crucifixes made of wood or metal. And there was an ornate carved cross hanging over her bed. Perhaps Mrs. Bernini hadn't been quite as sanguine about living with ghosts as she had appeared.

I snuck down hallways, opened door after door, and even went up into the empty attic. To no avail. The ghosts weren't talking.

Finally, I gave up. I found Zach in the solarium, where he was so intent on his photography he didn't even notice me approach. He did not, however, jump like a fool when I walked in. He was a much cooler customer than I.

"I don't suppose you've seen anything . . . untoward?" I asked him.

"Untoward?"

"Ghostly?"

He smiled. "Nope. You?"

I shook my head and kicked lightly at the baseboard with the steel toe of my boot. There was a disturbingly hollow sound that indicated either that it hadn't been built correctly in the first place, or that there was water and/or insect damage to the wood below. I was betting on the latter. I made a mental note.

"I thought ghosts roam around mostly at night," said Zach.

"I'd like to try that, if I could figure out a way to get the Propaks out of here. But I saw the first ghost during full daylight. I think she just doesn't want to talk. Hey, do you know this song?" I started to sing, *"With garlands of roses, and whispers of pearls . . ."* I couldn't remember the rest of the words, so I "la-laed" the rest.

An odd expression passed over Zach's face. He looked confused. Pained, even. "That's a song?"

"Yes," I said, feeling rather defensive. I love to sing, but I stink at it. I mean, *really* stink at it. I had been banned from my local karaoke bar. "Okay, it's possible I'm not conveying the tune adequately. But how about the words, recognize those?"

He shook his head. "Sorry. I'm more of an alt-rock, indie sort of guy. A little blues maybe, oldies, Motown—"

"Never mind." I let out a sigh. This was a bust. Some crack ghost buster I turned out to be.

"Hey, don't get downhearted," Zach said, laying a hand on my shoulder and squeezing gently. "I'm sure if you try hard, you'll be attacked by ghosts soon enough."

"I'm not going to be *attacked*," I mumbled, shrugging off his hand. Except for occasional evenings to keep my dad company, I never watched television, and rarely saw movies. Apparently I was missing out on an entire oeuvre that depicted ghosts as being ferocious. Now that I thought about it . . . perhaps that was best. "I know what. Let's try the basement."

"I don't really like basements."

"*No* one likes basements. They're liminal spaces, like attics."

"Excuse me?"

"It's an anthropological term. Liminal places are in between: not a living space, but not wild, either. They're always a little spooky." I led the way to the basement door off the main hallway. We both gazed down the steep wooden steps. I couldn't find a light switch, so I used the tiny flashlight on my key ring and focused the small beam into the dark void. "Plus, basements have the added benefit of being dark and dank. Also, they're often fear cages, filled with high EMF readings from pipes and wires, that sort of thing."

"I have no idea what that last bit means."

"Ghost buster talk," I said oh-so-casually, trying to talk myself into being jaded about the whole thing as I started down with care, the steps creaking under my weight.

When I reached the bottom, something metal slapped me in the face. A chain. I pulled it and a single bare bulb blazed to life.

Zach remained at the top of the stairs. "See anything interesting?"

When he spoke, his voice reverberated through a vent in the wall. I heard him through the vent more clearly than from the top of the stairs. It was common in old houses to connect rooms to one another through vents, windows, and transoms in order to increase air flow. It also increased the possibilities of eavesdropping.

"Come on down. There will be some great shots for Kim's haunted house book, I guarantee it."

I started poking around. Water was seeping in through cracks in the concrete. There was a grime-covered workbench, tools stacked willy-nilly, shelves made of bricks and boards holding a bunch of rusting cans of paint and solvents that needed to be carted down to the hazardous-waste recycling center. A few crumbling cardboard boxes, some plastic bins. On the damp concrete floor were scattered beer cans, some cigarette butts, and even a dead mouse.

The visible plumbing was ancient, mostly lead pipes that were too small in diameter. The electrical was actively frightening; there were wires threaded through old gas pipes, and the knob and tube system common to old homes was frayed in areas, and had been spliced.

A massive utility sink had several taps coming straight out of the wall. One dripped with a slow *tick-splash*, *tick-splash*; a couple inches of brackish water in the bottom of the deep basin indicated a very slow drain.

I reached out and tightened the grip. The water stopped dripping.

An ancient water heater had solid iron doors stamped with a decorative scrollwork design. Back when it was made, manufacturers figured if they were going to make something, whether it be a vase or a water heater, by gosh it was going to be pretty. I opened one heavy door. The pipes ran in a coil around the central heating element. It probably still worked, though inefficiently.

Speaking of ancient appliances, a hulking furnace filled one entire corner of the large basement room, its many arms reaching octopus-like up into holes in the ceiling of the basement. While walking through the house I had noticed there were heating vents in the main living rooms and parlors. But upstairs, only the nursery had heat. As was customary in these old places, most bedrooms had no heat source, as a person was meant to warm up under the covers.

But central heat at all was rare in such an old house.

I did a quick check to make sure the furnace exhaust pipe was intact, but despite its obvious age it still seemed to be in order, and had even been wrapped in insulation. I found a date of installation written on a small plaque: 1911.

There was some evidence it had been worked on recently. I made a mental note to get the name of the Propaks' heater guy. I worked with a great HVAC crew, but it was always good to have a backup or two when schedules got tight. And a lot of contractors hated working on old devices, much less crawling through aged walls and replacing venting in areas that weren't up to modern code. I was always on the prowl for folks who actually understood the majesty and beauty of historic homes, and who were willing to be flexible—in more ways than one.

If I was ever able to begin restoration of this place in earnest, I would follow all the ductwork through the walls, probably tearing out the original to replace it with new metal for the sake of safety and cleanliness. Still, modern venting was essentially the same technology as we had used for decades. In construction there were many things that hadn't changed since they were invented: cement, brick, wood framing. Maybe that was why I liked it so much: The ancient Romans built using many of the same principles, and even materials, as we did today.

Energy efficiency, on the other hand, had made great

strides in recent years: alternative sources of power, insulation, weather stripping, double-paned windows. And safety devices—I noticed there was no carbon monoxide alarm anywhere in the basement—nor did I see an outlet to plug one in. I had also noticed a lack of smoke detectors throughout the house. That was a simple fix—I should bring some over and mount them just for the sake of being a good person. This was the kind of task that might seem daunting to someone unfamiliar with working with their hands, but if you owned a drill and didn't mind standing on a ladder, they took about seven minutes, each, to install.

Peeking behind the heater, I saw a door that looked as though it hadn't been opened for some time.

My heart raced. This was the exciting part of historic homes: the treasure hunt aspect . . . or the horror movie aspect. What could be behind such a door?

I grabbed a crowbar from amid a bunch of rusted tools and forced the portal open.

It creaked, loudly. A puff of cold, musty air blew by me. The flashlight beam revealed an intricate, ancient system of wells, tubs, and lots and lots of pipes. The old waterworks, I presumed.

Also stored in this underground grotto were half a dozen antique hospital beds.

"Okay, now, *that's* not creepy at all," Zach whispered as he trailed behind me, clicking photos the whole way.

"The original owner ran a maternity hospital here. It's not that strange."

"Uh-huh. Because you'd keep the beds?"

"Some of us have a hard time letting go. . . . Oh, cool!" I was distracted by several old glass-paned cabinet doors, propped up off the damp floor, leaning against one wall. Beside them was an old wooden box full of what looked to be original doorknobs, light fixtures, and hardware such as drawer pulls and hinges. "Check it out!"

At Zach's questioning look, I explained.

"This is the best thing about basements and attics: You never know what you'll find. When people tear out original fixtures, or doors and windows, that sort of thing, they often store them rather than throw them out," I said, starting to poke around the stacked boxes and containers more seriously. "It's perfect when you're renovating— you just clean it up and reinstall. And usually if they're installed in their original location, they don't even have to be brought up to code—though when it's a safety issue, of course we do it anyway."

Zach stared at me for a moment. "I've got to hand it to you, Mel. You truly are focused on your work."

The drip started again, sounding louder than before, its noise seeming to echo in the room we were in. I stepped on something, and I looked down to find a small glass ball.

Again with the marbles.

I thought I heard a child's giggle.

"Do you hear that?"

"The dripping?"

"No ... laughter?"

He shook his head.

But then ... footsteps coming down the creaking stairs.

"I hear *that*," he whispered.

Chapter Nineteen

"Hello? *Helloooo?*"

It was Kim Propak. *Darn it.* Just when the ghosts were making contact. Zach and I hurried out to the main basement room, emerging from behind the furnace.

"Hello, Zach! And . . . *Mel*? What are you doing down here?"

"Oh, well, you know . . ." I could feel Zach glaring at me. "Remember I was going to drop by sometime and take measurements for the proposal? I just happened upon Zach here, and thought I'd come in and get started. . . ."

"But I thought Marty said . . ." She trailed off, frowning a bit as she looked around the room. "Good gracious, it's a bit *icky*, isn't it? I've never been down here. What's that?" she asked as her eyes alighted on the open door behind us, yawning into nothingness.

"That would be your subbasement," I said. "I was checking things out, looking for sagging or damaged floor joists."

"Subbasement? What's a subbasement?"

"You see them occasionally in old structures like this—they wanted to keep a decent basement for canned goods, even wine, and the heaters, but they kept some utilities and stored things like root vegetables or fermenting spirits out of sight."

"Oh," said Kim.

"Could I just say . . . if you're really going to buy this place, you and Marty should really hire an inspector and look through every nook and cranny. It's a huge responsibility. This furnace alone, what with its removal and installation of a new, efficient unit that can heat the whole place, will run you a pretty penny."

"I leave that sort of thing to Marty. I'm sure he's seen it. But . . . it's so icky down here."

There was no denying the creepy factor. But if you're going to buy an old house . . . ? There's some inherent creepiness. Not to mention the fact that Kim Propak was knowingly walking into the idea of establishing a *haunted* B&B.

"A lot of that is the dampness. It's a common problem around these parts, and the only solution is multifaceted: good gutters, proper drainage that slopes away from the house, and a French foundation drain along the perimeter. A dehumidifier would be great down here, as well. And, of course, there's caulk."

Zach and Kim both looked at me in silence.

"I really can't overstate the importance of caulk."

"Did you get pictures?" Kim asked Zach.

"Of the subbasement?"

"Sure, it's perfect! If that doesn't scream 'haunted house,' I don't know what does. Listen, Zach, I wanted to let you know Marty and I are going back to Indiana for a few days to take care of some paperwork."

"Didn't the police ask you to stick around?" I asked.

"We're not running off to the Cayman Islands or anything," she tittered. "Just going home for a few days. We'll be back by Monday." She fixed Zach with a look. "Here's my problem: This news story . . . well, it's stirred up some interest. And someone's been messing up rooms . . . or maybe it's the ghosts, maybe they're angry with us. Do you think that could be?"

"I noticed Mrs. Bernini's bedroom was tossed. You're saying you think the resident ghosts were responsible?" Poltergeists, maybe, but why would Anabelle trash the place?

"No, that was . . . that was me," she said, tears filling her eyes. "I . . . I don't know what to do. I've been looking for a more recent will. Portia has a handwritten one, but I've been hoping to find an updated version somewhere that might specifically say she wanted me and Marty to take ownership of the place. We have a copy of the purchase agreement, but it seems Portia doesn't have to honor the arrangement."

A single tear fell prettily down her cheek.

"And now with the Kirkbrides and Mountain going at each other . . . and people coming by to lay things on the shrine, and some of them trying to look over the wall to the gardens where it . . . *happened*, I really don't want to leave the house empty. Zach, dear, I don't suppose you'd be willing to house-sit for us? Starting tomorrow?"

Zach shook his head. "I'd love to help you out, Kim, but . . ."

"Of *course* Zach will house-sit," I said. "He'd be happy to. Wouldn't you, Zach?"

"Oh!" said Kim, clapping her hands together, tears forgotten. "That would be so lovely! You sure you don't mind?"

"Mind? Are you kidding?" I said. "You should see Zach's place. Poor fellow lives in a studio apartment the size of a shoe box."

After a long moment, Zach finally said: "Sure. I'd be happy to."

"And while he's house-sitting," I said, "would it be okay if I came by, as well, and took some measurements and whatnot to work up a proper job bid for you?"

"Oh, Marty said you had talked about that. I suppose there wouldn't be anything wrong with that. . . . My only concern is that you include dear Josh. We wouldn't want to leave him out, now, would we?"

"Of course not."

Before we left, Kim told me she was *so* excited about the architect's new drawings she simply *had* to show them to us. She brought out a huge roll of blueprints and conceptual drawings, and laid them out on the dining room table.

"But these don't exactly fit in with the historic quality of the house," I said as I looked them over. There was some fun, Alice-in-Wonderland-type stuff, curvy shapes and asymmetrical walls. But this house was historic, with its own distinct style. I hated to be a stickler about it, but I don't understand why someone would buy a Spanish-style house and then try to make it look French, or tear out the wood paneling in an Arts and Crafts home. What was the point?

Architects were a mixed bag in my book. Many were true artists, with inspired ways of imagining both form and function. But they rarely actually took part in building anything and without such hands-on experience, they often made suggestions and drawings that made little sense for history, much less for the sanity of those of us implementing their designs. On the other hand, architects might complain, with some justification, that contractors were focused on maintaining construction schedules to the exclusion of all else.

I didn't recognize the architect's name, but that was no surprise. There were probably more architects than contractors in the San Francisco Bay Area.

"Well, we would like to be *creative* with this project," Kim said.

"When we first talked, Marty said he would like the house to be eligible for the AIA award in renovation. With these kinds of changes . . ." I shook my head, appalled at the idea of stripping out the house's unique charm. "It would be like a whole new house."

"Josh liked the idea," Kim mumbled as she rolled up the blueprints, her lips pursed in anger or disappointment, or both. "He was the one who recommended the architect."

"Looks great to me," Zach said as he placed his hand on the back of my neck and steered me out the front door. "Great to see you, Kim, as always. I'll call you later."

Out on the sidewalk, Zach said, "You've got a real way with people, you know that?"

"It would be a crime to make those kinds of changes to this house. Why don't they go rip apart a house in a development somewhere, or build something new? They would be free to do any sort of zany project they wanted with a new house. I know an artist up in Calistoga who built an ersatz Roman villa with corrugated metal and cement. It's incredible."

"Plus, you made her cry."

"I *didn't*!"

"Where's your car?"

"Over near Castro Street," with, no doubt, a fifty-five-dollar parking ticket. It dawned on me that I had blithely left it there all day, lured into a false sense of security by the two-hour parking. Rats. They got me again. My parking fines, I was sure, amounted to a significant contribution to the working budgets of the various Bay Area cities.

"I'll give you a lift."

"I can walk."

"No, you can't." He clicked his key ring and an old Honda Accord lit up. "We have to talk. Get in."

I got in.

"Did I miss something here?" Zach asked as he drove. "Last time I looked, I didn't work for you."

"That's true."

"And yet you just promised Kim that I would house-sit for her. What was that about?"

"Your place really is tiny. Think what fun it will be to have a little space."

"Yes, except now you'll be sharing some of this space?"

"Be a pal, Zach. I'm not going to hurt anything. Besides, I figure if a person kidnaps another person and traps her in a salvage yard, he owes her. Plus, I got you this job."

"Hey—I helped you out on your last murder. That made us even."

"As I recall, your information didn't actually help me find the woman I was looking for that time, so it didn't *really* make us even." I looked at his handsome profile; he was clenching his jaw. "Listen, I'll call Marty and make sure to get the go-ahead from him, okay? In fact, I'll offer to house-sit and let you off the hook entirely, if you prefer. Although you should think about what you're missing: the possibility of ghosts and the certainty of really good pizza. What's not fun about that?"

I called my dad to let him know I wasn't going to make it home for dinner. He told me Stephen and Luz had dropped by to visit with Caleb. Dad was, of course, already starting to cook a huge meal for the whole gang.

I felt a little left out. But I was glad they all got along so well—this way I didn't feel so guilty about spending the evening in the city and foisting the care and feeding of my stepson on my dad.

Olivier's store was in an old building in the Jackson Square area off Montgomery Street. Brick was rare in San Francisco because it did a real number on folks when the earth decided to shake, which was a common occurrence here on the Pacific Rim. If you see a real brick building—not those fake facade brick-tiles— you've likely found a place that dates back to the city's Barbary Coast days. This four-story building had a plain, unembellished facade and enough blackening of the bricks to indicate its age. Three steps led to the simple front door, painted black.

Montgomery Street used to be waterfront until land-fill created several more city blocks before the piers along what is now the Embarcadero. Every once in a while ruins of old ships would be discovered when crews excavated for a new office building. I was always hoping to find a way to poke my nose into one of those finds, and put my anthropology degree to work. But I never was a great archaeologist, and cultural anthropologists don't have much legitimacy for sticking their noses into ancient buried finds.

Unless, of course, there was an otherworldly presence that only a professional ghost buster could deal with. *That* was another good reason for getting a better handle on what I was doing.

The store sported a painted shingle that hung like a pub sign from an iron rod. On it was a stylized skull and crossbones reminiscent of what one might see in old cemeteries; I remembered going out into graveyards with my mother and rubbing a crayon over paper atop similar gravestone motifs.

The sign read:

Galopin's Ghostly Goods
(A Spirit-Hunting Supply Shoppe)

Oh, brother. Another Shoppe, and this one to serve all my ghost-busting needs.

"Ah, Mel!" Olivier greeted me as I walked through the front door. Several customers turned around to check out the new arrival. "My dear ghost-talking friend, do come in."

"This place looks great, Olivier. I'm really . . . impressed."

"Please, do look around and I'll be with you momentarily. Serve yourself wine, and take some hors d'oeuvres." He turned back to a pair of rapt-looking women.

I followed orders, poured myself a glass of Bordeaux, and munched on some puff pastries as I poked around the shop.

Scary boy-choir music played softly in the background as I perused bookshelves along exposed brick walls that held books and DVDs. I noticed old broad-planked floors that, unless I missed my guess, were likely made from lumber salvaged from old ships, back in the day. Glass display cabinets held enough high-tech gadgetry to put me in mind of RadioShack, which made an interesting contrast to the plethora of Celtic imagery, crystals, incense, crucifixes, candles, and talismans from various cultural traditions. I noticed plenty of Saint Christophers along with Buddhas, and the Virgin of Guadalupe held pride of place right next to Quan Am, an Asian bodhisattva.

Another table held crystal balls, pyramids, tarot cards, and bags of marbles.

"Help you?" asked a tiny old man wearing a Grateful Dead T-shirt. His gray hair stuck out in random tufts from his head.

"What do people do with the marbles?"

"It's a method of divination. Like tarot, or runes. Same-type deal."

I had assumed the marbles at the Bernini house were Ezekiel's toys. Could there be something more to them?

I veered off and checked out some fun stuff that looked like it had been salvaged from post-October sales at the Halloween Superstore: tombstones and witches and ghosts and the grim reaper. A corner hutch housed a whole slew of baseball caps and T-shirts with the shop's logo, name, and address.

"*Mel!*" Olivier joined me. "What can I help you with? You are dealing with homicidal ghosts, you say? Or dare I hope this is a social visit?"

"I did want to check out your shop . . . but you're right, I also need to ask you a few questions, if I may."

"Of course. Dingo, would you watch the register for a moment, please?"

"'Course," said the older man.

"His name's Dingo?" I asked in a low voice as I followed Olivier through a doorway and up a steep set of dark stairs.

"Yes. Dingo. This is his name. Why?"

"That's a, uh, wild dog in Australia."

"Oh?"

I was guessing he'd never seen that movie about the baby and the dingo. Not worth going into.

The stairs opened onto a large room lined with the high multipaned windows common to buildings of this era, which valued natural sunlight. There were two conference tables, lots of folding chairs, and a screen set up in front.

"This is our classroom," said Olivier. "Ghost Busting 101."

"Seriously?"

"It has had a very good response so far. People are interested in how to go about such investigations in a sane and rational manner." He gave me a significant look. "We're starting a new course next Thursday night."

"Oh . . . um, yeah. I'll think about it." One of my problems with accepting myself as a ghost talker, or whatever you wanted to call it, was that I had a hard time with a lot of the believers around me. I wasn't sure how to handle that aspect of my talents yet. I found out only after my mother's death that she had some ability to see the beyond. I wished I could have understood earlier and spoken to her about it—specifically, about how she dealt with it around other people.

We both took seats at the big table, and I gave Olivier an abbreviated version of what had happened in the Bernini house.

"What I don't understand is why Anabelle won't just speak to me, tell me what happened."

"She may not have witnessed the recent murder. And as to her own demise—it's common for ghosts not to know what happened. I think of it like head trauma; when someone is hit on the head hard enough to lose consciousness, their memory right before the event can be erased." He shrugged one shoulder and pushed out his chin in the nonchalant way that only a French person could pull off. "And when you ask her about it, she might grow frustrated or upset because she does not know, and does not want to think about it. In fact, she might be appearing precisely because she's trying to figure it out, or now hoping you will help."

"What about her parents? From what I can tell, they

died at the same time, the whole family together. I've seen evidence of the boy, but nothing from the parents."

"Anyone's guess. They might not be powerful enough, or sensitive enough. The same reason that Anabelle appeared to you in full body apparition, while her brother, apparently, only sends signs: the marbles and the writing on the wall, the playfulness in the nursery."

I thought about the movements in the nursery, and how they had sent us all fleeing in terror. Playfulness, indeed.

Olivier's eyes dropped down to my chest.

"I like your teacher."

"My . . . what?"

"Your teacher. 'Measure twice, cut once.' I have heard you say this before. It's a saying from the building professions?"

"Um, yes. Yes it is. But . . . do you mean T-shirt?"

"That's what I said. Teacher."

I smiled. I couldn't *wait* to get to Paris.

"I think you should try to make contact with the parents, to understand what happened there."

"How do I contact the parents?"

"You might want to practice a bit, somewhere where you are not emotionally involved. Graveyards, for example. Or even here—you could walk around upstairs in the middle of the night. This was an old brothel. Lots of activity."

"I'm feeling a little time pressure in this case. Could you come and check out the house with me?"

He blew out a breath and ran one hand over his nearly bald head. "I am sorry to say that I am booked out for more than a month. Dingo has been promoting the shop, and my services. I am exhausted, to tell you the truth. In fact, I could use your talents, if you were to become a bit more polished. You would be well paid to contact spirits."

"I thought you were gunning for a reality-TV show?"

He waved off the idea. "They are very 'Hollywood,' as you say. Nothing but wanting to exploit this sort of thing. I became disenchanted with this idea."

Part of me was ready to accuse Olivier of exploiting the beliefs and fears of those around him. Interesting to think Hollywood was too much of such a thing for him.

"Anabelle's always singing a tune. Do you think there could be a clue there?"

"Could be."

"You're not as much help as a person might hope for, you know."

"What is this tune? Sing it for me?"

I gave it a go.

He laughed. And cringed. And shook his head. "Sorry, I don't know this. But do not make the mistake of thinking everything a spirit does is significant. She is first and foremost a child. But Anabelle sounds very good at taking advantage of the energy around her. I wonder whether she might have had some special abilities when she was alive. A psychic talent of some sort. That would explain why she is able to appear to you so easily, while the others aren't."

Olivier's cell phone beeped, and he read a text. "I am sorry—they need me back downstairs."

"Of course." We both headed down the stairs. "By the way, the radio on my car is playing music of its own accord. Is that normal? I mean, is it paranormally normal?"

"Very much so. Radios work on different frequencies

than the human ear. Sometimes spirits are able to use this."

Before I left, Olivier and I agreed on fair compensation for the equipment he had lent me, and then he outfitted me like a real ghost buster. On impulse I grabbed a Saint Christopher medal and a little statue of Quan Am. Just in case.

Olivier raised his eyebrows at that, but just smiled as Dingo tallied up the price of my new equipment. In addition to the EMF detector and the EVP monitor with external mic, I bought a red lens flashlight—doesn't interfere with night photography—a new digital camera, and a thirty-five-millimeter infrared camera with eight-hundred-speed film. Also a compass, because the needle moves erratically in the presence of spirits. The only recommended item I didn't buy was a first aid kit—I had that part handled.

I even purchased a couple of business-type things: standard release forms and investigative checklists. According to Dingo, there was no actual ghost-hunting license required by the state; however, I was bound to pay taxes like any other independent "consultant."

"In this case you're a spiritual consultant," Dingo said.

"That makes me sound like a priest. Do I have to wear robes?"

Dingo didn't crack a smile. As he was placing the boxes into a big paper bag with the store's logo and GHOSTS written on the side, Olivier gave me a few last-minute tips for a legitimate ghost hunt.

"Write down everything, no matter how trivial it may seem. There are spirit encounters—as you well know—but a lot of what we see comes in the aftermath, studying the results of the EVP and the like. So write down any sounds you hear, from outside and in. You sneeze, you write it down so you'll be able to note it on the recording. A car pulls up, anything."

"Okay." Folks were milling around, a few glancing over at Olivier with expectant looks on their faces, and I realized I'd been monopolizing the charismatic star of the show. "I'll let you get back to your guests. I just have one final question—maybe the most important question: Can ghosts hurt people?"

There was a long pause. I hated that.

Whether he was doing it for the sake of theatricality or because he was choosing his words carefully, I wasn't sure. But everyone in the store stopped what they were doing and observed him.

"There are three kinds of hauntings. First, the earth-bound spirits of humans who have passed. Typically these are only as mean or kind as they were in life—our soul does not change markedly upon moving from one dimension to the next.

"Second are residual hauntings. These are like a scene that is played back endlessly. Especially on sites of old murders, suicides, traumatic events. These cannot hurt you."

He paused again, and everyone in the store seemed to unconsciously lean forward so as not to miss his next words. Gone was the happy-go-lucky Gaul; when he spoke, he was very serious.

"And then there are spirits that are not human. These are bad news."

"Not human as in, what?"

"Evil spirits. They were never human and cannot be prevailed upon the way a human ghost can. This is important: Never, *ever*, invite them to stay, or wish them into a building. Calling on them, even to answer questions, can be very dangerous."

"And do these ever appear as children?"

Yet another long pause. I was about to kill me one blue-eyed, ghost-busting Frenchman.

"Almost never. These almost never appear at all. I myself ... perhaps in all my investigations I have seen such a thing once, or twice. Many ghost professionals do not believe in them at all. Be resolute, Mel, and you should be just fine."

I thanked him and turned to leave.

"Oh, and Mel? Look up the history of the place. You should have done that first thing. Perhaps this will answer all your questions."

Chapter Twenty

I was going to take Olivier at his word when he said the demon stuff hardly ever happened. I had seen and felt nothing that would indicate some sort of pure evil. If Anabelle had been a demon, wouldn't there be, I don't know . . . *Exorcist*-like signs? Of course, a movie I hadn't seen since I was a teenager wasn't, perhaps, the most trusted source of information.

But still, knocking a defenseless old woman down, then hiding the body in the well, sounded much more humanly crass than diabolically clever.

And besides, it had taken me some time to wrap my mind around the concept of a thinning of the veils between the earthly and spiritual dimensions, and the occasional crossing over of energy. Demons and evil spirits on the other hand . . . unless forced to do otherwise, I would leave all of that to Hollywood.

By the time I climbed behind the wheel, my head

abuzz with paranormal possibilities, all I really wanted was to go to bed. I checked my phone: It was a little after eight. I was pathetic. I remembered a day when I used to stay out until the wee hours, dancing and enjoying. But that was back when I was a student, not when I got up at five every day to hit the jobsite.

As soon as I slammed the car door behind me, my phone rang.

It was Luz. "What's up?" I asked.

"Thought you should know that Stephen, Caleb, and I are on a stakeout."

"I'm sorry?" I must have heard wrong. "You say you went out for steak?"

"On *stakeout*. We're outside your ex-husband's house. Your ex-house."

"*Why?*"

"Caleb says his dad and the missus took off—they're out of town until tomorrow night."

I heard some laughter and excited chatter in the background. A sense of foreboding came over me.

"Luz, you aren't by any chance out drinking with my underage stepson?"

"Get real, *chica*. You were a little caught up with your other haunted house, and anyway, we talked it over and have decided this place isn't haunted. It's probably the workers screwing around since they can't stand Valerie. Hell, she makes *me* want to vandalize her and I'm an upstanding citizen. By and large."

"Luz, I really don't think . . ."

"Besides, poor Stephen was traumatized by the other night with you, so he had to get right back up on that ghost-busting horse. Right, Stephen?"

"This wasn't my idea!" I heard Stephen shout. *"I'm a hostage!"*

Then another burst of laughter. I was annoyed, but there was no denying I loved to hear Caleb laugh like that, the way he used to before he became a sullen teen.

"We might go in and check it out."

"No, you will *not* go in and 'check it out.' What are you, cat burglars now?"

"We weren't going to *take* anything. A bottle of wine, at most."

Now Caleb shouted toward the phone: *"It's my house, too. We're not breaking in."*

"Not sure Daniel would see it that way," I grumbled.

"And Valerie even asked for your help," Luz said. "So, we're helping. We want to find out what happened to Caleb. If there are ghosts, wouldn't they be out at night?"

I blew out a sigh. "Just promise me you won't do anything until I get there."

"She's on her way," I heard Luz say to her companions, before clicking off.

"I can't believe you dragged me into this."

"Dragged, nothing. I mentioned we were here and you felt you had to come rescue us. Because that's what you do. Accept it."

Caleb had let us into the house and disarmed the alarm system. Stephen and Caleb had a grand old time ripping into my packages and playing with the new devices—the EVP recorder, especially. Then the four of us did a quick walk-through of the house, from top to bottom.

I sensed nothing out of the ordinary: no sounds, no chills, no cold spots. Nothing out of the corner of my eye, no unexplained shadows or ectoplasmic mist. And if this house was haunted, wouldn't I have felt something in those years I lived here? I disliked Valerie, and Daniel for that matter, but I couldn't imagine they had killed someone and stashed the body somewhere in the intervening years, leading to a haunting.

Predictably, after forty-five minutes of clowning around with the equipment—I had the sense I would be treated to some unsavory, *South Park*–style jokes and sounds when I listened to the tapes—Caleb got bored and went to his room to text his friends and play video games.

"Can't blame him," said Luz, who was strutting around and talking a big game now that she was free of any lingering doubts that she might actually encounter a ghost. "Hey, let's check out the wine cellar."

"We are not going to break into the wine cellar," I said with a nervous chuckle.

"After everything the Worm's put you through?" she said with a slight East LA head waggle. "He owes you a bottle of merlot. Besides, no one's breaking in—Caleb showed me where Daniel hides the key."

She held up a tiny key.

"I'm not saying the man doesn't owe me. But after all . . ."

But then I remembered something. Back when I lived here, I had bought myself a case of lovely twelve-dollar French Bordeaux. Daniel always stashed a copy of *Wine Spectator* by his bed, and in keeping with his vision of himself as a connoisseur of California wines, he wouldn't touch a bottle under fifty bucks. So my contribution to the wine cellar had never been brought out in mixed company; unless Daniel had poured it down the drain, my stash was probably sitting where I'd left it.

Luz opened the small door to the cellar under the stairs. There it was, in the corner: an old cardboard box whose contents didn't even merit a place on the shelves. It looked like Daniel hadn't touched a bottle since I'd left—there was practically half a case remaining. I took one specimen out of the dusty box.

Beside my wine was a pile of tools, presumably left by one of the workers for safekeeping. That was peculiar—tools were expensive, and crucial to the job. Those of us in construction usually kept our tools with us, treating them with the care one would a child. I wondered, could Valerie be on to something? Was this the sort of ghostly prank they'd been experiencing on the job?

I paused and tried to open myself up to anything otherworldly, but felt nothing. After a few moments, I shrugged it off and joined Stephen and Luz, who were hunkered down on the floor in the darkened foyer, their backs against the wall, legs splayed in front. I opened the bottle and we passed it back and forth like a trio of overgrown juvenile delinquents.

"I gotta say, Mel," said Stephen, "it's hard to imagine you living here."

"It looked a little different back in my day. This may come as a shock to you, but I've never been much of one for the 'many shades of beige' school of interior decorating."

"Maybe I just envision you in that old farmhouse in Oakland," said Stephen.

"This place doesn't suit you, is all," said Luz with a nod, taking a swig from the bottle and handing it back to me. "I think maybe the best thing Daniel ever did was dump you."

"He didn't exactly *dump* me. It was a mutual parting of the ways."

"If it's so mutual, why has it been so hard to move on?"

"I'm moving on. I'm dating, for heaven's sake."

"You're dating?" said Stephen. "That's news to me."

"You're not giving Graham much of a chance," said Luz.

"I'll have you know we walked on the beach just the other day."

"Walked on the beach. And . . . ?"

"And nothing. We walked, and talked. It was nice."

She and Stephen exchanged glances. They were sitting on either side of me, so this necessitated them both leaning forward. Flanked as I was, I was beginning to feel like this was a planned intervention of some sort. Lord knows what they had been plotting while they were in the car together, before I arrived.

"Okay, okay. I know I haven't given Graham that much of a chance. It's just that . . ." I took another sip of wine. "It isn't Daniel per se. It's that I showed such awful character judgment that I can't trust myself anymore. I think maybe I should stick to houses. It's what I'm good at."

My phone rang. Speak of the devil: Graham.

"Hi," I said, hyper-self-conscious in front of Stephen and Luz.

"Your dad's worried."

"I told him I was having dinner in the city."

"It's nearly ten."

"What am I, sixteen?" I said, aggravated. Good Lord,

I was pushing forty and my daddy was still checking up on me? "And why didn't he call *me*? Why'd he call you?"

"I think he's worried since you brought a man home the other morning."

"I told you: That was no man; it was Stephen."

"Hey!" Stephen interjected with a frown.

"You know what I mean."

"Shall I take it that's Stephen with you now?"

"Sort of." Why was I feeling guilty? Nothing was going on, and Graham and I weren't exactly going steady.

"Could I ask what you're doing, or is it none of my business?"

"It's a little weird. . . . Actually, I'm at my ex-husband's house with Luz and Stephen and Caleb. And we're, sort of . . ."

"On a stakeout," shouted Luz in the direction of the phone.

"On a stakeout?" I heard a soft chuckling. I couldn't help but smile at the sound. "You're going on stakeout and you take those particular friends with you?"

"Laugh all you want. Fact is, we found out some valuable information. In my newly minted role as a professional ghost buster, I can confidently say that Daniel's house shows no signs of being haunted."

"That's a shocker."

"Oh, here's some good news: Starting tomorrow I'm going to be house-sitting the Bernini house." No response on the other end of the line. Both of my wine-sipping buddies, however, stared at me. "It'll give me a chance to have a real chat with the ghosts there. I hope."

"Tell you what," Graham said in a quiet, careful tone.

"How about I meet up with you tomorrow? I'd love to talk more about this, in person."

"Don't you have a business to run?"

"The joy of being self-employed: I'm my own boss."

"Is my dad putting you up to this?"

"Mel?"

"Yes?"

"I'll meet you tomorrow. How about I take you to lunch? Taco truck?"

"Big spender."

"Nothing but the best. I'll call you tomorrow."

I hung up.

"Don't do that eyebrow-raising thing, Luz, I'm begging you. I can't deal at this late hour. I get up very early, you know."

"What do you *mean* you're house-sitting at the Bernini house?" Stephen's voice went so high it squeaked. "Weren't you with me the other night, when we were terrorized by *ghosts* and an old woman was *killed*?"

"Of course, which is precisely why I have to go back, I— "

The knob on the back door turned. Someone was fiddling with it; I could hear the rattle plain as day, and a quick glance at my companions confirmed that they heard it, too.

From where we were sitting, we had a clear view to the door off the eating nook in the rear of the kitchen. We were sitting in the dark, but that area was illuminated by the neighbors' back porch lights.

While we watched, the door opened slowly inward.

Chapter Twenty-one

A man crept in, quietly closing the door behind him. Somehow in all our stakeout antics we hadn't factored in the possibility of actually capturing anyone. Luz was the first one up, standing in a single, soundless move. Using the wall between the foyer and the kitchen as a screen, she held the EMF detector up as if it were a gun, and flipped on the lights.

"Hold it!"

The man froze, thrusting his hands in the air. "Don't shoot!"

Once it was clear he wasn't armed, we all crept out from behind the wall. Luz stood tall, EMF detector held out in front of her. Stephen and I tried to follow her confident lead and flanked her. Luz was of average height, just a tad shorter than I, and slim to the point of skinny. Stephen was, well, Stephen. I had more body mass and muscle than either of my companions, but the man before us, though small of stature, had the ropy, hard muscles common to construction sites. Somehow I couldn't imagine him quailing at the sight of any of us.

On the other hand, Luz had an in-your-face attitude she'd used to claw her way out of the neighborhood she grew up in. She wasn't scared of anything human.

"What in holy *hell* do you think you're doing?" Luz began, going on to say something clearly threatening in Spanish. She was speaking too quickly for me to follow with my rudimentary language skills, but her tone of voice was enough to get the gist.

The man looked young, probably no more than twenty years old. He stood with his hands thrust in the air, his chin quivering, and he seemed like he was about to cry. He started to shake all over, then started speaking rapidly in Spanish to Luz.

"English, please," demanded Luz. "I want my friends to hear whatever lame-ass excuse you're coming up with."

"I'm sorry, I'm—I just wanted to get my tools. My things. Not to steal anything. Just my things."

"At this hour?" Luz said, glancing at me.

Though my heart was still pounding, I finally found my voice. "Were you on the construction crew, then? With Avery Builders?"

"Yes, construction. Avery Builders. Who are you?"

"No importa," snapped Luz. "It doesn't matter. We're asking the questions here."

"Este . . . Mrs. Burghart is not here?"

"Valerie? No. Why? Are you here to see her?"

"No! This is why I come like this, when she is gone.

She hates me. She took my tools. And then she called *la migra* on me."

"Valerie called immigration?"

He nodded.

"Why would she do that? Are you . . . ?"

"I have my green card. I am legal! But she does not want to pay for work I did in the kitchen, right here—these cabinets." His hands were still in the air, but he gestured to the cherry built-in with his head. "She drew plans herself, told me what wood to use. I buy supplies and make them exactly as she wants. But when I install them, she say they are not big enough for serving trays. This is not my fault, I do not know about her serving trays, I say her. I cannot redo without more money. But then she tells Avery I must be fired. Plus, she keeps my tools."

Valerie wasn't my favorite person, but this was ridiculous. Keeping a construction worker's tools threatened his livelihood. And then calling in Immigration and Customs Enforcement, otherwise known as ICE? A very low blow. ICE had broad powers of authority; they were much freer than the police to detain people without charge, for instance, and yet they moved at the glacial speed of the typical bureaucracy. Once a person was detained, it sometimes took months or even years to resolve the legal issues. Not to mention money.

Sad to say, the young man's story had the ring of truth to it; I remembered Valerie going on about the cabinets herself last time I was here. And I would imagine he was the owner of the tools hidden in the locked wine cellar.

"Listen, I am Ignacio Gutierrez, but everyone calls me Nacho," he said, his tone ingratiating. "Please put down the gun. Really, I am not here to hurt anyone, or to steal anything."

Luz lowered the EMF detector, but kept her stink-eye on him.

"Are you responsible for the strange things happening here on the job? The damage to the dining room table, the clothes taken out of the closet and spilled on?" I asked.

"Got to hand it to you, Nacho," muttered Luz, "that bit was particularly inspired."

"My friends on the crew, they were angry. It was wrong, they know this now; I have spoken to them, telling them we must pay her back for the table. They were also angry at Avery because he has not been paying proper overtime, so they wanted him to pay for the table. But I say if we pay a little each month, each of us, we can make that right. But then the kid was hurt—"

"That was *you*?" I said, any compassion I had been feeling immediately replaced by fury.

"It was an accident! I'm a father myself. I would never hurt a kid." He licked his lips and looked nervously at Luz, who had once again raised the EMF detector in his direction. "Caleb is a good boy, very nice. He has nothing to do with this. That piece of the toilet was set there to fall off and break on the stairs, not to hurt anybody. They were just trying to make Mrs. Burghart unhappy."

"Look, I don't blame you for being angry, but my son was seriously hurt. And it could have been much worse. There's no excuse for that."

Luz launched into another long, rapid-fire tirade in Spanish. Nacho answered, his tone passionate. They lost me after the initial sentences, though I did understand

Luz threatening to call her sister, the cop. Luz's sister was low on the police totem pole, a rookie who was mostly assigned to crowd control, but Nacho didn't have to know that.

I took a deep breath to calm myself, and noticed that Nacho had started shaking again. He looked so young. Just a few years older than Caleb, really, but already with a family of his own to support. What Valerie had done, if true, was reprehensible and demonstrated her lack of understanding of what it was like to work for a living. And there was something in his voice . . . I believed him when he said he hadn't hurt Caleb on purpose, and that he was trying to undo what he—or his friends—had done.

I glanced at Stephen, who had remained quiet throughout this exchange. He was good at reading people. He gave a subtle nod, indicating he believed Nacho, as well.

"Tell me about Avery," I said. "What do you mean he wasn't compensating you properly?"

"Before, I worked for Thomas Avery, who understands more. I don' like this Josh as much. He only sits in his fancy office, never comes to work with us. I think maybe he doesn't understand how it works when you are on the job."

That was a standard complaint of workers toward their bosses. It wasn't the way I ran my business, but it wasn't criminal behavior.

"Wait," he said, picking up on my interest. "I . . . I can tell you a secret about Josh Avery."

"We really don't care if he's got a secret love child stashed somewhere," snapped Luz.

"What? No, nothing like that. But he's not who he says he is. He isn't really Thomas's nephew."

"What are you talking about? Then who is he?"

"I don't really know. I hear this from one of my friends, Chewy."

"Chewy? How could I get in touch with him?"

"I . . . I don' know. I could find out."

"All right," I said. "I'll make you a deal. If Caleb backs up your story, and you agree to contact this Chewy fellow and get him to talk to me about Avery, I'll let you go."

"You not gonna charge me?"

I met Luz's eyes. She raised her eyebrows and gave me a strange twist of the mouth and inclination of the head.

"Show us your ID," Luz said. "I'm going to give my sister, the *policía*, all your information, and you come up at all, for anything, your ass is mine."

He swallowed, hard, and handed over his wallet so Luz could write down all the pertinent information. Then we marched him down to Caleb's room, and my stepson vouched for him and corroborated the parts of the story about Valerie he knew. We helped Nacho collect his tools—they were marked with his name—and brought them out to his truck.

"I will call you, I promise. Chewy will talk to you about Josh Avery." His eyes flicked over all of us. "Thank you, thank you so much. And, Caleb, I'm so sorry for what happened to you."

"Ah, it's whatever," Caleb said with a shrug. "I'm gonna come up with a good story to tell the girls."

Nacho looked a little confused, but smiled. "Okay, then. Thank you again. I will call you, Mel."

We stood and watched the taillights of his truck, speeding down the quiet residential street.

"You suppose there's any chance he'll actually call me?"

"Nah," said Luz.

"Probably not," said Stephen.

"Still, maybe I really should have my sister follow up, just to keep him on his toes. He seems a little arrogant for someone named after snack food."

I gave her a look. "Really? You're going to go there?"

"Love the cultural sensitivity," said Stephen.

"Cultural sensitivity's for outsiders. I'm Latina, so I get to say whatever I want."

"Is that true?" Stephen asked me.

I glanced down at the EMF reader she still clutched in her hand. "As long as she's holding that deadly weapon, I guess whatever she says goes."

After the excitement of our impromptu stakeout, I was relieved to see my bed and get some much-needed sleep. The next morning I met with some prospective clients in Sausalito, and then headed over to the California Historical Society on Mission. I was eager to research Anabelle's family to see if I could learn any pertinent information. Olivier was right, I should have done my historical research on the house, first thing.

I'd been through this drill before, so I pulled the file on the address, looking up blueprints, newspaper clippings, tax rolls. Anything I could get my hands on.

The original builders of the house were Franklin and Elizabeth Bowles. They built the house in 1902. Bowles came from money, but became truly wealthy when he set up a waterworks for the rapidly growing—and thirsty—

city of San Francisco. A man of science, he was a physician and built the house to live in as well as to serve as a maternity hospital. It was one of the first of its kind in all of northern California.

"I remember that story," said Trish Landres, who had become a friend over the years. Trish was the very picture of a librarian, with her reading glasses on a beaded chain, short-cropped no-nonsense hair, and wool cardigan. But I happened to know that underneath that staid exterior was a rebel who loved salsa dancing, believed passionately in the cause of certain Latin American countries, and regularly brought medical supplies to Cuba with a group called Pastors for Peace.

"You really are amazing," I said. "Do you know the story of *every* old family in San Francisco?"

"Of course," she said with a grin. "No, seriously, I remember the scandals, mostly. This story was huge for the Castro. The Bowles Water Works was wildly successful and financed his innovative maternity hospital until this other fellow bought the acreage up the hill, and siphoned off the water. Let me see, . . ."

She went back behind the reference counter and started tapping on her computer keyboard. "Uh-huh . . . uh-huh . . . not that . . . ," she muttered under her breath, tilting her head back to see through the lower lens of her bifocals.

"Aha!" she cried out in victory.

"Did you find it?"

"It's still on microfiche." She looked around to be sure that the handful of patrons were taken care of by the other librarian on duty. "Kai, I'm going in the back for a few."

She headed through a door marked EMPLOYEES ONLY and gestured for me to follow. I love all libraries, but especially adore the back rooms like this: stuffy and musty, shelves crammed with papers and ephemera that hadn't made it onto computers yet. This was where you felt the history, a sensation impossible to get from a scanned picture on a computer screen.

"I didn't realize you still kept microfiche," I said. "I thought everything would be computerized by now."

"Funny story, that," Trish said as she stood on a step stool and started pawing through cardboard boxes sitting high on a metal storage shelf. "We started converting our whole collection over to computer, scanning in documents and entering the information for easy accessibility. Problem was, halfway through the project our funding was cut, and we couldn't afford to staff computer experts to make sure the data wasn't lost. *Here* it is." She yanked a box off the shelf, which released with a puff of dust. She sneezed.

"Gesundheit," I said. "Here, hand it to me."

"Thanks," she replied with a sniff. "So anyway, at that point we stopped scanning in the microfiche, but luckily we have the old machines, and they still work perfectly well. All they needed were new lightbulbs. Our budget covers that, at least. Just barely."

I put the heavy box on the desk with a thump.

"I always wish I could earmark my tax dollars to pay for things like libraries," I said. "And fire departments."

"Good idea," she said with a smile. "Want to know the worst part? Turns out, since we didn't have the resources to keep updating the computer programs, now that data is hard to get at."

"You mean lost?"

"I certainly hope not. Some of us are pretty committed to keeping hard copies, so there's always that. And I don't think the data's irretrievable for someone who knows what they're doing, just for us mere mortals who simply want to look up a historical document."

"I thought computers were supposed to make our lives easier."

"Ironic, isn't it?" she asked as she rummaged through the little rectangular boxes within the larger crate. "It's great to have searchable databases, of course, that sort of thing. And it's a wonderful service to let people do research remotely. But there are definite drawbacks to the information revolution."

I was enough of a Luddite to be secretly pleased when I heard about computer conversions failing, or mucking things up much worse than when they were on paper. What can I say? I like old stuff. As I told Caleb ad nauseam, real live books, the old-fashioned kind that you hold in your hand, never run out of battery or have their hard drives fail. Heck, drop a book in the bath and once it dries out, it is still readable. Try that with an e-reader.

Of course Caleb, sensible twenty-first-century lad that he was, would nod to placate me while he whipped out his smart phone to download a movie or communicate with someone in Madagascar.

"*Aha,*" Trish said, holding up a small carton in triumph. "Let's get this one on the machine, and you can do a little reading. Find some interesting tidbits, I have no doubt."

It didn't take long to find references to the Bowles house, or, as it was known, the Bowles "Folly," because it was so large and so remote from Nob Hill, where people of wealth and privilege built their homes. But when it came to that, at least, the Bowles family had the last laugh. The 1906 earthquake and fire destroyed most of the buildings on Nob Hill, while the Folly survived with only a few toppled chimneys.

The Folly was also famous for all the innovations Bowles installed: energy-saving devices, a newfangled water heater, a speaking tube. Franklin Bowles spent most of his family money on the construction of the manor, so he put in the waterworks to finance the city's first maternity hospital. Most women at that time had babies with the help of midwives, or their female relatives. But Bowles tended to the wealthiest citizens of the city, accumulating yet another fortune.

A little shiver went up my spine when I read:

> *On nights when the coastal fog creeps down over Twin Peaks and the nearby hills with long white fingers, the huge house looms darkly out of the weblike mist. The occasional clops of horses' hooves on cobblestone streets and the clanking of carriages signal a new arrival to the hospital.*

I thought back on the sounds Claire, Stephen, and I had heard when the pizza arrived. With a flash I remembered the strange smile on Mrs. Bernini's face and her comment that she had heard that sound numerous times. She had not been afraid.

I returned to my reading. Owen Campbell was the neighbor who siphoned off Bowles's water. Campbell, for his part, accused Bowles of malpractice, and the unhygienic treatment of patients. At one point, Campbell even accused Franklin and Elizabeth Bowles of mistreating their two young children, Ezekiel and Anabelle. Campbell managed to cut off most water to the Bowles house, effectively shutting down the hospital.

When Franklin Bowles filed suit and tried to take his neighbor to court over the water rights, the hotheaded Campbell challenged him to a duel. Bowles refused, calling the practice barbaric.

And then one night the physician's entire family—Franklin and Elizabeth, Anabelle and Ezekiel—all perished in their beds. Actually, in one single bed.

Angry neighbors suspected foul play, and in two separate articles Campbell was accused of "some sort of foreign witchcraft" and "abominable island customs."

Campbell, for his part, insisted on his innocence. He noted that Dr. Bowles had been on the verge of losing the house because of financial troubles, even suggesting that he might have poisoned his own family because of those finance woes. And he was quoted as denying "the use and application of any kind of magic, barbaric or otherwise."

"How's it going?" Trish asked.

"There's plenty of information, but it's pretty depressing. Franklin Bowles said Campbell cut off their water access. Meanwhile Owen Campbell accused Bowles of malpractice, and child abuse."

"Interesting. Child abuse wasn't a common accusation back then—'spare the rod' and all that. And the man of the family was given free rein when it came to dealing with his wife and children."

"Is it possible Campbell was trying to intervene in an

abusive situation, but none of the other neighbors would support him?"

"Possible," she said with a nod, pushing her glasses higher on her nose. "I imagine most folks would have told him to stay out of it."

I thanked Trish for all her help and walked back to my car. Even if Campbell had killed the family for some other reason—say, to get full control of the waterworks— that didn't explain why their ghosts would be hanging around the house. Trying to exact revenge? Their sworn enemy was long gone, had died decades ago. Or maybe they were just a tragic group, not understanding what had happened, and haunting their house forever? My visit to the archives had turned up interesting historical tidbits, but as I left I didn't feel any closer to discovering what the ghosts wanted from me ... much less who had wanted to harm Mrs. Bernini.

I begged off lunch with Graham and asked him to meet me at the Cheshire House jobsite instead, where I was responding to a panicked phone call.

He arrived with doughnuts and coffee for the whole on-site crew.

"Trying to be the popular kid?" I asked.

"Always." He handed me a paper cup full of strong black French roast. My favorite.

"So, tell me about house-sitting at the haunted scene of a recent murder."

"Gee, when you say it like that, it sounds so ... dashing of me."

"'Dashing' wasn't the first word that came to my mind."

"Oh, I haven't even told you what last night's stake-out revealed." I filled him in on what our nocturnal visitor told us about the events in Daniel's house, and then the suspicion he cast on Josh. "Right now I have to settle a skirmish between the plumber and the bidet supplier, and then meet with the landscapers, but then I want to go have a little chat with Tom Avery. Dad tracked him down at the Jack London Marina in Oakland."

"I'll drive."

"You can't just follow me around, you know," I said. I liked the idea of having Graham with me, but it also made me nervous. And if this was all a wild-goose chase—which was likely—I would feel foolish. "As I was pointing out last night, you have a fledgling business to tend to."

"Yes, but I have an evil plan. I'll neglect my own work in favor of protecting you, and then when I go out of business, you'll feel so guilty you'll be compelled to sleep with me."

"Very funny."

"It's all your fault, anyway. You're the one who suggested I give up my lucrative government career. And I had such high prospects for climbing the ladder."

"The Cal-OSHA ladder? Please." Graham used to be an inspector for California's Occupational Safety and Health Administration. Though worker safety was paramount, we builders had a few snide things to say about the necessity, and especially the efficiency, of OSHA.

He shrugged. "It was a real job with regular hours, and benefits, even. Now I'm just a poor self-employed man, living on a shoestring, trying desperately to keep my business out of receivership. . . ."

I glared at him. He smiled.

Since starting his green building consultancy, Graham had tapped into a very affluent, environmentally conscious elite clientele. They paid scads of money for him to tell them what they could have figured out by reading a book or two: put in solar panels, conserve and reclaim water, insulate, and install double-paned windows. There was no denying Graham was gifted at developing designs, coordinating workers, and liaising with generals like me. But when it came right down to it, he was being handsomely paid to have a lot of nice lunches and assuage the guilt of the Bay Area wealthy.

I got the sense he was having trouble filling his time. I would bet good money he was going to start flipping houses soon, in addition to consulting.

After I settled the bidet dispute, we headed across the Bay Bridge. Just as we were passing through the tunnel at Treasure Island, my cell phone rang.

Wonder of wonders, it was Nacho. He gave an address and a name: Chewy Garay, who lived in the Bayview, and was expecting my visit this afternoon. Nacho begged me to tell "the mean woman with the gun" that he had held up his end of the bargain. I assured him I would.

Ten minutes later we parked on the street near Oakland's Jack London Square, a waterfront area that had been "redeveloped" several years ago. There were numerous shops, a hotel, a parking garage, and a theater in addition to the marina. I rarely came here, since the eateries seemed like the kinds of pricey restaurants you would take visiting elderly relatives to, each offering similar expensive fish entrées and great views of the estuary. Today hordes of people were milling around at a farmers' market, and several artists had brought out their wares, setting up their easels and display tables in the sunshine.

We walked past row upon row of yachts and sailing rigs. I noticed a building that advertised showers, laundry, and toilets. A man held a big plastic bucket under a spigot, collecting freshwater. Funny to think that you might *live* on the water, but still be so dependent on access to freshwater.

"Could you see yourself living on a boat?" I asked.

"Seems a little cramped to me. But if you have the sailing bug, I guess it would be great to feel as though you could escape any time you wanted." He gave me a sidelong look. "Head out for Paris, maybe."

"I don't think you could quite sail all the way to Paris."

"Don't they call it *Île de Paris*? *Île* means 'island,' right?"

"You're thinking *Île de la Cité*. But even so, it's not an actual island," I retorted, noncommittal. Seagulls screeched overhead, and a snowy heron stood solo on the dock, white tendrils of feathers blowing in the wind off the water.

"Speaking of Paris, what's up with your plan to run away and live in a Left Bank garret?"

"As of now, the idea appears to be on semipermanent hold. The dream is not dead, however."

"Ah. And this dream depends on what, exactly?"

I sighed. "I don't think I could leave Caleb. And there's Dog to consider."

"Your dad loves dogs."

"Yeah, but I feel bad. I sort of foisted Dog on the household. Also there's the business, of course. And Dad."

"Your dad's fine, Mel. He's almost back to his old self."

"I don't know. He's not as young as he used to be. And if anything were to happen to him, what would Stan do?"

"Mel." Graham put his hand on my arm, stopping me. He smiled down at me with an almost tender expression on his face. "Let's go over that misanthrope thing again. Tell me how much you dislike people and want to jettison all your baggage."

"I—" I cut myself off as a man in a wheelchair rolled over to us.

"Hey there, Princess."

"Stan? Hey, we were just talking about you." I leaned over to give him a hug. "What are you doing here?"

He looked a bit sheepish, and his eyes flickered toward the docks. I followed his gaze to see my father down on the floating pier, talking to a man on a yacht.

Chapter Twenty-two

"Bill and I thought we'd come have a chat with Tom Avery," said Stan. "See what he could tell us about his nephew."

"Oh, that's . . ." Sweet, was what it was. But it was also aggravating. First Stephen and Luz decide to investigate, with my stepson no less. And now this? "That's not Tom he's talking to now, is it?"

It had been a few years, but the Tom Avery I knew had been short and stout, while this fellow was tall and thin. And from what I could tell at this distance, he had a full head of blond hair. Either retirement had been remarkably good to old Tom, or this wasn't our guy.

"Nah. His boat's gone."

A young woman in Bermuda shorts carrying a big laundry basket set her load down to open the locked gate. Graham hurried forward to give her a hand, then held the metal gate open for me.

After depositing the woman's basket on her sailboat named *Lettie*, Graham joined me and we headed down toward my dad. The dock floated and wobbled with each step, making me feel off-kilter. Daniel and I once went on a bay dinner cruise, drank too much champagne, and danced until the wee hours, oohing and aahing over the lights of the city as seen from the water. It was a nice memory. Generally speaking, though, I prefer land.

"Hey there, babe, what a surprise," said Dad as he noticed us walking toward him. He beamed, no doubt because Graham was by my side. Dad excused himself from the man he had been speaking with, who ducked back into his boat. "Graham, good to see you."

The two men shook hands.

"What brings you two down here?" Dad asked.

"Same thing that brought you, I think. We were looking for Tom Avery. His boat's gone?"

He nodded. "Looks like he took off."

"Any idea where to?"

"That's what I was trying to get from his dock mates, but he didn't say anything to anyone. Just disappeared one day."

"And why are you asking around?"

"Old times' sake. You were wondering about his nephew, so Stan and I thought we'd come on down and take the man out for a beer, see what we could find out."

"Let's try the harbormaster's office," said Graham. "Maybe they've got more information on him."

The man behind the desk was in his sixties, bald on top but with longish white hair on the sides of his head. He smoked a pipe with flagrant disregard for the NO

SMOKING signs, and wore a baby blue polo shirt with the logo of Jack London Public Marina on it.

"What can I do you for?"

"We wondered if you could give us any information on Thomas Avery, who's usually in slip number thirty—"

"—seven," the harbormaster finished my sentence.

"Right, thirty-seven."

"Hadn't moved that boat in, I dunno, years. Then the bastard slipped out the other night, still owes me three months in back moorage fees."

"Slipped out? Any idea where?"

"Don't know and don't care. All's I want is my moorage fees. People fight over these spaces, you know. There's a waiting list. Not like I'm gonna wait around for some old man doesn't pay his fees. And he was living on that boat, too. That's extra if you're gonna be using the facilities while living here."

"Don't boat operators have to file a sailing plan, or something?" I asked.

"You're thinking of pilots of small planes, probably. Nope, there's nothing like that required. 'Course it's a good idea—in case you get caught in a storm, we can notify the Coast Guard. But one reason why we like sailing," he said with a significant glance, "is to get away from people asking too damn many questions."

"But—," I began.

"Thanks for your help," said Graham, and I felt a subtle but insistent hand on my shoulder.

I noticed the man picked up the phone as soon as we closed the door behind us.

"You suppose he's calling someone about us?" I asked.

"Could be that, or a whole lot of other things," said Graham. "But yes, could be he's letting someone know we're asking questions."

"Or he's just going about his business," said my dad as we joined him and Stan. "And he's right, no reason he should tell us anything about old Tom, whether he knows it or not. We're strangers to him."

"How about a beer at Heinold's while we think this through?" Stan suggested.

"Great idea," said Graham. "I do love being self-employed."

I returned a couple of work-related calls as we walked toward the bar. Then I checked in with my foreman on each job, just to be sure. The foreman at Matt's house asked me to stop by this afternoon and check supplies with him, but otherwise everything was running smoothly, so I felt justified—though still guilty—about sitting around having a beer in the middle of the day.

Only two buildings had been exempted from the Jack London Square makeover: the eponymous author's purported Alaskan shack, and Heinold's First and Last Chance Saloon.

Jack London's shack was a one-room log cabin with a sod roof. Apparently a group of devoted fans found the shack he once lived in up in Alaska, dismantled it, brought it back to the Port of Oakland by ship, then reconstructed it here to honor the author who was born and raised in Oakland.

Sometimes it felt to me as though we Oaklanders were reaching. Still, it was an incongruous little sight at the side of the parking lot, and its oddity always brought a smile to my face. Visitors threw pennies in through the barred windows as though it were a fountain to be wished upon.

The shack sat right next to Heinold's First and Last Chance Saloon, which opened in 1883 and was said to be the oldest bar in Oakland.

"This place would never pass inspection," Graham said, quite unnecessarily. "Not exactly up to ADA standards."

The saloon was rumored to have been constructed from the timbers off a whaling ship. According to legend, the clock on the wall stopped during the 1906 earthquake, and the floor tilted to its current steep angle at the same time. Supposedly Jack London studied as a boy at the same tables that sit in the bar today, and he wrote part of *Call of the Wild* while imbibing at First and Last Chance.

In his wheelchair Stan would have careened to the low side of the tilty bar, so we decided to take our seats at an outdoor table. It was January, but the sun blazed and there was only a slight breeze off the placid estuary.

I gave everyone my version of the mystery as it stood.

"I suppose it would be jumping to conclusions to suggest that Josh Avery—or whoever he really is—knocked off his alleged uncle at sea in order to cover up some deep dark secret?"

"Hold on just a second, there, Mel," said Dad. "Some disgruntled worker you caught breaking into a house—a house you yourself had broken into, but I'll let that slide for now—tells you Josh was skimpy about overtime, and from this you decide he killed Tom Avery?"

I shrugged. "If the man was capable of throwing a woman down a well, there's no telling what else he might be capable of. Maybe Tom found out about what happened to Mrs. Bernini and Josh had to . . . keep him quiet."

All three men sipped their beers and remained silent.

"Okay, okay. It's a wild accusation. I'm just brainstorming—work with me. Maybe it was as simple as Josh wanting the job. He seems pretty in cahoots with Kim Propak, but I think Mrs. Bernini liked me better."

"If you're right," said Stan, "and this Josh guy killed a little old lady to get a job, then took his favorite uncle out for an ocean cruise with no return, what makes you think he's going to skip you?"

That was an excellent question.

"Sounds to me like it's time to call the cops," said Dad.

"I talked to Inspector Crawford just yesterday. But I don't have anything real to go on, do I? Graham and I are going to go talk to one more man who works for Avery, see what he has to say. If we come up with anything, I'll call the inspector and tell her what I've found out, see if it fits in with her investigation at all."

"What about the spirits in the house?" Stan asked. "Can they tell you anything?"

My father harrumphed and excused himself to use the men's room.

"Not so far. Strange, isn't it? You'd think the dead would be able to spy on folks, that sort of thing, but in my limited experience they don't seem to know much of anything. It's very frustrating."

"So in a scant few months, you've gone from thinking you're going crazy, to excitement, to feeling frustrated by your ability to see ghosts. I never thought ghost hunting would seem so banal," Graham said.

"Right?" I returned his smile. Our gaze held. I started to feel tingly; my heart sped up. I lost track of time. My lips parted, but no words came out.

"So," Dad said as he came back to the table, breaking the mood. "What's all this garbage Graham tells me about you house-sitting at the Bernini place? I thought a woman was killed there a few days ago."

"The crime scene was out in the garden," I said, glad to have my focus pulled away from Graham, however momentarily. "So the police already did whatever evidence collection they needed to, and they've released the house."

"Okay, but that still doesn't explain why you're going to be there."

"The Propaks are going out of town for a few days, and with all the media attention and all . . . well, it's a busy neighborhood. They're afraid to leave the place uninhabited."

Graham and I gazed at each other again. This was ridiculous. I might as well be sixteen again, with a crush.

"And Graham's going with you?"

"I —" I was about to say no, but our eyes caught again and I couldn't help it — I smiled.

"In that case," my dad said. "You two need protection."

Good Lord. Were we that obvious? My cheeks flamed.

"Geesh, Dad, we haven't even gotten around to . . . that, yet. And we're adults, we've got it covered."

All eyes were now on me. My father grimaced. Stan chuckled. Graham grinned.

"I wasn't talking about *that*," Dad grumbled. "As you know, I wouldn't mind another grandchild, but since no one listens to me anyway, I'll leave that up to you."

He got up from the table and strode to his car in the adjoining parking lot. He grabbed a leather bag from the trunk, came back, and deposited it on the table.

"That's a present for you two."

I opened it and peered in. A handgun. And two boxes of cartridges. "Gee . . . thanks."

"You need protection, as in a *gun*."

"Thanks for the offer, Bill," said Graham, "but I'm not a big fan of armed combat."

"I'll take it," I said, slipping the gun and ammunition into my oversized bag and handing him back the leather case. "Thanks."

Graham and Stan exchanged looks, raising their eyebrows.

"What?" I demanded.

"You can't just walk around with a concealed weapon," said Graham. "In fact, this is California. I don't think you can have a gun in your possession at all without a license."

"I'll pick up an application next time I'm at city hall."

My father wasn't what you'd call in favor of gun control. I was, at least theoretically. But frankly, the idea of staying another night at the Bernini house, though I had finagled it, was enough to make me glad of a little firepower.

Maybe I was my father's daughter after all—I already felt better with the cold weight of the weapon in my bag.

Chapter Twenty-three

Chewy Garay lived in a squalid apartment building that looked like it had once been an old motel. A pack of kids were playing soccer in the parking lot that served as a courtyard.

"Number seventeen," I said, leading the way toward the second-level catwalk.

The soccer ball flew toward our heads. I ducked, but Graham leaned into it and bumped it off his forehead toward the boys. The children laughed and yelled in response, and Graham said something impressive in Spanish.

"You speak Spanish?"

"Enough to get by. You know how it is, working in the trades."

Wow. Now I *really* felt like a schlub. I needed to get back to those lessons. Add that to my growing list of late New Year's resolutions.

"And you play soccer?"

He nodded. "Saturday mornings in Golden Gate Park. Nothing fancy—just a bunch of us getting together. I only started a couple of years ago and a lot of the guys are from Latin America, so I look pretty pathetic in comparison. But we have a good time, and it's a nice excuse to go out for a beer afterward."

The man made time to learn languages and play sports and hang out drinking beer with friends. He'd even had a girlfriend before I inadvertently broke them up. Whereas I . . . what? Worked. That was pretty much it.

I have got *to get myself a life.*

I knocked on the door of apartment seventeen. No response. I cupped my hands and tried to peek through a small opening in the curtains, whose inner lining was torn and sun damaged, lying in long peels along the sill.

Graham peeked in over my shoulder. "Doesn't look like anybody's home."

"He got taken in. *La migra*," said a young woman walking by with two children, one on her hip and the other holding her hand. She looked like a teenager, wearing skintight low-riding jeans and a bright red sweater over a baby-doll T-shirt.

"Taken in? When was this?"

"Just this morning."

"Were they doing a sweep of the neighborhood?"

"All I saw was that they took him. His wife went down to look for him, but they don't have to tell you anything. My sister got picked up once after work, but all we knew was she didn't show up for her kids at school. We thought something happened to her. . . . She finally called us after she got sent back to Mexico."

The little girl in her arms reached up and pulled her

hair. She shrugged and pulled away. "Now we know if someone disappears, we can go down to immigration and ask about which jail ICE keeps people in, and if you file papers and ask for a name, they'll tell you if they have 'em."

Were we supposed to consider that progress?

Graham played soccer with the kids for a few minutes; then we headed back to San Francisco.

Employing illegal aliens was a big issue in the world of construction. Most of the people I knew who flooded to California from Mexico and Central America, and beyond, were hardworking, otherwise law-abiding folks just trying to make a living for their families. Some were fleeing truly desperate economic and political circumstances. But it was true that we didn't have open borders where anybody who wanted could come in, and the trade in illegal border crossings had bred a dangerous but powerful smuggling business.

But when it came right down to it, I needed skilled, hardworking employees and a lot of Latino immigrants, especially the ones from small towns, had impressive carpentry skills and mechanical savvy. And, as a group, their loyalty and willingness to work couldn't be beat.

Clearly, I was a little muddled on the subject. From time to time issues of legality had come up for us at Turner Construction, and there were a few cases when I had filed papers and gone to court to try to help friends and employees gain their green cards or resident alien papers. But by and large, I tried to avoid the issue by hiring only verifiably legal workers.

"Let me guess," said Graham. "You're thinking maybe someone called in *la migra* before Chewy Garay could tell you whatever he knows about Josh?"

"It's possible. I've known employers who call just because they owe their workers wages, and they have them deported before payday."

"It would be pretty far-fetched to imagine Josh called ICE on his own guys. Regulations are pretty tight these days. Any employer who doesn't check documents is in for fines and reprimands, if not more serious consequences. It wouldn't be worth it."

"Unless he had something very serious to hide. Oh, and what about this? Dad says Tom Avery had two sisters. So how does Josh have the Avery last name?"

"I know you're not wild about this guy," Graham began in that oh-so-rational tone I was already familiar with, "but just to play devil's advocate for a moment: Not long ago, you thought a perfectly nice man was a murderer because he married a foreign woman he met online."

"I just found it odd. I *still* find it odd that a heterosexual man can't find a woman in this city. I mean there are, what, four or five eligible women for each guy?"

"*I'm* not married. And last I checked, I wasn't a murderer, either."

"That's different. Neither am I. You and I are both battle-scarred and bitter from our failed marriages. There's a reason we're afraid of commitment."

Silence.

I finally turned back to find him watching me, once again.

"What?"

"Speak for yourself. *I'm* not afraid of commitment. Nor am I particularly battle-scarred."

"Um . . . I should probably get back to work."

Graham chuckled and shook his head. "Whatever you say. Let's stop by the taco truck on the way. I believe I owe you lunch."

Graham was at his charming best as we sat on a low cement wall in the Goodwill parking lot, eating our *carnitas* and *carne asada*. I began to wonder whether his goal was to make me laugh so much I would forget about my plan to occupy the Bernini house, much less to move to Paris.

The tacos were delicious as always. I doctored mine up with cilantro and serrano peppers and salsa so hot my lips and tongue felt a pleasant burn, even as we pulled up beside my car half an hour later.

"So what time are we moving in?" Graham asked as I reached for the door handle.

"Moving in?"

"To the Bernini house."

"You can't just assume you're coming with me, Graham. We don't have that kind of relationship."

"So you're planning on staying in that haunted house alone? With a murderer on the loose? A murderer who might believe you know something, and that you're a threat?"

"Well, Stephen has offered to stay with me."

"Stephen. This guy's really beginning to get on my nerves."

"I thought you liked him."

"I *do* like him. But I don't like him spending nights with you . . . especially if I don't get to."

"Oh, and Zach will be there."

He pinched the bridge of his nose as though he had a sudden headache. "Please tell me you're kidding. What is your obsession with that . . . *boy*?"

"He's not a boy." Although I called him that, myself. "And I'm certainly not 'obsessed' with him. If I were, I would have accepted his multiple offers to take me out."

"Are you trying to make me jealous?"

"No, but I sort of love that you are." I smiled and shrugged. "Zach's my excuse. He's the official house sitter; I'm just the hanger-on. Kim Propak wasn't all that wild about me being back in the house. . . . Do you suppose they want to keep me from learning the truth from the ghosts?"

"Or maybe they're just putting things on hold for a while because there was a murder there. Do the Propaks even own the home? I thought you said the inheritance was in dispute, which might mean that the purchase agreement is voided, right?"

"Maybe so. Which is actually a good point: It's not the Propaks' place, so they don't really get to say who can be there and who can't."

"It may not be *their* place, but it's certainly not yours."

"Are you always this argumentative?"

"Only when provoked."

"I'm just saying, it does not bode well. I have it on good authority that I'm rather provocative."

His eyes fell to the low-cut line of my shirt. "Mm-hmm."

"Be serious."

He smiled. "This is all very new to me, Mel. If I hadn't experienced what I had with you in that attic a while ago, I probably wouldn't buy any of it. But as it is . . . you do seem to have an extraordinary ability to be where this sort of thing is going on."

"The Propaks called me because they wanted a haunted B&B, so I knew I was walking into a possibly haunted scenario. It's just . . . I don't know. All I'm planning to do is stay in that house for a night or two. Just long enough to talk with a couple ghosts and figure this whole thing out. I'm now armed, and there will be at least a couple of manly—well, manly-*ish*—men there with me. And as for whether you get to stay there or not . . . I haven't decided. It might depend on whether you keep annoying me."

He had the audacity to grin. "Of course I get to stay there. You need me."

"Oh? How so? We're not in the market for a windmill or solar panels or whatever other new green technology you might have up your sleeve."

"I seem to remember that you and I once developed a special ghost-busting technique. One that involved mouth-to-mouth contact in order to arouse the supernatural energies—"

"*Stop.*" I punched him in the ribs. Not hard, but he let out a satisfying little *oof*.

Then he pulled me to him, and his mouth came down on mine.

Yes, it had been a while for me, but that wasn't the whole explanation for the magic I felt in his kiss. It was a hot, searing connection. Sensation zinged through me, all the way down to my toes and into secret corners of my soul. I lost track of anything but the feeling of his wonderful mouth, his strong body. The feelings were so intense that after a few soul-tilting moments, I pulled back with a jerk. Graham kept his strong arms wrapped around me, so I didn't get far.

"Okay," I said, wincing a little at the breathless quality of my voice.

"Okay what?" he asked. I was gratified to note that his voice wasn't all that steady, either.

"You can stay over."

A grin spread across his face and he kissed the tip of my nose. "One kiss and I get what I want? Maybe I really *do* have secret supernatural powers."

"Very funny."

"What changed your mind?"

"I decided that the more people overnight in the house, the better."

"Meet you there this evening?"

I nodded. "I should be there by seven."

He gave me one more long, lingering kiss; then I climbed out and watched as his truck disappeared.

After taking my friend and client Matt tile shopping—for the fourth time—I returned to his house and met with his architect, who had drawn up plans to lift the roof, presuming Matt could manage to get the neighbors to approve his plan. He asked me to put together a detailed bid based on the new blueprints, so I took the heavy roll with me to analyze in more depth at home. Finally, I went over the supplies order with the foreman.

Then I returned to the Castro, to check out the house where Owen Campbell once lived. I wasn't sure what I expected to find there, but it seemed worth a look.

Notwithstanding recent murder and mayhem, this was a pleasant, relaxed neighborhood. An elderly couple passed me on the sidewalk and nodded their hellos. A woman in the Victorian next door was working in her postage stamp of a yard planting bright red begonias. Two men sat on the porch of the house across the street holding steaming mugs and talking.

The old Campbell house was perched upon a hill, but it had not been built on a grand scale. In fact, it could have been the servants' quarters to the Bernini house, the kind of place that was built for practicality rather than to establish social status. It was one story, and though not small, its wraparound porches and low overhanging roof made it seem more suited to the colonial steamy tropics than frequently foggy San Francisco.

Adding to the tropical feeling of the place were the plantings: several different types of palms, ferns with fronds that reached at least ten feet, and two mature, thick-leaved banana trees flanking the broad wooden stairs that led to the front porch.

I paused out on the sidewalk, half hoping to see Owen Campbell's ghost relaxing on the old porch swing, or meandering through the overgrown garden paths. I couldn't help thinking it would simplify matters if I could just get some straight answers from a representative from the spirit world. At this point I wasn't picky about which one.

The house's wood trim had once been painted a blue green, but it was so faded and peeling it looked as though a faux finisher had been at work. As I crossed the porch to the front door, I saw four mailboxes, four doorbells. The house had been split into apartments. That helped explain the condition of the place. An absentee landlord, or family ownership where no one took full responsibility—

those were the sorts of things that explained such obvious neglect.

Something rustled in the garden, and a verdant stand of thick undergrowth started to shake.

Then a booming voice rang out: *"Who's there?"*

Mountain emerged, looking as he had when I first met him: big hands in leather gloves, pruning shears stuck in the pocket of his overalls. He did not seem all that pleased to see me.

"It's Mel Turner," I said. I was wary of him, but with all the neighbors around I felt safe. "We met the other day at Mrs. Bernini's. Do you remember?"

He pulled up short.

"Oh, yeah . . ." Recognition dawned on his florid face. "You surprised me, is all. I wasn't expecting anyone. When I get digging and weeding and pruning and planting . . . I lose myself in this stuff."

"Oh, sure, I understand. I love to garden."

That was a half-truth. I love the *idea* of gardening, and I appreciate the heck out of beautiful gardens. How much digging I actually did, though . . . ? My father would have a thing or two to say about that. Currently I was trying to convince our Oakland neighbors that our yard was an experiment in growing "California native grasses."

I wasn't fooling anyone.

"So . . ." He inspected the underside of a leaf and picked something off. "How're you doing?"

"I'm . . . okay. So very sorry about what happened to Mrs. Bernini."

He pinched his nose and sniffed loudly. There were tears in his blue eyes. "Can you believe it? I really can't . . . I mean, who would do such a thing? I know we live in a city, and things happen . . . but this neighborhood feels so much like a home, you know what I mean? We all know each other. Everyone knew Mrs. Bernini. Everyone loved her."

"I understand you were working on the gardens for her?" I hesitated, then added, "For free?"

"I was bringing them back from the brink, I like to say. I've got a green thumb. I'm actually a Web site designer by day, but it's always been my dream to work with plants full-time."

"And . . ." Again, I hesitated. How could I ask him about the will—or multiple wills? "Did you do it out of the goodness of your heart, or was Mrs. Bernini compensating you for all that work?"

"She told me it would all be mine one day. It seemed like such a far-off thing when we talked about it. I mean, the last thing I wanted was for her to . . . to pass on. I don't care about the house, but the gardens . . . they're a different story."

"It's quite a big lot, but— "

"The house needs too much work. Personally, I think it should just be razed." He reached into a thick patch of ginger plants and pulled out the smallest by their roots. "What this neighborhood really needs is a park. Imagine how beautiful it would be. I could expand Campbell's plans—I have some of his original drawings—and bring his dream to fruition. Set up waterworks, fountains, in addition to the gardens. The way it was supposed to be."

"It's a historic building, Mountain," I said as soon as I found my voice. The mere *idea* of razing such a beautiful place took my breath away. "It needs work, yes, but it's not that far gone."

He shrugged and snapped off a few sprigs protruding from a young palm.

"It sounds as though there are other claims on the house ... ?"

"You mean *Portia Kirkbride*?" He said her name in a nasty, singsong tone of voice. "With her whole antiques shtick ..."

He met my eyes, and seemed to catch himself.

"It might be a moot point anyway. ... I don't have a copy of the will." He shook his head and moved toward a potting bench at the side of the house. I followed. "Mrs. Bernini promised me things, but it seems like she never wrote it down. I've been looking. ... I asked the Propaks if I could search the house for it, but they refused." He started inspecting a row of potted orchids sitting on a rustic bench. "I've known Mrs. Bernini for many years. It's possible she ... I dunno. Maybe she promised something to the wrong person."

I couldn't get a handle on this guy. He seemed like a really nice fellow, until he didn't. And since I was looking for someone coldhearted enough to throw an old woman down a well, I couldn't be too careful. I glanced across the street to see that the two men on the porch had been joined by a third. Surely I was safe with all these people around. And having Mountain expound upon his favorite subject was as good a way as any to get a better feel for him.

Not that I'd shown any particular talent for sniffing out murderers. But it was worth a shot.

"This garden is so lovely. I'm surprised, though, that San Francisco is warm enough for a tropical garden."

"Not for everything, that's for sure," Mountain said as

he removed an orchid from a pot it had overgrown, its thick roots protruding, reaching out for new territory. "They do love the heat and humidity, of course. But Campbell had a hothouse for the more delicate flowers, which he coaxed indoors and brought out on sunny days. And the rest of them . . . they might not love it here, but they survive. We don't have much frost to speak of, and since the ground never freezes, their roots are protected."

"It's really beautiful. I wonder why Campbell settled here if he missed the tropics so much."

"He was here for business reasons, I guess. Not sure. And anyway, he built this place for his wife, Tallulah. He brought her here from the West Indies."

"And he wanted her to feel at home?"

He nodded, finding a larger pot for the orchid in his hands and filling it, not with potting soil, but with a mix of bark and mulch. "I don't think it was easy for her. . . . San Francisco was always more progressive than many parts of this country, but she was . . . well, he called her 'Hispanic' so they could marry. But . . . I saw a painting of her. . . . I'm not sure how well she fit in around here, even with the Barbary Coast folks."

"They could only marry if she was Hispanic?"

He nodded. "Hispanic, or white, of course. Antimiscegenation laws weren't overturned until 1948."

"Seriously? In California? I don't know why I'm so surprised. . . . We just always seem more progressive than that."

"The state was so large and wild that there wasn't a lot of law to go around, so laws weren't always enforced. Maybe that's what gave the state a reputation for being liberal." Mountain set the orchid in its new pot down on a tree stump, and lifted another one onto the potting bench. "But the laws here were just as racist as anywhere else. Over time the state was filled with so many immigrants, and attitudes changed, so it didn't really count anymore."

"You seem to know a lot about Owen Campbell."

"I did some research when I first moved into this house. And then I found Campbell's journal in the basement."

"Did you happen upon any information on his relations to the family in the Bernini house?"

"Oh sure, they were the only two real houses out here back then: Campbell's and the Bowles Folly. And as neighbors they . . . didn't really get along."

"Any idea why?"

"There was an issue over water rights. They'd both sunken wells, but Campbell was upstream. He set up a pipeline and started selling clean water to the city. There was a huge demand."

Mountain yanked another orchid out of its pot, bark flying. For someone who loved plants, there was something apparently brutal about it. But then, I had observed that a lot of plants appear to be masochists—roses, for instance. The more you cut them, the more they bloomed.

"Do you know anything about Bowles's maternity hospital? Campbell wouldn't have cut off water to the clinic, would he?"

"Seems like it got pretty nasty. From what I've read, Campbell thought Franklin Bowles was unreasonable, and suggested he was mistreating his patients. And at one point he wrote that the little girl who lived there was a real 'witch.' Tallulah had a difficult pregnancy, but according to Campbell, Bowles wouldn't help her." He shrugged. "Bowles was doctor to the city's finest citizens. Maybe that didn't include a nonwhite woman from the islands."

"I heard someone refer to him as 'Evil Campbell.' They suggested he was responsible for the deaths of the Bowles family."

"Yeah, I know people say that. But frankly, I think Campbell got a bad rap. From what he wrote in his diary, he seemed like an ambitious man, though he became distraught over the death of his wife. But to suggest he'd turn around a few months later and kill an entire family, with kids? From what I can tell, there was never any evidence. So it was all just conjecture."

"And . . ." I tried to think how to phrase this. "Did he write anything about using magic of some sort? Voodoo?"

Mountain stared at me for a long moment, then shook his big head. "I see you really *have* been listening to neighborhood gossip. Campbell never mentions anything having to do with any of that."

"Do you think I could take a look at the journal?"

"No. It's very fragile."

"I would be caref—"

"No."

I took a step back.

"Sorry." He wiped his eyes with the back of his sleeve. "I . . . was thinking I might take it to get preserved."

"I know a librarian down at the California Historical Society. She would know how to preserve it."

"I'll think about it. I'm sorry, but I really want to get back to my gardening. I still have a day job, so the daylight hours I'm home are precious."

"Just one more thing: about the painting you mentioned? The one of Tallulah? I think I saw it in Portia's antiques shop, right?"

He nodded. "They refuse to sell it to me. Or any of the other things Portia's been milking from the Bernini place. Portia has this thing about only selling stuff to a proper home, or some nonsense like that. All I know is, for months now, that truck pulls up and hauls things off—I doubt they ever paid her what anything was worth. They're like vultures."

"Tallulah's portrait used to be in the house?"

"I guess Mrs. Bernini found it when she was cleaning out the attic. I didn't see it until Portia had already taken it, unfortunately."

"If the Bowleses despised her for her heritage, why would they have kept a portrait of her?"

"Beats me. I've always wondered that, myself."

Chapter Twenty-four

When I walked into Kirkbride's Antiques, Portia was speaking to a young couple about an Empire-style dining room table. Though she noticed me, she didn't pause in her discussion, so I meandered around the shop, paying special attention to those pieces Edgar had told me had come from Mrs. Bernini's house.

The polished walnut sideboard had a price tag that declared it was "on sale" for almost twenty thousand dollars.

Was that enough to kill over? Maybe not one single piece, but once several such antiques were tallied up?

I started sliding open the drawers. Mrs. Bernini wasn't the most organized person in the world—what if she stashed an updated will in a drawer somewhere, and then Portia brought the piece of furniture here and discovered it? Of course, if Portia had found it, she would have told the police—or if she was, indeed, after the house, she would have hidden or destroyed it already. In any case, the drawers contained nothing but the slight scent of wood and shellac, common to old furniture. Then I spied the leather-bound chest that looked like the one I had seen in the playroom. It sported a tag that said NOT FOR SALE.

"Could I help you with something? Are you looking for a sideboard? That one's quite expensive."

"I was just looking at the trunk—didn't I see one just like this in the playroom at Mrs. Bernini's house?"

She nodded. "It's not for sale, though. Our assistant took the wrong chest—he was supposed to get the one from the master, but he retrieved that one instead. It's still full of toys."

"Wasn't that radio part of the Bernini estate, as well? Is it for sale?"

"It's *very* expensive."

Usually I'm not insulted that hoity-toity shop owners don't think I can afford their boutique prices. The fact is, whether I could swing the money or not, they were right to doubt me. But Portia was ticking me off.

"May I ask how much?"

She looked worried. "It's a very special radio."

If Mountain was correct when he said Portia's credo was to sell only to "proper homes," I was betting I didn't meet the criteria.

"Can I ask . . . does it play of its own accord?"

"What?" She gave a disbelieving laugh. "No, of course not. It's an old crystal radio, handmade. It's very valuable. It's simply not for sale."

"I was just thinking that if the Propaks restore the Bernini house, it would be wonderful to bring back some of the original items." Portia gazed at me, unblinking. Right about now I would trade some of my ghost-talking skills for a little interpersonal psychic sensitivity: I wished

I could get a handle on this woman. "How did it work, you selling off Mrs. Bernini's pieces? Did you pay her a percentage for each piece?"

"I brought them here on consignment, sold them, and we split the proceeds. Just like I do the property of any estate."

"But now that Mrs. Bernini has passed, where does the money go?"

"The estate."

"And the estate is . . , who, actually?"

Portia's stiff face managed to look very displeased. She tucked a sleek lock of hair behind her ear and pressed her lips together

"Mrs. Bernini left her home and all its belongings to me, with the specific wish that I use a portion of the proceeds for a few of her favorite causes: the foster program that she used to work with, and to provide Mountain with a living in exchange for his continued work with the gardens. Unless he can produce an actual will, I don't think there is any further question about it."

"The Propaks still insist they have a legitimate purchase agreement."

Portia shrugged and produced a bottle of Old English scratch cover and started rubbing the already gleaming doors of a tall armoire. Her strokes were vigorous and steady. This would be the perfect occupation, I thought, for someone who felt the need to clean whenever anxious or angry. Me, I just stormed around and used power tools. Or stuck my nose into other people's business.

"I guess . . . I don't know. If they had a legitimate purchase agreement with Mrs. Bernini, letting them turn the place into a B&B might be the best solution. It would be good for the neighborhood. . . ." She shook her head. "I can't *believe* she did this to us. Why would she have made so many commitments she had no intention of keeping?"

It was an excellent question, for which I had no answer. I kept thinking about the players involved as self-interested, even grasping, but it would be devastating to find that someone who had promised you so much had been lying or, at best, unclear with her intentions.

"I heard from Mrs. Bernini's foster son the other day—Homer? And now even Raj seems to think he's entitled to something," she muttered as she finished with the doors and knelt to polish the base trim of the furniture.

"Raj? He thinks he's inheriting the house?"

"Not the whole place, but he said Mrs. Bernini promised to help him with his mother's medical bills. He's . . . I don't know. He's sort of obsessed with that house. About a year ago he was arrested for breaking in there, but Mrs. Bernini refused to press charges and got him that job at the pizzeria instead. She was the queen of lost causes."

I remembered something: When Raj delivered our pizza on Saturday night, he mentioned we should check the basement for water, as though he was familiar with the place.

"I understand Raj works for you, as well?"

"He does some odd jobs for us."

She didn't elaborate, and I thought it best not to push the subject. Especially since I had one more request to make of her.

"I know this might seem out of line, but could I see your copy of the will?"

She slammed down the bottle of polish and the stained rag.

"*Why?* Why do you keep coming around here, asking all these questions?"

This was an entirely legitimate query for which I had no good answer.

"Mrs. Bernini asked me to communicate with the ghosts in the house. I was there the night she was killed. I guess I just feel sort of . . . responsible. I'd like to help sort things out, if possible."

Portia gazed at me for a long moment, then took in a deep breath and blew it out, as though willing her body to relax. Finally, she used a small key to unlock a filing cabinet, reached into the top drawer, and brought out a manila folder. From this she extracted a photocopy of a handwritten note detailing Mrs. Bernini's last wishes, exactly as Portia had recounted them. And at the bottom of the paper were the names and signatures of two witnesses: J. D. Casey and Raj Deepak Singh.

Raj's signature was beautiful and flowing. His script reminded me of a scroll. I had seen such handwriting before.

Upon exiting Portia's store I saw the friendly red, white, and green storefront of Sylven's pizzeria. After my frustrating interaction with her, I could use a more approachable source of neighborhood information.

"Can I ask you something? Do you know Portia well?" I asked J.D. after he welcomed me, once again, with open arms.

He tsked and shook his head. "Something that thin doesn't eat pizza, girlfriend, I can tell you that much. Edgar has to sneak over when he wants a slice, because she tells him to watch his cholesterol."

"But you signed as a witness on her will?"

"Oh sure. That was back when Mrs. Bernini used to come by on her walks, and they asked me to sign. Why?"

"I was just wondering about Portia's connection to Mrs. Bernini."

"Just that she was helping her to 'catalog' her antiques, which seemed a lot more like Portia moving stuff out of the house if you ask me. Every few days you see Edgar's big old HVAC truck out there, unloading stuff into the shop."

"Edgar's truck? He's an HVAC technician?"

"Yup. He's a nice fellow — Raj used to work with him, as his assistant. Edgar was training Raj, taking him around to his accounts. Now Raj keeps our clunky old pizza ovens running smoothly, doesn't he, George?"

"Real smoothly," said George gamely, methodically working a big ball of pizza dough.

"That first night when I came in to use the phone, the night that Mrs. Bernini died, you mentioned there had been a fight here in the store. 'Fisticuffs,' you called it."

J.D. smiled and ducked his head slightly. "Ooh, George teases me about using that word. I just hated to call it a 'fight,' because that sounds so serious, and it was more . . . a scuffle, really."

"Who was involved?"

"It was Edgar, as a matter of fact."

"Edgar, and who else?"

"Mountain. Who, even though he's got size on his side, doesn't know much about fighting, does he, George?"

George said, "Not really, no."

"Neither do I, though," J.D. said with a little laugh. "I just flapped around ineffectually — it was Raj who stepped in to break it up. I don't know what we would do without that boy."

"Portia mentioned that Mrs. Bernini got him this job? That he broke into her house?"

J.D. gave a reluctant little nod. "I believe in second chances. He was a screwed-up kid, but he became a good worker. Mrs. Bernini did like to take on young people. They were her projects."

"Where is Raj now, do you know? I'd like to speak with him."

"You know, it's the strangest thing. He's usually quite reliable, but lately you can never pin him down." He glanced at the big clock on the wall, in the shape of Italy. "He was due in for work nearly an hour ago, and he didn't even call to say he'd be late."

I called Inspector Crawford and was surprised when she answered on the first ring. It was cowardly of me, but I had rather hoped to be bumped to voice mail.

"You're suggesting Raj was the one who wrote the threatening note?" Crawford demanded after I told her what I had seen in Portia's shop.

"Um . . ." *For the love of all that is holy, Mel, get a grip.* It was clear Crawford considered me a rather dubious informant, and something about her attitude of utter certainty made me wonder if she might be right. Who was I to cast aspersions on Raj? After all, I was no expert in the field of handwri—

"Are you trained in handwriting analysis?" asked Crawford, finishing my thought.

I took a deep breath and pushed my case. "Portia also mentioned that Raj knows the Bernini House and once broke into the place. Far be it from me to suggest how

you do your job," I added quickly, "but I thought you
might want to know. That's all."

"Yep, okay, we'll bring him in for a chat. Thanks. Anything else?"

"Nope, that's about it." I briefly considered mentioning the "fisticuffs" in the pizza shop, but Crawford already
knew about the tension between the Kirkbrides and
Mountain over who was inheriting what. Besides, I was
already wrung out by my brief exchange with the inspector. I wondered whether Ghost Busting 101 included any
helpful information on how *not* to act like a suspicious
nervous wreck around hard-nosed police officers.

After hanging up, I headed over to the Bernini house
and pulled into the drive. A tall, pale man stood on the
front stoop, knocking on the door.

Homer.

"I'm really glad to see you," he said after I parked
and joined him at the door. "In fact, after the other day
I realized I didn't have any way of getting in touch with
you, and I just wanted to let you know, to let the whole
neighborhood know, that we wanted to schedule a memorial service for Mrs. Bernini on Saturday."

He handed me a flyer with the information, and a
sweet picture of Mrs. Bernini, smiling her warm smile.

"That's a wonderful idea," I said. "If you give me a
handful, I'll take them to the pizzeria. She has a lot of
friends there."

"I don't even know how to get in touch with the people
who want to redo this place—the Propaks?" said Homer.
"I've really been out of touch. I thought ... I don't know
what I thought. I guess I figured we would have more
time. I should have spent more time with her."

"I think we all feel that way when someone passes." I certainly did when I lost my mother. Death was so final. For most. "The Propaks are out of town for a few days, so I'm house-sitting for them. I can give you their number if you'd like," I said, finding it on my phone and writing it down for him.

"Oh, yes, please. I was hoping we could have the memorial service here in the house, if the Propaks don't mind."

"I can't imagine they'd mind. . . . In fact, the Propaks aren't exactly the owners of this house, at this point."

"Yes, I know. Mountain told me the inheritance is still being contested. I tried to talk with Portia Kirkbride about it, but hit a dead end." Homer stepped back a little and looked up at the facade of the gracious old house. "This place . . . the ghosts, or whatever they were, scared me when I lived here. But everything else was great—Mr. and Mrs. Bernini changed my life. They gave me a sense of myself. Moving in with them was the luckiest moment of my life."

"I could let you in," I said. I had never returned the key to Zach. "Would you like to go take a look around?"

"*No.* I mean, no, I'll go in for the memorial service when there are a lot of people around. I know it sounds crazy, but the place really does make me nervous. Anyway, I'm going to take these flyers to some of the neighbors," Homer said. "It was good to see you again."

"You too. I'll see you at the memorial."

Just as he left, a black Chevy truck pulled up. Josh Avery reached into the back of the cab, threw his duffel bag over his shoulder, and approached the front stoop. We eyed each other warily.

"What are you doing here?" I asked.

"I told you, I want this job. Whatever it takes."

"You can't just move in, Josh."

"Isn't that what you're doing?"

"How did you even know about this?"

"Kim mentioned it." Josh dropped his bag and fixed me with a look. "You think if I get Kim on the phone, she won't say I can stay here, too? I think you underestimate my charms."

"This isn't a game, Josh. I was going to share all my measurements and photos with you. There's no reason we couldn't both come up with thorough bids. And with the legal challenges over the will I think it will be quite some time before *anyone's* actually allowed to work on the place." I paused, then added, "Believe it or not, I'm here tonight to look for ghosts."

"Like the supposed ghosts that are screwing up the jobsite at your ex-husband's place?"

"Actually, since you brought it up, I'd love to talk to you about that." I felt for the reassuring weight of the gun in my bag. It was nearly seven, so I was expecting Graham to show up any minute. He was almost always on time. "Such as what happened to my stepson. And fair trade practices. And where your uncle might be."

"According to Valerie, 'ghosts' hurt Caleb." His sarcastic tone left no doubt as to what he thought of that hypothesis.

"That house shows no signs of being haunted. But your employees there are unhappy."

He put his hands on his hips, angry. "Are you accusing my employees of something?"

"Who's accusing who?" said Graham in a calm, quiet voice as he came up behind me. He rested one arm along my shoulders. It was a relief having him, quite literally, at my back.

Josh glanced at him. "Your girlfriend here seems to think my employees injured her son."

"Not at all," I said. "I think it was an accident, but accidents are much more likely to occur around disgruntled workers."

"I tell you what," said Graham, his voice low and slow. "I brought a bottle of cabernet. Why don't we go in, pour ourselves a drink, and talk about this like civilized people?"

Josh gave a curt nod, but then he seemed to relax. "Oh, my . . . friend's here. This time I brought my own entourage. Kim said the more the merrier."

Striding over to join us on the stoop was Braden, the young receptionist from the fancy office of Avery Builders.

"Isn't this *great*? What a fabulous old house, and in such a neighborhood!" he gushed, wrapping his arms around Josh. It wasn't the kind of embrace one expects to see among men who are simply friends or work buddies.

Well, *that* was interesting.

We all filed into the kitchen and Graham filled a few mismatched juice glasses with wine while I told Josh the essence of what Nacho had told me about the goings-on at Daniel's house, leaving out any names.

"Wow, that's . . ." Josh took a deep sip of wine, placed it on the table, looked at Braden for a long moment, then ran his hands through his hair. "I can't believe things have gotten that bad with Valerie. You're absolutely right, I should have been on top of that situation. And as to the overtime pay, we'll have to check into it. I hate to say it, but it's possible he's right."

Braden didn't add to the conversation, but he brought a small notebook out of his bag and started a list that began:

(1) Check into overtime.
(2) Figure out Valerie Burghart.

"Payroll can be tough to figure out, what with workers' comp and the like," I said. In this business, meeting one's monthly payroll obligations, at all, was challenging. It was a delicate balancing act that depended on the flow and wane of project revenues and outlays. Lucky for me, Stan took care of the majority of those issues for Turner Construction.

Josh nodded. "I have to admit it's been a pretty tough learning curve. Obviously a few things have fallen through the cracks."

"Couldn't your uncle give you a few pointers?" I asked, oh-so-innocently.

"He hasn't spoken to me for weeks."

"Oh? Where he's gotten to?"

He shrugged. "Tom invited me here to work with him, brought me into the business, treated me like his own son. It was good at first—I dealt with client relations and PR, while Tom kept on top of the jobsite crews. I even took on his last name, just to keep things consistent. But then when he found out that Braden and I are together, he really lost it." Josh looked down into his glass of wine.

Braden dutifully wrote down:

(3) Find Uncle Tom.

"By the time it all came out, I had several big upcoming projects under contract, and the clients loved me. But

Tom didn't want to deal, so he basically walked away. Early retirement, I guess. I begged him to come back and help, told him about this project. But then he actually *sailed* away somewhere just to get away from me. Braden is trying to help, but office work isn't his strong suit. We're a little overwhelmed."

"Mea culpa," said Braden, holding up both hands in surrender. "I was a theater major."

"That's . . . quite a story," I said. "I'm so sorry to hear about your uncle's reaction. For both of you."

"I don't know why I thought everything would be different out here." Josh looked at Braden and they shared a sad smile. "San Francisco has such a reputation for openness. . . . I just thought things would be different."

"Just to be clear," said Graham. "You didn't happen to call ICE on a fellow who works for you, goes by the name of Chewy?"

Josh frowned and shook his head. "Chewy got picked up? I would never do that."

"He told me he was having a few . . . paperwork issues," said Braden. "But I didn't really know who to talk to about it. I thought immigration was still called INS, that's how behind *I* am." He wrote:

(4) Help Chewy.

"You know, in terms of the workload and certain basic practices—I could help you out with some of that, if you want. My office manager, Stan, could give Braden some pointers. And we could talk about loaning you some good workers until you get things settled."

"Seriously? You'd do that for your competition?"

"Avery Builders is a good company, and you employ a lot of people. I'd hate to see all that put in jeopardy because your uncle is acting like an irresponsible jerk." I noticed Graham smiling at me, and I tried not to get distracted. "One more thing I'm curious about: How was it that you happened to be working on my ex-husband's house, and I met you here? That's such a coincidence."

"Well, I . . ." He tilted his head and gave me a smile that was, I'm sure, meant to charm me. "Marty Propak's brother, the AIA guy, was a visiting professor at UC Berkeley, so he was over at your ex-husband's place one evening when I stopped by with some paperwork. Daniel couldn't stop talking about what a great contractor you were—right in front of me, by the way. The guy was describing the Bernini house, and the job sounded incredible."

"So you poached the job?" Graham asked.

"I like to think of myself as practicing aggressive business tactics," responded Josh. "But Braden says I'm just acting like an ass."

"Uh-*huh*," said Braden.

"Wait, you're saying *Daniel* gave my name to Marty Propak?"

Josh nodded.

"My ex-husband?" I clarified.

"Daniel always speaks well of you. I've got to hand it to you both: I think I'd have a harder time learning to be civil after a divorce. I think it's great that you two are still friends, and you're both there for Caleb."

"I'm, uh . . ." I was saved by a knock on the door. My world was tilting on its axis, and I was just as happy to be interrupted. "I'll get it. Maybe that's Zach."

But when I opened the front door, Stan, Caleb, Dad, and Dog were standing on the front stoop.

"Hi, guys . . . What are you doing here?"

"We wanted to check this place out," said Dad.

"And make sure you're safe," said Caleb with a nod. He stood tall and held his arms out slightly from his body in a military stance, like my dad always did. I wondered if he even knew he was mimicking my father, or if it was unconscious, a male-bonding thing. He was taking himself very seriously, so I refrained from mentioning how adorable he was.

"The thing is, you guys can't stay here. . . . I mean, it's really not appropriate. . . ."

"We're not staying," said Stan. "But Bill was suggesting he do a walk-through with you, and help you start working up the bid."

Before his unscheduled hiatus, Dad was the best in the business at spotting construction issues and estimating time schedules and budgets. His knack for realistic assessments was responsible, in no small part, for the fact that Turner Construction had a reputation for doing excellent work in a timely manner, and without excessive cost overruns. I had to scramble to achieve anywhere near his accuracy with such things.

But far more important, was this a sign Dad was stepping back into the family business?

"And Dog?"

"I hated to leave him home alone," said Dad, patting the canine on his haunches.

"Oh sure, why leave anyone out?" I asked, standing back and letting in the crowd.

Chapter Twenty-five

J ust as I had when I was a kid, I trailed after Dad as he inspected the house and took notes of his mutterings and queries: Check for old oil tanks in the crawl space under the kitchen; replacements for the unusual mother-of-pearl push-button light switches were now available at Omega Lighting in Berkeley; the venting situation should be assessed as soon as possible, especially with the old furnace and water heater.

"The windows are unusually tight," said my dad. "Check this out, Graham. Nice work with the weather stripping, especially considering the age of the house."

"I noticed that, as well," said Graham. "Must help with the heating bill."

Except for when the ghosts show up, I thought to myself. Speaking of which, I kept expecting some sign of spectral inhabitants, but so far there was nothing.

After an exhaustive tour, Dad rejoined Stan and Caleb, who were talking about ordering pizza.

I asked Graham to help me put up the smoke detectors and carbon monoxide monitor I had brought with me. Graham hauled a ladder out of the shed out back, I grabbed the drill, and he and I started installing the smoke detectors throughout the house.

We had just finished installing a detector at the top of the stairs when we heard a sudden screeching, scraping noise, as though a piece of heavy furniture was being dragged across the floor.

The nursery door was ajar.

And there were fresh gouges in the floor, leading from the master to the playroom. When I peeked into the bedroom, it was clear to see the bed was pulled away from the wall. I had a sudden idea.

"I think . . . would you help me move this bed into the nursery?"

"Why?"

"I think they want it there. I think that's where the family died. All together."

"The ghost family? That's horrifying. How?"

"That part I still haven't figured out."

We wrestled the mattress and box spring off the frame, then awkwardly maneuvered the heavy old iron frame through the wide double doors. Luckily we weren't particularly concerned about scratching the hardwood floors, as they were already in such bad shape.

It screeched as we pushed it across the hall.

We managed to get the bed frame positioned in the nursery, then brought in the mattress, and remade the bed. I had a moment of near panic when our eyes met over the bed, and the domesticity of the scene struck a chord.

"Why don't you . . . uh . . . go get the pillows from the other room?"

Graham smiled a knowing smile. "Whatever you say, boss."

As I was leaning over and smoothing the bedspread, a wave of frigid cold enveloped me. I felt a hand tugging at my skirt from behind.

I turned around just in time to see a little dark-haired boy in short pants and a sweater running out the nursery door.

"Ezekiel? Come back—"

I stepped out into the hall, but there was nothing to see.

"What was it?" asked Graham from the opposite doorway.

"I thought I saw Ezekiel. The little boy. But . . . he's gone now. You didn't see anything?"

He shook his head.

"I think I'm making progress, at least. This was the first time he showed himself to me. Maybe Anabelle will show up soon; I have a few things to tell her." I said the last loudly, hoping she might be listening in. I still wasn't quite sure how it worked: whether Anabelle tracked my every move and word in the house, or she overheard only when she was near. "For now, let's go put up that carbon monoxide monitor down in the basement."

"That ancient furnace isn't working, is it?"

"No. But just in case . . . in a place like this, there could be gas sources that aren't obvious."

While we were in the basement, I startled when I heard disembodied voices. . . . But it turned out to be Caleb and Stan talking upstairs. We could hear them clearly through the vents.

And then I heard knocking—again, nothing eerie, just a pounding on the front door.

Surely one of my sizable posse was around to answer it.

More knocking.

"I guess I should get that. You okay here?" I asked Graham, who was screwing the detection device into the low, bare wood ceiling.

"Sure, go ahead."

I hurried up the stairs, down the hall, and into the foyer, where I spotted Dad, Caleb, and Stan in the doorway between the sitting room and the dining room.

"Are you guys suddenly deaf? Someone's knocking at the door."

They all stopped what they were doing to listen, but the knocking had stopped. Then I realized that not only had they been blatantly ignoring the person at the front door, but my dad had a tool in his hand and was prying off a piece of molding.

"What are you guys *doing*?" I asked.

"Pocket doors," said Stan.

"Pocket doors . . . ?" I parroted back.

"You believe this?" said Dad. "They had pocket doors here, of course, just like all these old homes, so you could keep the rooms closed to one another, or open them up to make them one—you should know that, Mel. Some idiot put up molding to hide them, so they couldn't be used."

He grunted as he shoved the crowbar farther into a small gap. The molding popped off with a splintering *crack*.

"You see 'em in there?" asked Stan.

"Certainly do," Dad replied, triumphant, peering into the opening in the wall.

"Um, guys? Hate to point this out," I said, "but this house isn't under contract. It isn't . . . it's still in legal limbo somewhere. We have no authority to start work on it yet. You have to stop."

"Then why are you here?"

"I *told* you, I'm house-sitting, and checking things out with the . . . you know. Spirits. Just in case they can tell me anything about what happened to Mrs. Bernini."

"Besides," Stan told Dad, "these folks wanted Mel to speak to the ghosts about opening a haunted bed-and-breakfast."

My father gave me the same look of confused disbelief I got when I told him I was going to study anthropology rather than, say, accounting or physical therapy "*or some damned degree with a shot at getting a job*."

"They *want* the place to be haunted?" He looked at Stan, who shrugged and nodded.

"Well, I'll be damned. So . . . they're paying you for this?"

"Well, not exactly. Not so far. Right now I'm just house-sitting."

"So let me get this straight," Dad said. "You don't have the renovation contract on this place. You don't have a ghost-hunting contract, either? If you're gonna get into the business, don't you think you ought to take it seriously?"

"I'm not 'in the business,'" I protested. "And I do take it seriously."

Sort of. Actually, maybe he was right. Rather than backing into one ghost project after another, maybe I should think them through the way I would any construction job: doing thorough research, talking to the experts in the field, and formulating a plan *before* encountering whatever spirits might be present at a house. And all that made me wonder—did ghost busters bid for jobs like contractors did? Did they have set fees, or charge by the hour? Or by the ghost? This was probably covered in Ghost Busting 101.

I heard the clopping of horse hooves, a whinny, the clanking of harnesses.

And the foyer lights flickered out.

And then . . . someone was trying the knob. My hand was on my gun as I approached the door. Standing to the side, I reached over and unlocked it.

The door swung open.

"Zach."

He jumped back when he saw the gun, his hands reaching for the sky.

"Mel! What *is* it with you and guns?"

I was beginning to think I wasn't a very good influence on Zach. When I first knew him, he had been a relaxed, smiley sort.

His gaze shifted to my father, who was holstering his own weapon, and Stan and Caleb, who were looking guilty, with a few pieces of splintered wood at their feet. Just then, Dog apparently woke up and realized he was supposed to be doing something. He ran in from the kitchen, barking loud enough to wake the dead.

Zach spoke in a low voice so only I could hear. "When you volunteered me for this gig, I thought you might, you know, stop by and look for ghosts, not move in your whole family and start tearing the place apart. It's like the Clampetts moving into Beverly Hills or something."

"I spoke directly with Marty Propak, Zach. He was fine with me staying here, especially since Josh is here, as well. In fact, you shouldn't feel obligated to stick around at all, if you don't want."

"No worries there, young fella," said Josh, thumping Zach's shoulder in a manly, let's-be-friends manner. "Kim told me we should feel free to bring our entourages, the more the merrier."

"And my family is just staying for dinner; then they'll leave," I said. "Like Josh says, no worries."

Zach sighed. "That pizza better be really good, that's all I have to say."

A young blond fellow made the delivery.

"Where's Raj?" I asked. In fact, I had ordered the pizza at least in part because I wanted to ask Raj a few questions, especially now that I had backup. I had told Graham about my suspicions concerning Raj, and he stood by my side, doing a pretty good job of looking menacing.

"He never showed up for work," said the new delivery fellow. "Weird thing is, I thought I saw his car on the next block over. Anyway, that'll be thirty-four fifty."

So much for the special discount prices from Sylven's Pizza. I paid the man and peered up and down the street, but saw nothing unusual.

"Let's batten down the hatches, just in case," said

Graham in a low voice so the others wouldn't overhear. "I don't like the idea that he's out there somewhere."

"The inspector said they'd bring him in for questioning. He's probably in custody already."

"Maybe. I'm not willing to bet on it."

Graham and I brought the pizza to the table, where my dad and Stan were regaling Josh, Braden, Zach, and Caleb with funny stories from their contracting days.

Once we sat down and poured drinks, we toasted the memory of Mrs. Bernini, and observed a moment of silence. I kept hoping to see her ghost, thinking she might enjoy seeing us with her favorite pizza, that she might even join us at the table. But so far, nothing.

True to his word, after we all ate our fill, Dad announced that he, Caleb, and Stan had a game to watch, and would be leaving.

"Why don't you leave Dog here?" suggested Graham. "Kim Propak didn't seem to mind having an animal in the house, and he could come in handy."

In case anyone was sneaking around the house, I imagined Graham was thinking.

"I should probably be going, too," said Zach. "Somehow I don't think I'm needed here, with all these overqualified house sitters."

"You really don't have to go, Zach, unless you'd rather not be here," I said as I walked him to the door. I imagined his decision had something to do with the nasty looks Graham was casting his way all through dinner.

He smiled down at me; then his gaze shifted over my shoulder to where Graham was no doubt glowering at him.

"I think you've got an admirer who would like you to himself. But thanks for the offer." He reached out and pulled on a corkscrew curl in the middle of my forehead. "Another time, I'd love an invitation to an overnight. But maybe without so many people around."

He winked, then slipped out the front door.

So it was just me and Graham, Josh and Braden. Like a double date. An overnight double date. I started to hyperventilate.

As I turned back to join the three men at the table, I felt a wave of frigid air.

Anabelle walked right past me. I followed her as she crossed the foyer and proceeded down the hall. Graham started to join me, but I waved him off. He watched as I continued into the study where the portrait of her and Ezekiel was hung over the fireplace.

"Anabelle?"

She gave no indication of hearing me.

I thought of what Olivier told me, that sometimes ghosts need to be approached obliquely.

"Hey! I've got a question."

She stopped, slowly turned around, crossed her little arms over her chest, and tapped her foot.

"How come you sing that song all the time? The roses song?"

"I like it."

"It wasn't written until 1949, but you died in 1912."

"I have ears, don't I? I can *hear* things. We used to have our own radio. Father insisted, when they first were invented. He's good with mechanicals. Gadgets of all types. We had the first gas water heater and furnace in the whole city."

"How do you know that?"

"Well, maybe just the neighborhood. I don't know. But it was very new and original. Father says science will bring progress to us all. Do you know where the radio is? I've been looking for it."

"I do know where it is. I'll try to get it back for you." I would prevail upon Portia one more time, with a specific request from a ghost. If nothing else, perhaps I could scare it out of her. "Anabelle, I don't suppose I could talk to your father?"

"He doesn't . . . he and Mother don't really . . . well, they don't think it's appropriate to speak to the newcomers. They say it's simply not done."

"Why not?"

"It's not right to speak when you haven't been properly introduced. And besides, they're afraid you'll make us leave."

"You want to stay?"

"Of course. This is our home. We're all together. It's such a beautiful house. Father had it constructed especially for us."

"What if the new owners of the place wanted you to stay?"

She searched my face. Once again I was struck by how real—how material—she looked. As though she were a little girl dressed in old-fashioned garb, not a ghost at all.

"Truly? You won't make us leave?" she asked.

I shook my head.

Gone was the snide look on her face, the slightly curled lip. Her lips parted, her eyes softened. She looked like the little girl she must have been, full of hope and excitement.

"They want to bring in guests, operate the house as an inn. But they'd love for you all to stay, and they want to restore it so it's a lot like it used to be, when you all lived here."

"We still live here."

"Oh, of course. I meant . . . before. We want to make it look a lot like before. Anabelle, can you tell me anything about what happened to your family?"

She shook her head.

"Was it your neighbor, Owen Campbell? Was he involved?"

"No!" Anabelle stamped her little foot. "I know the neighbors thought he was . . . but he was just sad about his wife, Tallulah. She died here; Father tried his best to save her and the poor little baby. It wasn't Father's fault. He even had a painting made of her, afterward, to try to make friends with Mr. Campbell. But he refused it, he was so angry. . . ." Her face crumpled and she started to cry. "The night, the night that things changed . . . I looked into the marbles, and I could see that there was great danger. I thought Mr. Campbell would come after us, so I insisted we all sleep together. Mother and Father finally agreed, because I was so upset."

"What happened?"

She shook her head and answered impatiently, "I keep *telling* you, nothing. It was very cold. I remember the new heater was installed that very day, and we put a bed in the nursery so we would be warm and cozy. We all went to sleep but then . . . things changed. And our puppy ran away. I wish I knew what happened. . . . I wish I could find our puppy."

I studied Anabelle for a moment, and started to put

things together. The family had just had their new furnace installed, and there was a vent directly from the basement to the playroom. The family had all slept together in that room, but then never awoke. Anabelle's lips were cherry red, as were her cheeks and ears.

I glanced back up at the portrait. In it she and Ezekiel both looked pale, with alabaster skin.

Such high color was a mark of carbon monoxide poisoning. I was willing to bet Anabelle was right, that poor Owen Campbell had nothing to do with their deaths. Instead, it had been a terrible accident.

"Anabelle, I think I've figured out what happened. . . ."

But as I looked back, she was gone.

I headed back to the kitchen but found Dog at the foot of the stairs, whining incessantly. He was fretting, anxious and panting, breathing quickly. It wasn't like him. Barking at nothing and being generally annoying, yes, but not this kind of fretful cringing and crying.

A marble came rolling slowly down the stairs. Roll, drop, roll, drop, as it made its way down the steps. At the bottom of the stairs, it turned the corner and came to tap at my boot.

And then, muffled crying from the second floor. Anabelle, as though her heart had broken. She started to wail.

Cautiously, I peered up into the dim light at the top of the stairs. Taking a steadying breath, stroking my grandmother's wedding ring on the chain around my neck for courage, I started to climb the stairs. I hesitated for a moment, wondering whether I should bring backup. All the men were in the dining room. But Anabelle hadn't appeared to anyone but me.

This was something I should do alone.

I ascended the stairs slowly, then paused and looked down the hall. There was a light shining out from the bottom of the closed playroom door. I heard the tune of the carousel, the clacking of the marionettes, and *I drive a dump truck.*

The door had been jammed from the outside with a metal bar under the handle. It would make it impossible for anyone—or any*thing*—to get out.

Who would have jammed this door? Had one of the guys gotten scared? Using my heavy boot, I started kicking at it. Finally the metal bar fell to the floor, clanking loudly.

I pushed the door in slowly. The carousel stopped, the little horses still rocking slightly. The puppets swayed in their ornate case.

And Raj lay prone, splayed on the wood floor.

"Raj!"

He didn't respond.

I hurried to kneel by his side. There was no blood, no obvious trauma. He was still breathing. But then I heard something. Not music this time—instead, a far-off beeping.

It was the sound of a carbon monoxide alarm. I could hear it through the heating vent.

"Graham!" I called.

"Mel?" I heard his muffled voice coming through the vent. He must have run down to the basement when he heard the alarm.

"Shut off all the gas to the house! And I need help up in the playroom!"

I grabbed Raj under his arms and started pulling him toward the window. I thought of trying to take him outside, but he was heavier than he looked and I wasn't sure I could manage it alone. He needed fresh air, immediately—as did I. I could already feel myself getting light-headed, and an ache was developing in my temples. I set him down for a second while I yanked open the sash window and took several big breaths. Holding my breath, I pulled Raj toward the window, hoisted him up, and hung him over the sill like a sack of potatoes set out to dry in the sun.

I stuck my own head out the window beside him and inhaled deeply.

Carbon monoxide doesn't smell, or taste, or give any indication of its presence other than the deadly symptoms. If Raj had known he was being gassed, he could have at least opened the window and breathed in fresh air. But he must have thought he was trapped in the playroom, maybe by ghosts. Another aspect of carbon monoxide poisoning was that it jumbled your thoughts and often made you see things. . . . Many alleged hauntings had been blamed on the presence of a small amount of carbon monoxide in the home's air.

But what was Raj *doing* here? I had been on the verge of accusing him of murdering Mrs. Bernini. He had motive, opportunity, and he seemed to know the house. That night when he delivered the pizza, Mrs. Bernini had told him we were going to renovate the house—had he panicked, thinking that Mrs. Bernini's promises wouldn't be upheld by the new owners? And then there was his handwriting, which I had recognized from both the will and the brick. I thought he had been searching the house looking for the other will, the one he feared left the house to Mountain.

Josh appeared in the doorway.

"There's CO in here! Could you carry him outside?"

Josh was already rushing over to us. He hoisted Raj over one brawny shoulder and ran out of the playroom and toward the stairs. I took a deep breath of fresh air through the open window, then ran out, closing the door behind me. I heard Graham meeting Josh halfway down the stairs and offering to take Raj the rest of the way, out to the garden.

If it wasn't Raj, who else might have been so invested, who also had access to this house? I thought I knew.

I ran down to the basement to double-check what had happened. Last I saw, the heater wasn't even hooked up. Or . . . had the heating service been here recently? There it was, a sticker with the heating service number. Kirkbride HVAC.

Dripping water from the taps. And another marble rolling along the floor.

I heard the far-off whine of sirens. Thank goodness there were competent folks here—I had been so enraged that I forgot to call 911, much less to carry my gun with me.

This was stupid. I turned to leave.

But Edgar was standing in my way.

"Why Raj?" I asked. I had assumed Edgar would run. Why would he hang around? Surely he knew the jig was up?

"It really wasn't my fault. He was going to tell. He left me no choice."

"It's not too late, you know. He's not dead. And I'm sure whatever happened with Mrs. Bernini, it was an accident."

"I was furious, but it was . . . it was just a little shove.

Barely a push, but she went down and hit her head. I panicked when I heard the doors fling open, and you were on your way out. But they won't believe me. Not now."

Fortunately he had no gun, but neither did I. Edgar was solid, and probably had at least fifty pounds on me.

"Go on, now, through the door there."

He gestured toward the door of the subbasement.

Feigning obedience, I turned toward the door, remembering the box of odds and ends I had seen when I was here with Zach. As soon as I passed through the low doorway into the pitch black of the subbasement, I crouched down and grabbed for the first substantial thing my hand fell on.

Still crouching low, I whirled and smacked Edgar as hard as I could in the kneecap with a heavy bronze hinge.

He went down, crying out in pain, clutching his knee. I tried to run past him, but he grabbed my ankle and pulled me down, hitting me on the back of the head so hard I saw stars. He yanked me up and then shoved me facedown into the brackish water at the bottom of the sink. It was only a few inches, but it was enough. I struggled and tried to kick backward with my boots, but he held me easily with his strength. The air I had managed to take in before he shoved my face in the water was running out, blackness forming at the edges of my sight.

Suddenly the pressure on my neck relented as Edgar backed off. With my last remaining strength I surged up and lurched backward, out of his reach.

Edgar was cringing. He looked horrified and shied away, stumbling into the furnace behind him.

Gulping in air, it took me a moment to understand

what was going on. I heard a clacking sound, then realized that Anabelle was holding up two marionettes—one in each hand—and making them jump and sway. I couldn't tell whether Edgar could see the ghostly girl puppeteer, or simply saw dolls floating in air, their limbs clattering as they danced.

I took advantage of his distraction and slugged him in the head with the hinge. He went down with a loud thud and I ran again, this time making it up the stairs, slamming the door, and locking it.

And then I collapsed.

Chapter Twenty-six

The entire neighborhood, it seemed, turned out for Mrs. Bernini's memorial service. The house was decked out with colorful bouquets in mason jars, almost all the flowers donated from neighbors' yards, rather than florist arrangements. Homer had suggested it, and their blowsy, homey look was just right to remember Mrs. Bernini.

No, she wasn't perfect. It seems Mrs. Bernini really had promised too much to too many people, and she hadn't been above doing what she had to in order to get what she wanted. But she was a tough old bird, had managed well by her foster children, and was generally beloved by her neighbors.

Raj was still in the hospital, but he had been cooperating with the police and eventually filled in the story: He knew how to break into the house, and Edgar had convinced him to search for an amended will so they could destroy it, lest it leave the house and grounds to anyone other than Portia and, since California is a community property state, Edgar. Raj had been methodically tossing the rooms, assuming we would blame it on the ghosts.

What Edgar hadn't realized was that Portia had already filed for divorce. He had been just a tad behind on his paperwork, and hadn't opened the envelope containing the papers yet.

The really sad thing is that there *was* no other will, at least none that any of us could find. One letter left on a crowded desk in the study, however, indicated that Mrs. Bernini wanted to include a provision in her will taking care of Raj's mother's medical bills, and had intended to honor the purchase agreement she'd made with the Propaks. Mountain never found anything in writing, but when he heard the terms of the holographic will in Portia's hands, he was content.

"So she took care of Mountain?" asked Claire.

"Yes," I said. "He'll be in charge of the gardens for as long as he wants the job, so he can develop them with the legacy of Campbell's tropical garden. Portia and he are working together now to open some of the gardens to the public as a small park. They're planning on razing one of the outbuildings to make room. Meanwhile, the Propaks will buy the house and the remaining land, and operate it as a bed-and-breakfast."

"That's great."

Behind her, I caught a glimpse of Anabelle. She didn't seem like a ghost, standing among all these people; if it hadn't been for her old-fashioned attire, she would have fit right in. But she looked sad as she gazed at the flowers and the photos of Mrs. Bernini through the years: as a smiling young woman in cat's-eye glasses with short curly brown hair—at her wedding, standing proud and stiff by Angelo's side, pretty white bouquet in hand.

I crossed the room to join the little ghost girl.

"Are you okay?" I asked.

She shrugged. "I'm sad. I've known Mrs. Bernini for so long. . . . I can't believe she's gone."

"She's . . . she's not with you now?"

"No. We asked her to stay—Mother and Father both invited her, and Ezekiel practically cried. But she wanted to go on. I guess she wants to find her husband. So it's just us again."

"I wanted to ask you something: that note on the wall of the playroom, the one Ezekiel wrote? Was he warning us to stay out for our own health?"

She gave me an odd look that reminded me of the first day when she'd opened the door. "Of course. What did you think he meant?"

"It seemed like some sort of threat, at first."

"Ha!" she said, and rolled her eyes.

"Is it . . . would it be weird for me to introduce you to the new owners of the house? I think they mean well— they want to make the place into a bed-and-breakfast, and many people will be coming hoping to see . . . people like you, from a different time."

"You can say it: I'm a ghost. I don't *feel* like a ghost. And besides, nobody really *wants* to see ghosts," she said with a cynicism far too old for her age. Then again, Anabelle was more than one hundred years old, I reminded myself. "Or . . . do they?"

"I guess a lot of people do. *I've* enjoyed getting to know you. Come on, follow me."

But when I arrived next to Marty and Kim and looked behind me, Anabelle had disappeared. I could hear only a disembodied, far-off lilting voice singing: *With garlands of roses, and whispers of pearls, a garden of posies for all little girls . . .*

"She was right here. . . . ," I said.

"That's all right, dear," said Kim, patting my arm as though she were my mother, even though she was no more than fifteen years my senior. But I supposed a little maternal attitude would go far in the hospitality industry.

"Kim, you seem to like dogs."

"Oh, I *do*!"

"How would you feel about getting a cocker spaniel puppy for the B&B? I have the feeling the ghosts would really enjoy that."

"Oh, you mean like the one in the portrait of the children? What a wonderful idea! Marty, Mel just gave me the most *wonderful* idea!"

I smiled as she hurried over to talk with her husband. With a little urging, the Propaks had agreed to leave the playroom just as it was, with the bed moved there permanently. We wouldn't alter it at all . . . except that now it wouldn't be receiving sporadic, low levels of carbon monoxide from the old heater, as it apparently had for years. That was one reason the children felt odd in the playroom—Claire and I had felt it, too. But I hadn't figured it out until it was almost too late.

The old furnace would be ripped out just as soon as possible. Even when it was new, apparently, it had never worked properly. In the interim, all gas to the house remained shut off, just in case.

And though Portia was distraught over what her soon-to-be-ex-husband had done, she brought the old radio as a gift to the Propaks—and to the house. It now sat up in the playroom, where I heard it cranking out scratchy old 1910s and 1920s tunes from time to time. She had also returned the oil portrait of Tallulah, and the Propaks planned to give it pride of place over the fireplace in the main entry, along with an explanatory plaque. It seemed right that she would be remembered that way.

I searched the room for Anabelle. The front parlor, kitchen, and entry were crowded with neighbors young and old. I recognized several guys from the pizza shop. And Homer and a dozen other adult foster children had returned to pay their respects. But no little ghost girl.

But then I reminded myself: Ghosts weren't here for our amusement, nor were they regular people anymore. They had their own agenda, their own sense of time and place, of right and wrong. I still had a lot to learn.

Maybe it was time to enroll in Olivier's Ghost Busting 101 class.

Graham came up behind me, placing his hands at the base of my neck and rubbing. I sighed in contentment.

"How are you feeling?"

"I'm okay," I said. After the exposure to the carbon monoxide—both in the playroom and then some down in the basement, as well—I was supposed to spend twenty-four hours in treatment at the hospital. Apparently I had not been the ideal patient. Once my time was up, they asked me to be more careful and not to come back.

"Thought I should warn you," said Graham. "I was talking with Marty about some energy-saving ideas to incorporate into the renovation of this place."

"I'll just bet you were."

Graham grinned. "It's a big job. It'll keep you busy for some time to come."

"I know. I might need to bring Avery Builders in on this, just for the sake of manpower. He's got a pretty big crew, and they don't have much to do at the moment. And we might just have a shot at that AIA award, now that we've got a new architect on the job. I think . . . I think Mrs. Bernini would be pleased, in the long run."

Not to mention the Bowles family, who would have been mighty upset if Kim Propak had implemented her Alice-in-Wonderland type of changes. I had worked out a deal with the pertinent parties: The Propaks would use Turner Construction to return the home to its historic roots while making a few essential updates, as well as the alterations necessary to make it a comfortable bed-and-breakfast. The ghost family, meanwhile, would not interfere with the construction process—as long as we didn't touch the playroom. We had put the toys back the way they were, and left the bed made up in pretty snowy white, old-fashioned embroidered linens.

Anabelle might appear from time to time if she felt like it, and Ezekiel would persist with his marbles and toys. The parents would be there, though from what I gathered from Anabelle, they didn't have much interest in what she called the New People. Rather, they preferred to carry on with their normal lives. Or post-lives. Or whatever it was called.

"So," said Graham. "Can I assume you're postponing running off to Paris?"

"I suppose so. Maybe indefinitely. I'm working on a new project, and I can't wait to see how it turns out."

"Another project?" Graham looked a little taken aback. "I thought your slate was pretty full."

"This is a brand-new sort of project for me." I rose up on the steel toes of my work boots, and kissed him softly.

A marble rolled across the floor and tapped at my boot, but I paid no mind.

About the Author

Juliet Blackwell is the pseudonym for a mystery author who also writes the Witchcraft Mystery series and, along with her sister, wrote the Art Lover's Mystery series as Hailey Lind. The first in that series, *Feint of Art*, was nominated for an Agatha Award for Best First Novel. As owner of her own faux-finish and design studio, the author has spent many days and nights on construction sites renovating beautiful historic homes throughout the San Francisco Bay Area. She currently resides in a happily haunted house in Oakland, California.

CONNECT ONLINE

www.julietblackwell.net
facebook.com/julietblackwellauthor
twitter.com/julietblackwell

Continue reading for a preview of
Juliet Blackwell's upcoming Witchcraft Mystery,

Tarnished and Torn

Available in July 2013 from Obsidian

"You're saying this is a palace . . . for cows?" I asked, casting disbelieving eyes over the huge Cow Palace, which sported a colossal banner that read: GEM FAIRE ALL WEEKEND!

Where I'm from in West Texas, the idea of a royal bovine showplace wouldn't have been entirely out of the realm of possibility. Here in the urban outskirts of San Francisco, on the other hand, it seemed rather . . . anomalous. If not downright preposterous.

"The C-O-W in Cow Palace stands for California, Oregon, and Washington," Bronwyn said, adjusting her new-to-her tunic, a rare, vintage 1960s find. The purple gauze, decorated with rune symbols and pentagrams, matched the violet sweet peas woven through Bronwyn's frizzy brown hair. "It started out in 1941 as a livestock showcase, and they have rodeos here sometimes, but they also have concerts and sports events. Anyway, the place has more in common with an airport hangar than a palace per se."

"Too bad . . . and here I had an image of cattle taking tea with the queen," teased our friend Maya.

"Just wait until we get inside, you cynics. I guarantee you, the Gem Faire will take your breath away," said Bronwyn with a cat-that-swallowed-the-canary grin.

The three of us were standing in a long line of eager shoppers waiting for the show to open. Multiple canvas bags were slung over our shoulders in anticipation of plenty of loot for my vintage clothing store, Aunt Cora's Closet. When Bronwyn first suggested we close the shop in favor of attending the Gem Faire this morning, I almost balked. After all, my customers had been so good to me—and my store—over the past few months that I hated to disappoint anyone who might be desperate for vintage clothing on a warm summer Sunday.

But then I thought: a huge trade show full of wholesale decorative jewels, stones, and ornaments?

Too tempting to pass up. Way too tempting.

One of the best things about my job was that I could do this sort of thing—pursue objects of great beauty and history—and call it "work." With friends by my side? Even better.

The doors opened and the crowd surged forward, through the entryway and into the main "palace," which was undeniably gargantuan enough to hold several herds of cows.

Jiminy Cricket, I thought as I looked around us. A thousand medieval knights might have worked for years to amass this quantity of goodies.

Display boards and cloth-covered tables were chock-full

of sparkling jewels, gleaming pearls, precious stones, glowing amber, fossilized wood, million-year-old ammonites . . . and then there were the pendants, necklaces, earrings, medallions, rings, anklets, and decorative tchotchkes from hairbrushes to tiny boxes. Hanging overhead were massive posters touting everything from coin necklaces for belly dancers to the health benefits of copper bracelets; half a dozen posters invited the public to "invite wealth into their lives" by learning to "fire dance." Its stars, as portrayed in the artwork, were dripping with jewelry.

It was chaos. Glittery, cacophonous bedlam.

"Glad I talked you into this?" asked Bronwyn as we started to meander through the aisles among gem-laden tables.

I nodded, dumbstruck.

"I'd say it's worth opening the store a little late on a Sunday," said Maya as she paused to stroke a long strand of polished garnets. The wine color of the beads as they reflected the fluorescent lights overhead was a perfect match to today's ruby highlights in Maya's black locks.

"You can say that again," I said. The crowd milling around us was mostly female—some appeared to be jewelry makers or wedding planners or artists, or dealers like me, but mostly they were shopping just for the fun of it.

For me, coming here today—going "shopping with friends"—was an important rite of passage. I had never before done such a thing.

We strolled by a dealer with tables piled high with strands of pearls in just about every color imaginable: sky blue, indigo, purple, pink, green, gray. In addition to the rainbow of color possibilities, the oyster-born treasures were offered in myriad different shapes, from the classic gleaming spheres to misshapen, elongated forms that looked like lumpy grains of rice or twisty coral.

The next booth specialized in Venetian glass beads, handmade and swirling with color. Strands of multicolored glass pieces hung from a long fishing line and created the effect of a beaded curtain; they twinkled beguilingly in the harsh lights of the exhibit hall. There were a few dozen finished necklaces and earrings hanging from display racks, but most were offered as loose beads in lined baskets.

Maya reached out to caress one piece after another, stroking their slick surfaces and rippling the beaded curtain with a pleasant *clickety clackety* sound.

Personally, I kept my hands tucked tight into the pockets of my vintage 1960s sundress. The buzzing crowd that surrounded us already felt just a mite overwhelming; I didn't want to add to my already overloaded senses by tuning in to an untold number of possible sensations emanating from the jewelry.

Not that I normally picked up much from metal or stone . . . but just to be on the safe side.

When it comes to witchcraft, as in the rest of life, I'm a bit of a misfit. For instance, I'm no good at scrying, or seeing the future in a crystal ball. Also, I tend to be at a loss in concentrating my energy to use magic in emergencies, though I am improving with practice. In the field of psychometrics I am especially weird: most sensitives are adept at feeling vibrations from metal and stone.

But *I* gather sensations from clothing. For some reason, the warmth of humanity shows itself to me through the everyday items we wear on our backs. Textiles talk to me. Stones, however, leave me cold.

"I think I should go find the vintage stuff," I told Bronwyn and Maya, both of whom were absorbed in their study of delicate hand-knotted necklaces made by a woman whose nametag read, appropriately, SAPPHIRE STONE. As for me . . . I have a finite supply of shopping energy. I wanted to spend it on items for the store. "How about I meet you two at the refreshment stand in an hour or so?"

"Sure. Let's see . . . here's the map," Maya said as she studied a brochure that included a map of vendors; before we left Aunt Cora's Closet this morning she had drawn red circles around a few names. "There are a few antique jewelry dealers in the back right corner, right in front of the big blue curtain."

"Thanks. I'll move that way."

I'm not much of one for crowds. There are too many sensations swirling about. Being outside is better, but in a confined space like this I can start to feel overwhelmed, jangly. Which might have accounted for the annoying, just-out-of-my-grasp inkling that something nefarious was up. Nothing specific, just a vague glimmer, like the "here one moment, gone the next" vision of a mirage on an insufferably long, straight Texas highway.

Slowly, I turned around three hundred sixty degrees, looking for something out of the ordinary: a practitioner with a blinking purple-gray aura, for example, or an out of control familiar. Or maybe a surprise appearance by Aidan Rhodes, a powerful witch who was the self-appointed godfather of the local magical folk.

But I saw nothing but grown mothers and daughters enjoying a day together, sharp-eyed merchants shopping for deals, artisans and jewelry makers in search of supplies. And mounds of gemstones, trinkets, and baubles on every horizontal surface.

Shaking off the vague, peculiar impressions, I made my way toward the back right corner, where a big sign announced: GRISELDA'S JEWELRY AND GEMS.

Behind the horseshoe display counter, I presumed, stood Griselda. A pawnshop's worth of gold chains and medallions hung from her neck; both wrists were manacled with dozens of broad bracelets and slim bangles; she wore sparkly rings on each finger; and multiple earrings and cuffs adorned her ears.

A snippet of an old poem my mother used to repeat came back to me: ". . with rings on her fingers and bells on her toes, she will have music wherever she goes . . ." I fought the urge to peek behind the counter to see if she wore anklets and toe rings.

Griselda's brocade-draped tables were loaded with antique gold lockets and brooches made of mother of pearl and bronze. A large tray lined with deep purple velvet held dozens of rings made of gold and silver, some of which twinkled with semiprecious stones and rhinestones.

At the moment, the only part of Griselda visible was the seat of her tie-dyed stretch pants straining across her backside as she leaned over, vigorously rooting through boxes. She jingled pleasantly with each enthusiastic move.

When two teenagers started looking over the display, *ooh*ing and *aah*ing over the fine old pieces, Griselda straightened and gave a welcoming, gap-toothed smile.

"This one's a beaut," said Griselda, speaking excellent English with a slight Germanic accent. She held up a silver chain with a dented and tarnished but stunning gem-encrusted silver medallion.

The girls seemed rapt, admiring the medallion.

"If you look deep enough into the opal you'll see the ocean." Griselda paused dramatically.

The girls giggled, teasing each other about what they saw in the depths of the opal.

"Could I try it on?" asked the younger of the two, a pretty, petite teenager who looked Latina, with almond eyes and straight black hair hanging nearly to her waist.

Griselda held the medallion out to her, but the other teen put out her hand to stop her friend.

"Wait, Marisela, *don't*. Don't you know opals are bad luck?" She was lovely, exotic-looking, with a glittering nose ring, and her hair was plaited into a multitude of braids. She had dusky skin, her eyes were a celadon green, and her hair was the light golden brown of clover honey.

"Seriously?" said Marisela with a smile. "I swear, Shawnelle, you're as bad as my mom with all the superstitions."

"Do what you want," Shawnelle replied with a shrug. "But if your teeth start falling out or whatever, don't come crying to me."

Marisela still smiled but hesitated. "Oh, I guess . . . yeah, seems like I've heard something like that before. Never mind."

Griselda snorted loudly, laid the medallion back on a special silk-covered stand, and, sensing she wasn't going to make the sale, turned back to unpack more boxes.

"Besides," said the green-eyed girl as she tried one ring after another on her long slim fingers, holding her hand out in front of her and admiring each in turn, "we're here on a mission, remember?"

"Oh, right. 'Scuse me, do you have any tiaras?" Marisela asked in the general direction of Griselda's backside.

"*Nein*. No tiaras," came the muffled reply. I could hear Griselda muttering something about opals and bad luck under her breath.

"Opals aren't necessarily bad luck," I said to the girls, unable to contain myself. I'm no gemologist, but opals are a very special kind of stone . . . and I hated for people to misinterpret old legends. "They're almost alive, and like any living thing they need proper care and respect."

Both girls' attention was diverted as a buff young man ducked through the massive blue curtains that cut off the show floor from the staging area. He was tall, large, and extremely fit, with short blond hair, a prominent nose, and light ice-blue eyes.

Impressive biceps bulged as he carried what appeared to be heavy cardboard boxes, one under each arm. "*Wo?*" he asked Griselda.

She gestured to a spot on the floor next to the half-unpacked one.

He grunted with the effort of setting down his burden.

"*Danke*, Johannes." She then asked him to bring in the rest of the boxes, as it was the last day of the faire. My German vocabulary consists of all of ten words, but I caught the gist of what they were saying.

The girls fell silent, shy and smiling in the presence of the handsome young man. He nodded in their direction and said something else in German to Griselda, who waved him off.

"You two lookin' for something special?" It wasn't as though there were hordes of customers pushing their way to the front, but some merchants hold a special disdain for browsers.

"I'm looking for a tiara for my sister," repeated Marisela. "It's her *quinceañera*. But mom doesn't want to buy a brand-new one; she wants an old one that looks like the one passed down through the family. It was stolen."

"How about a nice pendant?" suggested Griselda, holding out a shallow tray filled with a mishmash of tangled chains and medallions. "I got plenty with no opals. Or what about a ring?"

"It has to be a *tiara*, for a *quinceañera*."

"Don't even know what that is."

"You don't? Seriously?" asked Marisela. "It's, like, an awesome party when a girl turns *quince*, or fifteen. I had mine last year. It was awesome."

Akin to a "sweet sixteen" birthday, *quinceañeras* are a rite of passage common in many Latino cultures, a celebration of a girl becoming a woman.

"I have a couple of tiaras at my store," I said to the girls, handing them each a business card. "They might be rather poor replacements for a family heirloom, but they're pretty, and definitely not brand-new."

Marisela studied the business card I handed her.

"Vintage clothes? Cool. Hey, do you have any formal dresses that would work for a *quinceañera*? I still haven't found exactly the right thing yet, and it's, like, a week away."

"I do, yes." I smiled, thinking of the scads of taffeta, netting, and silks and satins hanging from the racks at Aunt Cora's Closet.

"Cool. Maybe we'll come check it out if we don't find what we need here."

"I look forward to it."

"Those rings look good on you," Griselda said to Shawnelle. "You have nice hands for rings. Men like that."

"I like this one," said Shawnelle, looking down at a large turquoise piece that sat in a setting of tarnished, worked silver. "But . . . I guess I should save my money."

Griselda snorted and, once again sensing she wasn't going to make a sale, turned her attention back to her unpacking.

Now that the object of their admiration had ducked back behind the blue curtains, the girls' enthusiasm had waned. They wandered off.

"Could I see the opal medallion, please?" I asked.

Griselda looked up from her unpacking, a decidedly skeptical look in her kohl-lined eyes. Though thousands of people mobbed the aisles, we were, for all intents and purposes, alone here in the corner.

She straightened, picked up the piece, and laid it in my outstretched palm.

I cupped the medallion in both hands, sharing my warmth with it. And feeling . . . not much. I really was at a loss when it came to most jewelry. But opals held water within their depths, which was one reason they were so fragile. I wasn't kidding when I said they were alive. There was a slight, tiny shimmer . . . like when I tried to scry by looking into my crystal ball. Almost . . . but not quite.

"You have some lovely items here. At my shop, Aunt Cora's Closet, I specialize in vintage clothing, primarily for women. I'm here hoping to score some nice vintage stuff. But your prices . . ."

"What's wrong with 'em?"

"I was just wondering whether you might consider a wholesale rate—"

"This *is* wholesale."

"Maybe a bulk rate?"

She smiled again. "You're a bargainer, huh? Tell you what, you come back later today, once the hungry crowds have been through, and maybe I'll make you a deal."

I handed her my card. She returned the favor and passed me a bright purple, shiny one with sparkles.

"Hey, you're on Haight Street?" she asked, perusing me again. "I'm staying at a bed-and-breakfast right over there."

Just then Johannes returned with another two boxes, one under each brawny arm. One was decidedly beaten up, and *Mull* had been written on it in black magic marker.

"Why do you bring this one?" Griselda chastised him. "It's junk—says so right there on the side."

"You want I put it back?"

"*Dummer Junge . . . Ja*, put it—" Griselda stopped mid-answer and appeared to reconsider. She looked at me out of the corner of her eye. "Unless you'd like to buy it. Give you a good price. You say you're looking for inexpensive items for your shop. There are some good pieces here."

Johannes still held the box, tilting it toward me. Griselda opened one of the top flaps so I could peek in to see the contents: a heap of tangled chains and medallions, rings, and beads. When I reached out to touch, she yanked it back out of reach.

"Fifty dollars for the whole thing, so I don't have to take it home."

"Thirty."

She frowned at me. "Forty, and I'll throw in the piece you were just looking at, with the opal. I think it likes you."

I smiled in return and peeled off two twenties.

Griselda quickly snatched the bills, gesturing to Johannes to hand me the box. It was heavy. Luckily the muscles in my arms and back were toned from the hours I spent washing vintage clothing—nothing like hand washing and twisting and hanging wet clothing to develop a little upper body strength.

Still, though I was sure I could make it out to the car with my burden, I didn't feel like walking around the Gem Faire with it. I considered asking Griselda if I could leave it with her, but her attention had already been diverted by a group of older women who were poking through her collection of antique school rings.

Sale completed, she had no more use for me.

I glanced down at my watch; I was supposed to meet Bronwyn and Maya at the refreshment stand in half an hour anyway.

I was anxious to paw through the contents of my mystery box. As likely as not, it was a bunch of plastic junk not worth five dollars, much less forty. But I slipped my new medallion around my neck, looked into the bright depths of the blue-green opal, and figured it was a good enough deal.

Might as well go grab a cup of coffee and take a gander at what I had.

As I made my way down the aisle, I could hear Griselda saying to the women: "Those are gen-u-ine sweetheart rings, all of 'em given to their girlies when the boys went off to war...."

I had to smile; I imagined Griselda had a dozen romantic tales to tell for every piece in her possession. What a character.

ALSO AVAILABLE FROM
NATIONAL BESTSELLING AUTHOR

Juliet Blackwell

DEAD BOLT
A Haunted Home Renovation Mystery

Turner Construction's latest restoration project is a
historic Queen Anne Victorian in San Francisco.
This time general contractor Mel Turner has to work
around the owners who insist on staying put—along with
some ghosts that insist in their own way that
the work stops...

The ghosts aren't the only ones standing in the way of
the renovations. A crotchety neighbor, Emile Blunt,
secretly wants this house, and could be behind some of
the disturbances. But when Emile is found dead, it's Mel
who appears guilty. Now she must restore the building—
and her reputation—before it's too late.

"A wonderful series."
—Fresh Fiction

Available wherever books are sold or at
penguin.com

facebook.com/TheCrimeSceneBooks